PARTY LIKE HELL

JON GARCIA

Copyright © 2026 Jonathan Garcia

Austin, TX

All rights reserved.

This is a work of fiction.

Names, characters, places, events, and dialogues are products of the author's imagination or are used fictitiously. Any resemblance to actual events or persons, living or dead, is entirely coincidental—unless they're famous, in which case it's probably a joke.

This book contains satirical elements and references to real-world figures, cultural touchpoints, and institutions. These are used for narrative, thematic, or humorous purposes and do not imply endorsement, involvement, or factual representation.

No part of this publication may be reproduced, stored, or transmitted by any means—electronic, mechanical, photocopying, recording, or otherwise—without the prior written permission of the copyright holder, except in the case of brief quotations used in critical reviews or scholarly work.

Cover design by Jon Garcia @RokrJon

ISBN 979-8-250-01497-7
ISBN digital 979-8-218-91338-0
Library of Congress Control Number: 2026900826

To my wife Jen,
for helping me craft my words and
making me the best old fashioned.

To Arya,
for being the furry angel at my feet while
I spent all hours of the night writing...
I hope we meet again on
that rainbow bridge.

This book is also dedicated to anyone
who has ever had their darkest
thoughts while sitting in a church pew.

This book is most definitely
NOT DEDICATED
to mega church pastors.
You're the scum of the Earth.

CONTENT WARNING:
Party Like Hell contains themes of death, grief, and suicide. While the story is grounded in empathy and hope, it deals with difficult emotional content that may be distressing to some readers.

Please read with care and prioritize your mental health.
You matter. Help is out there.

Chapter 1

Of course the Devil would be handsome. And charming. You don't tempt someone with a piece of fruit while disguised as a serpent unless you can really back it up with some choice words and dulcet tones. He had abs, too, but it's always about Jesus' abs, isn't it? You hear all about the Biblical muses inspiring arts and science but if you knew how many innovations were created from someone selling their soul, you'd most likely shit your pants. The "Rachel" hairstyle of the mid-90's? All him. The broad appeal of Coldplay? The Devil's work. The original Playstation? Yep. A sold soul, though, the Devil did return it once he played Tomb Raider. He felt the pointy breasts of Lara Croft and the subsequent sexual confusion they created in young males was worth more than any soul was worth. If you were ever aroused by the polygonal breasts of Lara Croft in her video game debut, you just got played by the Devil himself. He was also mad for the gameplay though don't get him started on the live-action film adaptations unless you have a few hours to kill.

In his current form, he liked keeping his skin a classic deep red color and enjoyed a loose man bun as he felt it really made his jawline pop plus the anger it evoked from everyone earned it bonus points in his book. His 7'5" frame was imposing but ever since attending the premiere of "Fight Club" as a guest of Meat Loaf back in the late 90's, he preferred a much leaner look. As of late, he'd taken an affinity to wearing t-shirts featuring WNBA teams because he felt their "fundamentals were vastly superior to the men." It was Friday in the human world which meant the Devil was partaking in his weekly tradition of Meryl Streep films and cocaine. Despite what you're thinking, the Devil had no part in cocaine. That was all the United States government. An entity even the Devil thinks takes things too far but he is grateful they're associated with Christianity and not him.

His sprawling office was circular with televisions mounted all along the 40 foot high stone walls that extended into the open-air ceiling. The sky was a constant deep gray with flashes of intermittent red lightning and the occasional screeching demon flying by. Surrounding the room was a moat of flames which intermittently shot up large multi-colored fireballs into the sky. The floor was a shiny, gloss white, constructed from the polished bones of the universe's most decrepit beings, mostly low-level politicians and mega church pastors. Between each television was a twenty foot torch with multi-colored flames dancing atop them. All of the televisions with the exception of the largest one showing "The Devil Wears Prada" displayed various humans having sex all over Earth. The Devil enjoyed the odd faces men made when they climaxed.

"God made one of the most complex nervous systems in existence and this is what he gave them to reproduce," He'd always say. "Tell me that crazy fucker didn't clock out early on Saturday before taking his Sunday rest."

As the Devil took a deep inhale of cocaine, he was interrupted by the sound of someone clearing their throat.

The Devil looked up to see the unamused eyes of his assistant and Chief Operating Officer, Asmodeus, staring indifferently at him.

For a crimson blood demon, Asmodeus had surprisingly delicate and androgynous features. Their horns were a deep, golden yellow and perfectly framed an angular face that evoked memories of Annie Lennox. Their silver mid-length hair was shaved along one side and tucked behind a single pointy ear. They wore a shiny sharkskin suit, perfectly tailored with tiny flecks of sparkling red scattered randomly throughout. The black horn-rimmed glasses that perfectly accentuated their cheek bones reflected a blood red color whenever the light hit them just so. As the Devil's chief operating officer, Asmodeus was privy to the wild mood swings and tantrums of the dark lord. They'd been decapitated numerous times and on more than one occasion, the Devil had transformed them into an anthropomorphic capybara. Asmodeus was loyal and knew the key to calming down the rage of the Devil was a shot of Jaegermeister and the music of Kings of Leon. Despite the vastness of the universe, the Devil loved the human world, in particular, all of their variety of entertainment and vices. Especially cocaine. God's little ones, abandoned and running amok, provided him endless joy.

"Sir, about this evening..." Asmodeus began, their voice even and monotone with a slight feminine tilt.

The Devil took another huge sniff and then grabbed a pile of cocaine with his two cupped hands. "Asmodeus, look. Look. I'm Lebron James."

The Devil took the cocaine and flung it into the air while

leaving his arms held aloft to his sides. He held them there for an alarmingly long time.

"Fascinating, sir. Just like all the other times. It never gets old. A true classic. I'm perpetually excited by your desire to mask indulgence with purpose."

"Fuck off. At least I'm bringing something to the table here. You just come in here with your shiny suits and your problems. 'Oh, your dark lord. The fire on the third level keeps going out. Kurt Cobain refuses to play. The Catholic priests won't stop crying.' It's always complaints with you. You never come in here with heroin or ketamine or solutions. Just complaints and that Daria Morgendorfer energy you use to light up a room."

"Well, I am your Chief Operating Officer, my dark lord. It's my job to make sure things run smoothly down here while you, and I quote, 'keep this party lit up.' And normally, I wouldn't dare interrupt your Meryl Streep Friday but your impending journey to the human realm requires extra special care. I need to make sure everything is taken care before your departure."

The Devil sighed and looked up, rolling his eyes. "I'll be gone one night. I doubt very little will happen. This happens every year. I go to human world, party my horns off, and I'm back. Usually with some poor bastard's soul."

It was true. Nearly every year since humanity first figured out how to ferment fruit and embarrass itself over fire, the Devil had taken a night off to revel amongst the living. He'd slipped through the seams of history in disguise, amassing stories, scars, and the occasional soul contract scribbled on the back of parchment or bar napkin. He was a chameleon of time, fascinated by the creatures designed to replace his kind.

Some blamed divine punishment or political unrest, but many global catastrophes could be traced back to a night when the Devil got a little too rowdy. The Great Fire of London? Too much absinthe. The invention of televangelism? A whiskey and heroin fueled rant about the lack of church taxation and the ease of television production. The Bush–Gore election? There's a reason he doesn't visit in the fall of election years.

The churches never mentioned that part, of course. They got the brimstone right, but left out the karaoke and the fireworks.

This wasn't about collecting damned souls. Not really. It was tradition. A tune-up. A reminder that no matter how deep Hell ran, the wildest heat still burned upstairs, fueled by the ones created in his image and pardoned by selling out his only son.

"What about the time the serial killers you were holding to incinerate escaped from their sub-level holding cells and proceeded to organize an orgy with all of the Christian youth pastors?"

"You're a broken record with that, Asmodeus. If I recall, most everyone had a really great time with that," The Devil replied, looking down at the pile of cocaine. With a toothy grin, he slammed his face into it like a baby's first birthday cake.

"Sir," Asmodeus continued. "I'm extra worried about this particular evening because in addition to your annual sojourn to Earth, tonight is also the 144,678th annual Bar Games sponsored by Dirty Chuy's Bathtub Vodka."

The Devil stopped sniffing and looked up at Asmodeus, eyes wide open. "I thought that was next week."

"It was but you moved it because your old roommates are stopping by next week. I warned you of the double booking but you told me that you'd, quote, 'handle that shit.'"

"Fuck. Okay. Okay. It'll be fine. You can handle it, Asmodeus. It practically runs itself at this point. The bars know what to do. The souls down here know what to expect. This is old hat at this point. Besides, it can't get any crazier than the time we held it the same night the Cubs won the World Series. Holy shit, what a party! And if it goes bad, I'll just eat your soul."

"I'm a crimson blood demon, sir. I have no soul."

"Shit. Then I'll kill you?"

"Again. Demon, sir. Killing me is, as you say, old hat. Regenerating is a bit of a nuisance, though, and your emails always pile up while I do."

"Fine," the Devil said, rubbing his chin. "If it goes bad, then when all of those edge lord Austin, TX comedians die, they all have to live with you. In a studio apartment. While you produce their podcasts."

Asmodeus looked up at the Devil and removed their glasses. "You are a perfect bastard, sir."

"I was made in his image, Asmodeus," the Devil said, furiously rubbing cocaine on his fanged teeth. "Now, is everything prepared for my journey to Earth?"

"Everything other than the human you require for the switch, my lord."

"I haven't picked my human yet? That's usually the first thing I do."

"Usually you do, sir, but this past week you spent an inordinate amount of time trying decide between the Charlotte Sting or Sacramento Monarchs t-shirt. The focus group alone took 9 days."

"Shit. You're right. No worries then. It can't be too difficult to pick a soul to replace mine down here for the evening. Plus, if it's an atheist, then bonus. I love fucking with those guys."

"I agree, sir. Though, if I can offer my opinion, I would thoroughly enjoy if you were to switch places with a militant Catholic. The look on their faces alone would be priceless."

"If only I could bottle that up and sell it," the Devil said, snapping his fingers. "But the pure soul rule kinda rules out most Catholics."

The Devil waved his hands lazily and without a trace of evidence, the cocaine disappeared, replaced by a pair of bright purple leather pants and a weathered, teal "Charlotte Sting" t-shirt.

"You're the keeper of the pure soul database," the Devil continued. "The last few decades of souls have been really good. You have quite the streak going so just use your best judgment."

The Devil walked up to his desk, hands on hips. As he

surveyed his clothing for the evening, he shook his head in disapproval. With another snap of his curved fingers, a large leather vest appeared next to the pants. He nodded his head and smiled, his white fangs glinting in the light.

"Tonight is going to be perfect," he smirked. "And if it's not, I get to keep some poor bastard's soul."

Chapter 2

"Did you get those dick pics I sent you this morning?"

Kally pulled her phone away from her ear and rolled her eyes. Her best friend, Maya, had recently joined an online dating site after turning 18 and despite not going on a single date, had amassed quite a collection of unsolicited photos of male genitalia. Primarily middle-aged and white. The kind of folks that if you did even a modicum of digging would find them proudly proclaiming the title of "Family Man" or "Proud Dad" on their social media profiles. The Christian ones were usually the most graphic. And she loved sharing them with Kally every chance she got.

"I did and thank you so much for that," Kally replied, switching her phone to speaker mode. "Nothing goes better with my Lucky Charms than a poorly lit photo of a middle-aged man's junk."

"General Mills is really missing a golden opportunity to

introduce that as a new marshmallow shape."

Kally set the phone down on her desk and snatched the bright yellow t-shirt that was casually draped on the back of her desk chair. A recent birthday gift from her parents, it still smelled faintly of silkscreen ink and the cardboard box it had been shipped in. She tugged it over her slim frame, the fabric catching for a second against her long neck before settling perfectly into place. The bold, black letters reading "Directed by Quentin Tarantino" stretched across her chest, and she smirked to herself. The golden shirt, hit by the early afternoon sunlight pouring through her large bedroom windows, cast a warm glow over her chestnut skin and lit up her wide hazel eyes, giving her the soft, electric look of someone born for the spotlight whether she wanted it or not.

Slumping into her well-worn, oversized white leather office chair, Kally slid her hands into her thick, coarse hair and fluffed it out until it framed her face like a deliberate, defiant halo. She'd only recently embraced her natural curls, a direct result of a 70s Blaxploitation film festival she and her stepdad spent three days at, where Pam Grier walked off the screen and rearranged her sense of self. The decision felt like armor and freedom all at once. She spun twice in her chair, the familiar wall of classic and indie film posters blurring around her in a swirl of color and ambition, before drifting to a stop at her desk.

"What the hell do you do with all of these pictures you're sent," she asked. "Other than send them to me."

"I store them on my 'D' drive, of course," Maya replied without missing a beat. "If the dude is married, it's usually pretty easy to find his wife and forward them to her. Sometimes I'll find them on Linkedin and endorse their photography skills. I'd be lying if I said I didn't really enjoy hearing them squirm when I tell them I'm still in high school."

"Well, you're not anymore," Kally said, grabbing a beat-up DSLR camera off of her desk.

"Yeah, I'm a high school graduate and I still don't know shit. What the hell did we learn in that school? What were our parent's tax dollars paying for? And how the hell do taxes work?"

"I know that 'a squared plus b squared equals c squared.' The mitochondria is the powerhouse of the cell. Chlorophyll is ...green?"

"Our health teacher was the fucking junior varsity baseball coach. It's no wonder so many uninformed girls got pregnant. He couldn't even coach those morons to turn a double play."

Kally laughed, a mix of delight and morose realization that Maya was actually right. "Wasn't he the assistant junior varsity baseball coach?"

"Of course. How could I be so disrespectful to the assistant coach of a team that didn't win a single game before having to forfeit their season when the entire team got caught cheating on tests."

"Another milestone in the proud legacy of Robert E. Lee High School. A school named for a traitorous Confederate general!"

"I expect nothing less from a place that claims disgraced Nascar Driver Billy Bonham and serial murderer Jackson Wayne Phillips as notable alumni. If this school district cranks out one more pedophile or sexual deviant, we might be eligible for some government grants."

"It's only a matter of time before they hang banners honoring them in the gym. But hey, for all the train wrecks and misinformation, that awkward 'Abstinence Awareness Week' included, we met Ryan and Eddie at junior high orientation," Kally said, a tinge of nostalgia in her voice. "Worth it, I'd say. Not as useful as learning how to do taxes or change a tire, but still."

"Speaking of those cheeky lads and tonight's festivities, tell me you're not bringing that fucking camera with you?"

The voice on the other end went silent. Sitting at her glossy white desk overflowing with overlapping post-it notes and cascading stacks of multi-colored index cards, Kally carefully snipped away the errant threads of the frayed rainbow strap attached to her weathered camera. An evening she'd both been dreading and looking forward to for months was upon them and by god, she was going to create magic from it. It was the last night she and her three best friends would be together for a very long time and the reality of its finality was ever present in her mind.

Kally lived for order and structure, an obvious coping mechanism brought about by the fact that she had lived in a new apartment of decreasing quality every single year from the time she was three until eleven. That was the year her mom met Vince, a 35-year-old white software engineer who frequented the deli she had worked at. He'd always leave her a big tip and after 6 months and 42 Italian subs with no tomatoes, he finally asked her out. He was a bit childish, wearing exclusively graphic tees and flannel, and adorned his face with the traditional beard favored by most elder millennials beset upon by anxiety-induced Peter Pan syndrome. But he was kind, brilliant, and gave Kally her enduring love of film.

Her mom and Vince had dated for about three months before Kally was finally introduced to him. He was clearly nervous but he looked her in the eye and didn't talk down to her like most adults did. Their first meeting was at an upscale cinema that cooked gourmet food served by waiters and had three screens dedicated to showing movies on film. Up to that point, money had always been tight and Kally hadn't been to a movie theater in years. She cringed with embarrassment when she thought about how often she had to miss out on movie outings with her friends because her mom couldn't afford it. The theater Vince took them to had felt like another world the moment she stepped inside. Too plush, too golden, and too big for a kid who shared a bedroom with her mom and thought "luxury" meant getting cereal in box and not a bag. Then the first flicker of 35mm film hit the screen. Kally sat, wide-eyed and enthralled. She didn't just watch "The Princess Bride" so much as fall through it. The projector hum became a heartbeat as the dancing dust in the light beam looked like tiny universes exploding into life.

As she fell in love with movies, her mom, sitting beside

her, completely unaware of the tectonic shift happening within her daughter, was falling in love with Vince. She would observe with quiet glee as Kally and Vince talked to the ends of the universe about the characters and the story and everything in between on the car ride home.

From that moment on, Thursdays with her mom and soon to be step-dad was officially movie night. As she got older, her friends and even their parents would join in on occasion, something both her step-dad and mom would admit they loved. Indie, horror, animated. They watched it all. She could always count on some type of limited edition Mondo film print or special edition steel-case DVD under the Christmas tree from Vince every single year. She'd always liked Vince, especially when she saw how he treated her mom, but it was the day she caught him watching YouTube tutorial videos on how to style African-American hair that she fell in love with him as her father. That day, at age 13, she stopped ever wondering where her "real" dad was and knew right then that he was down the hall, watching videos on how to style her hair while concurrently listening to D&D podcasts.

Kally looked down at the phone resting on her desk, slipped into a case designed to look like a blank T-120 VHS sleeve complete with a thin rainbow stripe running along the top — a gift from Ryan, an inside joke between them that meant more than it let on. Kally was both cursed and blessed with overt awareness and foresight. This made her live her life both in the moment but with overhangs of the nostalgia to come casting shadows on all she did. She would lose herself in moments of appreciation that rode sidecar with a subtle sadness that perpetually reminded her the moment was gone or soon would be. This is why film and the idea of capturing moments appealed to her. It was controlling the chaos and keeping a piece of it.

Kally's moment of reflection was broken by the heavy sigh emanating from her phone's speaker. Maya hated talking on the phone so it was telling that she actually called Kally directly.

"This is our last night together," Kally said, putting extra weight on the word "last."

"Yeah, it is. So why the fuck do you want to spend the entire time filming it?"

Kally prepared to respond but Maya continued. "I know how important tonight is and how much planning you put into it but I just want us to spend time together and I know you're going to spend so much fucking time getting b-roll and all of that other shit. And don't pretend like you won't, bitch. The three of us just standing around like jackasses while you whip around a traffic light like a Michael Mann movie or something."

"That's more of a Michael Bay move," Kally interrupted.

"Fuck off, Kally. I have so many more worse dick pics I could send you right now. There is an uncircumcised hog with some real nice overhead fluorescent lighting just waiting on deck. Real artsy shit. Pretty sure the dude shot it in that bathroom from 'Trainspotting.' I'm begging, can we please just go out and do whatever you have planned and, I don't know, just enjoy the night?"

Kally sighed and looked down at her camera.

"You fucking storyboarded the night, didn't you," Maya asked, already knowing the answer.

Kally glanced down at a stack of baby blue index cards on her desk before sweeping them into its matching glossy white trashcan.

"No," she lied. Even over the phone, her best friend could read her like no one else.

The friendship between Maya and Kally wasn't just unexpected, it felt almost statistically improbable. Kally, the hyper-driven, black cinephile who logged her life in Letterbox reviews, and Maya, the half-Asian smartass whose heart belonged to late-90s pop-punk and guitar distortion, didn't exactly scream compatible on paper. But somewhere between their opposing aesthetics and temperaments, something clicked. They'd known of each other since first grade, always orbiting but never colliding, until a sixth-grade oral report on the Louisiana Purchase changed everything. Assigned to work together by a disinterested teacher, it was Kally who pitched turning the project into a short film instead of a standard powerpoint slideshow. Most kids would've laughed or rolled their eyes at the idea. It wasn't the first time Kally had proposed something ambitious for a group project but it was the first time someone didn't flinch, didn't second guess her vision. From that moment on, they were a package deal.

"Heck, yeah," Maya exclaimed upon hearing the idea. "Let's do this!"

"I'm not sure it's allowed but I know we could make something really cool," Kally would reply nervously.

"Ms. Evans didn't say specifically that it wasn't allowed. My mom always says that it's better to ask for forgiveness than permission and that bitch is a CEO. And if we fail, we fail. Pretty sure this isn't going to tank our futures."

"I've never failed anything before."

"Then you're a failure at failing. Boom. We just popped your failure cherry. Let's just make a freaking movie, Kally! It would be better than anything else we could do. Plus, if I have to write another boring paper, I'm going to lose it!"

Using Vince's action figures and camcorder, they crafted a movie that had the entire class enchanted. The performance of Thor as William Clark was particularly noteworthy and powerful. Despite only playing guitar for about 6 months, Maya crafted a tour de force soundtrack (as far as 6th grade presentations went) utilizing only 3 chords on a used Fender Squier acoustic guitar that she had saved up for herself after spending her entire summer mowing lawns and doing errands for neighbors. Kally never understood why Maya loved that guitar so much until she realized that it was the first thing Maya had ever worked and paid for by herself. Maya was, and this is an understatement, incredibly wealthy.

"I'm not rich," Maya would say. "My parents are."

"Still. You call vacations 'holiday.' Only rich people and Europeans do that!"

"I say it as a joke," Maya said. "I don't want this to make

things weird."

Kally always knew Maya was wealthy, but it wasn't until about a year and a half ago that she realized just how wealthy Maya's family really was. When Ryan's dad passed, it was Maya's father who quietly covered the entire funeral and reception without a word of hesitation and even sent over a new suit for Ryan with the tags still on. That's just who Mr. Okada was. Quiet, generous, and unshakably devoted to his daughter. An immigrant from Tokyo, he came to the States as an infant and eventually made a fortune as a cybersecurity expert turned venture capitalist, helping startups go public and cashing in on stock options before most people knew what equity was. He moved from Chicago to Lawrenceville to help a dating app make its IPO run and ended up meeting Maya's mom, Olivia, during a company happy hour at an arcade bar. She repeatedly destroyed him, and nearly everyone else at the company, at Mortal Kombat.

"When she ripped out my spine, she also ripped out my heart," Mr. Okada would always say.

"I also ripped out his heart with Kano later that night," her mom would add, without missing a beat, a story they had clearly told more than once.

The first time Kally visited their home, she saw a

digital photo frame cycling through their greatest family hits, including a shot of their wedding cake: six tiers of blood-soaked fondant, topped with Sonya Blade and Sub-Zero locking arms mid-attack. Kally, a Tarantino disciple and defender of the Mortal Kombat movie's soundtrack and ambitious special effects, instantly felt at home. For years, the Okadas became her second family. They even started showing up at Thursday movie nights with popcorn and overly enthusiastic opinions about practical effects that Vince said gave them a lifetime membership to movie club.

But now Maya was leaving, heading to NYU, where she claimed she'd finally start a real band and leave the suburbs behind. She'd been talking about New York since seventh grade, when her Uncle Tony returned from an NYC trip with a CBGB t-shirt and a battered vinyl of "What We Do Is Secret" by The Germs. It became her origin story, the Big Bang of her love of music that she'd recite to herself in imaginary interviews for Rolling Stone magazine. For a while, it felt like they were building something together: Thursday night movies, high school punk shows, shared playlists, inside jokes, making movies together. But ever since she got her NYU acceptance letter and her dream slowly became real, something shifted.

Kally wasn't sure when the drift started. Maybe when Maya quit her band, the Manic Panic Dream Girls, a few months before graduation, saying she "didn't want to waste her last summer on nostalgia." It could have been when she stopped showing up to movie nights without explanation. All Kally knew was there a moment where Maya looked at her with a kind of distant affection, like she was already preparing to miss her.

They were still friends, still laughing, still in each other's orbit. But for the first time, Kally felt like she was standing still while Maya was already slipping gravity.

Kally had been planning this night from the moment their post-high school plans solidified. Maya was heading to New York at the end of the week. Her stuff was already there waiting for her in the apartment that her parents rented for her. Eddie was officially signing up for the Army on Monday and then heading out on a vacation with his family before shipping out. Ryan was staying behind because life always has to pick a person to fuck over. For the past year and a half, Kally couldn't help but see herself in Ryan, trapped by circumstances but utterly helpless to do anything but go limp.

"I'm filming everything for Ryan," Kally said. "After this past year and with everything that happened, I just..."

Kally began thinking of Ryan and the look on his face when he had to throw away his acceptance letter to the University of Oregon the very day he received it. He could barely afford college in the first place but when his dad passed away suddenly in the middle of his junior year, his choice was made for him. A community college scholarship was easy and at least provided him temporary purpose and no financial burden. The life insurance money helped but didn't go near far enough. One Saturday night in late December, after an evening at the arcade and movies, he came home to see his mom fretting over bills. That was the night everything changed for him. Work. School. Repeat. He had even fell asleep during their graduation ceremony a week earlier after working a double shift at the grocery store the night before. She wanted one more night that felt like the old days. Something to cling on to.

The night was going to start at his favorite restaurant, a dive bar called "Milly's" that had the best, greasiest cheeseburger around crafted by Big Mo, a former metal guitarist turned chef who once played in a band with Ryan's dad. It was the place Ryan and his dad would go to every

Friday after school from the time he was seven until he had passed away. Big Mo would always give them extra fries to take home to his mom. As Kally thought of this, she looked down and closed her eyes.

The Friday before his dad died, she had convinced him to skip his weekly father-son dinner so he could help her shoot a few scenes for her short film. The shoot ran late and Ryan got home exhausted. His dad let him sleep in. The next morning, while Ryan was still asleep, his dad left early to pick up donuts as a surprise. On a normal Saturday, they would have gone to their favorite Tex-Mex dive on the edge of town. But that Saturday, he went alone.

He never made it back.

The last time Ryan saw his dad was a passing glance as he left the house for school. He never got to say goodbye in person. Their last conversation was Ryan texting him to let his dad know he was helping her with the movie. She knew Fridays were off limits and still she insisted because Ryan always said yes to her. She carried that weight with her and though he never said it out loud, she knew Ryan blamed her for everything that happened. He looked at her out of obligation and acknowledged her out of politeness. Their text messages were short and to the point. He usually had to cancel plans because he was working or trying to catch up on homework. He was once her biggest fan and now he was just vapor.

"Kally," Maya said. "I know where your head is. You can't keep feeling bad. Ryan wanted to help you that day. His dad understood how much he loved working on your movies. He was in two of them, for god's sake."

"Yeah, I know, but you and I can go into the other room right now and hug our dads. He can't. He has to stay behind while the rest of us get to start our lives. How is that fair? He's not only stuck here but he's stuck here alone."

"Do you really think he'd enjoy you busting up the moment just so you can get a shot," Maya groaned, sprawled across the off-white faux fur rug in her now mostly packed-up bedroom. "Can't you just film it on your phone or something? It's always so weird when you bring the big camera."

Maya herself looked as transitional as her current bedroom did with her short, choppy auburn hair brushing just past her shoulders, her natural black hair grown in just enough to look accidental in a cool-chick way. Her jawline was sharp enough to look deliberate, though everything else about her seemed effortlessly thrown together. The soft

Japanese curve of her features contrasted with the Joan Jett edge she carried in her posture and the slightly husky rasp of her voice, a trait acquired from her very outspoken Southern California mother. Her eyes were dark and intense, always taking in more than she let on. She could read as judgmental if you didn't know her but really, she was just paying attention. Her bedroom was a shell of itself now, the bed stripped to bare sheets and the walls faded with the ghosts of old posters. A beat-up Gibson Hummingbird leaned in the corner like a retired soldier. The only real color came from the stickers and silver graffiti on the vintage ruby-colored Marshall amp where Maya rested her feet. As she tapped her heel against it, she noticed the golden streak of Kally's signature scrawled across the toe of her black Converse, a mark Kally added to her sneaker on a night when both, very high, watched "Toy Story 3" and had an emotional breakdown about starting their senior year.

She picked at the loose black rubber piping on her sneaker's midsole and tugged it off in one motion, like a scab she'd been meaning to pull for weeks. The stark white amongst the worn rubber reminded her of her bedroom walls, blank and stripped clean, waiting for someone else's life to happen in them. She had been hunting for any excuse to bail on tonight, to Irish goodbye her way out of the entire thing before it got too heavy.

But she didn't and she wasn't going to. Because there wasn't a real reason not to go and because she wanted to see them. Kally, Eddie, and especially Ryan, more than she wanted to avoid the ache that came with it.

She just wished she could do it without the part where they all looked at each other like the finale it was. Maya didn't handle finales well. She'd been digging through her parents' old photo boxes recently and realized how many faces in their youth had already dissolved. People who once mattered so much had become blurry strangers with bad haircuts and half-smiles swallowed by time. She didn't want to become one of those hazy figures or even worse, a random Facebook memory that pops up on a random Tuesday. But she feared she was already halfway there and if she was honest, she was the one speeding up the fade out. For someone who always stayed for the encore, she was now trying to leave the show early to beat the traffic.

She hated goodbyes. She felt too much and hid every inch of it behind sarcasm and a carefully cultivated shrug. She had songs in her bones, lyrics in her lungs, and a Doc Martens shoebox stuffed with half-written verses on napkins and receipts crammed under her bed like emotional contraband. Endings made her itchy. She once grinded for three solid months to avoid the ending of Final Fantasy X because she was so attached to the characters. Goodbyes made the endings real and real meant final. She'd cried herself to sleep the week leading up to graduation listening to Hootie & the Blowfish's "Goodbye" on repeat, quietly resenting the fact that a dad-rock band understood her better than she understood herself.

Kally wanted closure. One last perfect night to hold up like a mixtape memory. But Maya just wanted to slip out of the side door. Quietly, without the ceremony or the weight of anyone's sad eyes watching her go. Because if she stayed too long in the warmth of it, she might never actually leave. And leaving was the only thing she knew how to do without breaking apart.

On some level, Maya knew the goodbye had already happened. When Ryan's dad died, everything shifted. Something broke in Ryan. In all of them. There was still school, occasional movie nights, shared playlists and half-hearted, gif-filled texts as they limped to the finish line. That final thread had stayed intact just long enough to pretend the world hadn't changed. It was strained and weakened for sure but the heart of the four of them held it together. After tonight, even that thread would snap. She couldn't shake the fear that this night would be the last time she ever saw Ryan.

Ryan, dear god. It was stupid. And fast. But there had been something there. A moment, maybe two. It was just a week or two before his dad died. Driving him home, he made her laugh with a joke so dumb she actually wheezed. Then, out of nowhere, he told her he loved her laugh. His smile was different, like he'd suddenly noticed her as a whole person and didn't want to waste a moment not telling her. And for a flicker, she saw him differently, too. Where once she saw him as quiet, she now saw someone deliberate who only spoke when necessary. Always kind. Thoughtful. An observer of people who always remembered things that no one else would. A person of substance. A spark. Potential. The same feeling she had when picked up that Fender Squier acoustic for the very first time. Then the accident happened and everything froze.

She couldn't look at him the same after that, not because of pity, but because she didn't know how to. The old blueprint of who they were, who they could've been, had been swallowed by grief. She never said the right thing. So she said less. And then stopped saying anything at all. The guy in the car, the one who knew every single lyric to "Bohemian Rhapsody," was now a shadow of that. Steady and kind but not complete.

"How about this? I bring the camera but only to get one really good photo of the four of us," Kally said, snapping Maya out of her internal free fall.

Maya sighed and glanced at the signature on her shoe once more. Kally had held them all together the past year and a half. Like Samwise Gamgee dragging Frodo's happy ass to Mount Doom, Kally persisted. When they would all begin to drift apart, she'd bring them back.

"One photo? Are you capable of that?"

"One photo. I promise to do my best to keep the filmmaker hat off, ok? I just want something great to remember our last night together. I don't just want something on my phone. It needs to be special."

Maya sighed once more and looked over at the scrawny black cat loafing next to her. She dangled the rubber string from her shoe in front of the cat as it unfurled a single paw and lazily batted at it.

"What do you think, Joan Jett? Can we trust her?"

The cat made brief eye contact, yawned, and then

walked away.

"Oh, man," Maya said dramatically. "She's walking away. I don't know."

"You know that cat fucking hates me. Why are you asking her?"

"She doesn't hate you."

"The little asshole threw up in my bag the last time I slept over. And she's pissed on my shoes at least a dozen times."

"That doesn't mean she hates you. I've thrown up on you at least three times and I love you to death. She just doesn't like it when you come into my room and immediately start organizing everything. How would you feel if you went into your room and your catnip clownfish toy wasn't where you left it? Or what if I fucked with your camera?"

"Fair enough."

"Well in the spirit of friendship and as amends for the piles of cat puke and piss you've endured over the years, you can bring the camera."

"Thank you," Kally said softly.

"For one goddamn picture!"

"One picture."

"I swear to whatever god you believe in that I will muff

punch you if I see you so much as reach for the video setting on that camera. And I'll know if you do."

"No video mode. I promise."

"Good," Maya said. "Now I'm actually excited. Let's tear this shit hole town a new one. I know Ryan will appreciate it. Eddie needs it, too. Caleb really did a number on him. Getting dumped by text the morning of graduation? Brutal."

"I read the text. It was so cold. It's like he had an AI write it for him so he could avoid it entirely. And Eddie can't even be sad at home because his parents get so weird when he brings up his love life."

"Those are the Catholics, for ya."

"Real fast and loose with that sanctity of marriage thing but god forbid you love another dude, right?

"No hate like Christian love," Maya chirped.

"I'm still proud of him for at least coming out to them even though we told him it would not go well."

"Remember when he came out to us? We'd just finished up volunteering at that pet shelter and we told him that college dude was asking about him."

"Skyler. That dude was hot," Kally added. "Eddie was so nervous like we didn't already know."

"And when he told Ryan," Maya continued. "The relief Eddie had when Ryan said it changed nothing between them and then took him to get a burger."

Maya remembered that day vividly, watching from her sideview mirror as Eddie told Ryan about who he really was in the parking lot outside of the soccer fields. She didn't hear the exchange but she remembers seeing Ryan embrace Eddie with no hesitation, a huge smile on his face, and a look of relief on Eddie's.

"That was a great day until he went home," Kally added.

"I try to empathize with his parents but I just can't. Eddie is such a good person. He's kinder than all of those fucking racist hypocrites in his family. Which is why I don't understand the fucking Army thing at all. Like, why?"

"His dad all the way back to his great grandpa were in the Army. He's just following the family tradition."

"His family tradition also includes fathering a child the old-fashioned way but I'm pretty sure that's gonna end with him. And now he's joining for what? It makes no sense."

"Please don't bring up his family while we're out. You know he hates that," Kally pleaded.

"I'll try my best but it's not easy."

"I suppose that's growth for you."

"I am a high school graduate, you know. I'm part of an elite group of people who've accomplished the bare minimum in life with the promise of prestige and success by following an archaic and outdated system."

"We all remember your yearbook quote."

"I stand by it."

Kally wrapped the rainbow strap around her camera and carefully placed it into her vintage sun-faded yellow camera bag, a Christmas gift from Ryan. His mom had told her he found it at a consignment store and worked two double-shifts over the weekend to pay for it. She snapped it closed, picked up her phone, and held it near her face.

"See you in a few hours. Tonight is going to be perfect."

Chapter 3

A proper pre-party starts with light beer around the 4 o'clock hour. Anyone who tells you differently is an amateur and will most certainly be crying on the floor of a Taco Bell bathroom before the clock strikes midnight. And not the "good" Taco Bell, either. Most likely the one that dimly sits off the interstate between a gas station Subway and a shuttered Cracker Barrel. The Taco Bell the road to rock bottom makes a long pitstop at. You know the one.

Kally grabbed a can of Westerly's Own Light Beer from the beat-up red and white Igloo cooler sitting in the trunk of Ryan's 2010 Toyota Corolla. Westerly's wasn't a particularly good beer but it did feature the mascot of Ol' Lady Westerly, an elderly mountain woman with the posture of a jumbo shrimp, a missing tooth, and a shotgun resting on her shoulder over the backdrop of a monochromatic blue American flag. It also cost only $3.99 for a 6-pack.

The gang had been drinking Westerly's Own since 9th grade when Maya absolutely lost her mind at the image of Ol' Lady Westerly on the can and shoplifted a six-pack from Benny Boom's Convenience Store. For the next 4 years, Maya would dress as Ol' Lady Westerly for Halloween, a joke that no one but her friends understood but amused her to no end. She'd even drunkenly written a song called "Old Mountain Cunt" that became a running joke.

Kally held the can away from her face and popped open the can, baptizing the asphalt in cold suds.

"Easy there, Ms. Westerly," Kally exclaimed, sipping the foam from the top of the can.

"Ol' gal is a squirter," Maya said, pulling a can of her own from the cooler. "The pride of the Appalachians."

Maya gently tried to open hers, the tab not budging an inch as her hand began to lose feeling against the cold. She tried again, grimacing, clearly trying not to ruin the manicure she'd gotten two days earlier "just for fun" but had lowkey fallen in love with. Before she could ask for help, Ryan was holding her can, his hand overlapping hers, and popped the top with ease. Maya blinked. A beat too long.

"Thanks," she said, softer than she meant to.

He gave a shrug and a smile, almost bashful. "Didn't

want you to chip a nail. They look good."

She turned away before he could see her expression change. He looked down at his own can, popping it open loudly and letting the fizz of his own beer fill the silence between them.

The unseasonably cool evening in the high school parking lot was empty with the exception of the four individuals standing around the weathered maroon sedan. The paint on the car was faded with spots giving way to the gray base coat underneath. The hood on the driver's side was scratched and dented. It wasn't in the best of shape when Ryan's dad handed it down to him but it was never the same after Kally attached a makeshift camera rig to film some driving scenes for her mumblecore short film the summer after sophomore year. The sideview mirror on the driver side was duct taped to within an inch of its life, the result of both a riveting argument over who the most attractive fast food mascot was and miscalculating the turn into a Wendy's drive thru. It's Colonel Sanders, by the way.

"Why do you make such a production out of opening your beer," Ryan asked Kally, laughing.

"Because your car shakes more than Eddie's parents when we talk about his love life in front of them," Kally replied.

As she finished speaking, Maya spit up her beer laughing. Eddie, one hand in his coat pocket, took a sip of beer while shaking his head.

"Never gets old, does it?"

Eddie Arevalo was tall, slightly over 6 feet, but you couldn't really tell with the way he stood and carried himself. His posture always seemed borrowed from someone more timid. A soft slouch, shoulders slightly curved inward, as if trying to fold a powerful frame into something smaller and gentler. His black hair was short and unfussy, the kind of cut you got because it was easy, not fashionable, and it stuck up in places from how often he ran his hand through it. His features were soft, almost delicate despite his broad build, and his eyes had a quiet, soulful weight that made people trust him without knowing why. He was strong, built more for lifting cousins at family parties than posing in mirrors, all solid muscle without vanity. Years of being the biggest kid in elementary school had made him a magnet for teasing, and being the tallest and youngest in his sprawling family earned him the nickname "Bebe Gigante," a name that once embarrassed him but now felt like someone else's memory.

When he came out to his family during his sophomore

year, they reacted the way most Catholic Latino families would. First came the Bible quotes. Then came the silence. Finally, the isolation. The daily texts from his mom slowed. His dad, who coached every team he had ever been on, only wanted to talk about sports, enlistment papers, and the family legacy. He knew it was broken forever when his favorite cousins excluded him from the annual "walk" they all took prior to Thanksgiving dinner. The color and chaos of his family gatherings would drain from the room whenever he walked in. Where once he couldn't stand being called Bebe Gigante, now he would kill for someone to say it to him just one more time.

Ryan placed his hand on Eddie's shoulder and tapped his beer can to Eddie's, snapping him out his brief stupor. "You in your head again, bud?"

Eddie laughed, grateful for the ease Ryan brought with him. He paused, then glanced at Ryan with a softer expression, taking a long pull of his beer.

It had been like this since the first day of fourth grade, when Ryan, half his size but somehow bigger than life, plopped into the empty seat beside him in homeroom and complimented his Jurassic Park T-shirt. No mockery. No hesitation. Just a crooked grin, shaggy brown hair, and a very long winded conversation about dilophosaurus versus velociraptors. Eddie may have said all of five words in that first exchange.

Ryan had always made it easy. He never asked Eddie to be anyone else. Never teased him for being quiet or awkward or the kind of kid who cried after reading "Perks of Being a Wallflower." He thought Eddie was cool, something Eddie himself had never believed, not even a little.

After Ryan strong-armed the introverted Eddie into coming to his house after school, they became inseparable. Sleepovers. Vintage video games in Ryan's living room. Fistfuls of popcorn and Milk Duds during horror movie marathons. Ryan's dad always made room for Eddie at the dinner table and always tossed him an extra controller like it was nothing. And maybe to them it was nothing. But to Eddie, it was everything.

So when sophomore year came and the weight of his secret became too much, it wasn't a question of if he'd tell Ryan but when. They were leaning on Ryan's car after soccer practice, drinking gas station slushies and listening to a burned CD Maya had made them called "High School Is Bullshit Vol. 3," when Eddie finally blurted it out. No build up. No apology. Just:

"I like guys."

Ryan didn't flinch. Didn't smirk. Didn't make a joke. He just nodded, set his drink down, and hugged his friend.

"I can't imagine that was easy, buddy," Ryan would whisper to him.

And that was it. No drama. No fanfare. Just the same safety Eddie had always felt when Ryan was around, like the world could tilt a little off its axis and he'd still be standing perfectly balanced with his hand held out. Eddie smiled at the memory.

"Happened right over there," Eddie pointed.

Ryan pushed his hair out his face and glanced to the fence that lined the soccer field.

"I don't know why I was scared to tell you," he whispered.

Ryan gave him a look that was part shrug, part soft smile. "You never had to tell me anything, bud."

In a world full of conditions, expectations, and fine print, Ryan had always made love feel simple. Maybe that's why Eddie carried the burden of not thinking he'd done enough for his friend when his father was taken from him. Eddie looked down at his drink, swirling it a little and taking his time in the memory.

"I knew you'd be cool but there was still this small thought that made me worry everything would be different."

Ryan nudged him gently with his shoulder. "It would have broke my heart if it all changed. Would have broke my dad's, too. Man, did he love when you'd come spend the night and we'd game with him."

Eddie's voice dipped, quietly remembering the father figure who loved him more when he finally spoke his truth. "I still remember how he gave me a ride home that first weekend I told you, and he didn't say anything about it. Just talked about how Matchbox Twenty was more deep than people gave them credit for. Then he took me for a burger before taking me home."

Ryan chuckled. "Pretty sure my dad is the only person who's love language is burgers. He did blame you for eating most of the fries he brought home to me."

"Oh no, I totally ate those. I would have eaten all of them but I filled up on the onion rings we also got you."

"Can't blame you for that one," Ryan laughed. "I wish your dad was that cool. Sucks that you aren't as close as you used to be."

"He is trying," Eddie replied, thinking of how lucky he was that his dad was still up the hall from him even if he avoided his son like the plague. "Those old-school Mexicans have a lot of bad habits they have to shake. He always looks like he's about to say something to me and then he mumbles something about the Astros and walks away. At least he isn't like my uncles. Especially Nacho, that chubby fuck. I'll take silence over his fucking rants any day."

"Ugh, that guy is a piece of shit," Maya said, wiping the beer from her face. "He still drops the n-word like he thinks if he says it enough, he'll finally win the lottery. Or that he'll grow a neck. He does know that there are other exercises than the shoulder press, right?"

"Yeah," Eddie said. "Still don't know why he showed up to the graduation party. He's family but I can't fucking stand him. I'll miss my mom and dad when I leave but I'll be glad to be away from the rest of them."

"He also called me a cunt that one time," Maya interjected.

"That's basically his nickname for you," Eddie said. "You, too, Kally. Though you do have the n-word prefix added to you."

Kally laughed as she took a big sip. "Still doesn't top him calling you a 'fag' during his toast at your graduation party."

The phrase lingered. It wasn't the first time they'd heard

it, but it always landed differently.

Eddie flinched. Subtle, but everyone saw it.

"Sorry," Kally said, throwing apologetic looks to her friends. "I hate that word, too. I'm sorry I said it even though I was quoting an asshole."

"It's okay."

"No, it's not," Kally said, shame running the length of her spine. "I'm really, really sorry. I know you hate it. I shouldn't have even let it into the air."

"Thanks, Kal," Eddie said, taking a nervous sip. "But really, let's move on from my terrible family. This is the last night we'll all see each other for a really long time and I don't want to dwell on that stuff. That shit bums me out and I'm determined to have a great time tonight."

"Exactly," Kally said, her eyes widening in excitement. "Which is why I have this evening planned down to the minute to achieve maximum fun."

"Maximum fun? Then why did we start in the parking lot of our high school," Maya interrupted. "We're done with this place."

Maya sucked down her remaining beer and crushed the can with an animated stomp of her Chuck Taylor. She picked up the smashed can and sidearmed it in the direction of the school. It echoed loudly as it skidded across the empty parking lot before settling near a tire-marked banner that read "ConGRADulations!"

"That is exactly why we're starting here," Kally said. "This place, as much as it sucked, is a part of us. If not for the shit we went through in that very building, we wouldn't be as close as we are now. We're saying both thank you and good riddance to this place before we move on to bigger and better things."

"Well, bigger and better things for most of us," Ryan chimed in.

"It's a bump in the road," Kally said.

"Lots of those lately," Ryan quipped, cracking open another spraying beer away from his face. "Fuck, I wish the shocks on my car were better."

"You've had a rough one, man." Eddie chimed in. "And shocks aren't the pressing issue with ol' Betsy here."

Ryan punched Eddie on his shoulder and placed his can on the roof of the car. He turned and walked over towards the graduation banner and picked up the can that Maya had thrown. He examined the crushed mass of aluminum in his hand and turned back to the group.

"Well," he yelled back. "At least it can't get worse than

being stuck in this town."

As he finished his sentence, a path of flames shot up from the asphalt and encircled him, rotating violently and growing higher into the sky. Ryan crouched down and covered his face, feeling the heat engulf his entire body. The flames rotated faster into a vortex, turning white hot and shooting large embers outward. The heat grew so intense that the group could feel it over 50 yards away. Before anyone could react, the flames spun back into the asphalt and disappeared in a instant, leaving behind a large ring of smoke that continued spiraling into the air.

Kally was the first to break their shocked silence. "What the fuck was that?"

Eddie slowly bent down and gently set his beer on the ground before slowly making his way towards the billowing smoke. Maya grabbed a clump of his jacket and followed closely behind.

"On your left," she said softly, hiding behind his large frame.

The dark smoke dissipated into the air and all that remained was a dark black circle singed into the parking lot, steam rapidly escaping from it.

"What the fuck was that Dr. Strange shit," Maya asked,

looking around. "And where is Ryan?!?"

As the burn mark in the parking lot still sizzled, a bright red light began pulsing like a heartbeat from within when suddenly, a light burst forth into the sky.

Eddie instinctively wrapped himself around Kally and Maya as they shielded themselves from the brightness.

The winds began to whip violently causing Kally to clench onto Eddie and Maya with a vice-like grip.

"What is happening," she yelled over the howling winds.

"I am happening," a deep, booming voice said, accentuating every word as it reverberated throughout the empty parking lot and into their very souls.

Kally shielded her eyes as she turned back, blinking wildly as the winds began to die down. As the air began to settle, a large red blur began to gradually come into focus.

Maya was the first to get her sight back completely and glimpse the demon towering before them, smoke billowing off his gargantuan, sinewy body.

The Devil looked down at the three humans and smiled. He dramatically threw his long black hair back and tied it into a loose bun. As he dusted off the errant fire embers from his leather vest, Asmodeus elegantly stepped out from behind him. They pushed their glasses up the bridge of their nose and gave a long look to Kally, Maya, and Eddie.

"Hello, I am Asmodeus. Chief Operating Officer of Hell and liaison to all subsequent Hell franchises located in all galaxies with intelligent life. I am also the Devil's personal assistant," they said, matter of factly. "If you haven't yet ascertained, this is the dark lord himself. Some call him Lucifer. Some call him the Devil. Others just 'his Dark Lord.'"

The Devil proudly put his hands on his hips, puffing his chest out and looking smugly towards the sky.

Kally looked over at Maya and Eddie, wondering what could possibly be going through their minds.

Maya couldn't take her eyes off the Devil and mindlessly sipped on her beer loudly. The Devil peered down and caught sight of Maya drinking.

"Is that a can of Westerly's Own," he asked, his voice raising an octave, breaking the facade of an all-powerful deity.

"Yeah," Maya said meekly.

"Holy shit on a stick," the Devil exclaimed. "I haven't had Westerly's Own since I attended some backwoods bonfire in Alabama back in the mid-70's. It's so fucking good!"

"It is. Would you like one?"

"Does the pope secretly make virgin sacrifices to me? Fuck yeah, I want one."

"In the cooler," Eddie said, motioning behind them towards the car.

With a large plume of red smoke, the Devil vanished and instantly reappeared at the trunk of the car. Grabbing a can in each hand, he punctured both on his horns and proceeded to let the cold, low alcohol brew run down into his mouth.

"He'll be over there awhile," Asmodeus chimed in. "While he is occupied, I'm sure you all have many questions."

"Yeah! Where the fuck is our friend," Kally yelled.

"Hell," Asmodeus replied flatly.

"What do you mean he's in Hell? Like he's dead," Kally exclaimed.

"No, not dead. He's got a temporary day pass. His soul is fully intact in the depths of Hell while his human body is in a stasis form where it will remain until his Dark Lord gives us the word to release both body and soul back to the human realm."

"I don't understand this," Eddie said. "Why is he in Hell? And why are the two of you here?"

"That's quite easy to explain. Tonight is the Dark Lord's annual visit to the human world to engage in a night of partying and debauchery. He's been doing it since humanity learned to walk upright. There was a brief moment in time in which he experimented with visiting other realms with intelligent life but the gluttonous and feverish ways in which human beings partake in life amuses him to no end."

Kally looked back at the Devil continuously pounding beers and then back to Asmodeus. "Partying and debauchery? That doesn't explain why Ryan is in Hell. He's like the nicest guy in the world. Why didn't you take me? I literally just dropped a homophobic slur."

"Or me," Eddie replied. "I'm gay. Doesn't that get you to Hell?"

Asmodeus looked at him puzzled. "In what world would that put you in Hell?"

"Um, this one. The Catholic one."

Asmodeus rolled his eyes. "The Catholics. That word is a slur if I ever heard one."

"I knew it," Maya exclaimed. "But really, why Ryan? I can't think of any reason for him to be chosen over any of us. I steal candy, like all of the time. I couldn't tell you what a Kit-Kat cost but I can tell you that I had four last week."

"You're still stealing candy," Kally asked.

"If they're going to make me scan my own groceries, I'm gonna take a little something for myself."

Kally glared at her friend, momentarily removed from their present circumstance, before looking back at the stoic blood demon standing before them.

"So why is our friend gone and we're all here," she asked.

"It's quite simple," Asmodeus explained. "For the Dark Lord to visit Earth, a human soul must be exchanged in his place. Your friend, Ryan Clark Phillips, is the soul that was chosen."

"Still doesn't answer our question," Maya asked.

"In order for the transfer to work, the soul sent down must be pure. Not innocent per se but pure and untangled. A pure soul holds its shape in Hell the way a diamond holds under pressure. It doesn't warp, doesn't fracture, doesn't feed the place more than it should. Think of your friend as a counterweight. If the Devil sets foot in your realm, something of equal but opposite nature has to stand in his. Otherwise reality buckles. His presence up here, your friend down there. Two forces of the same system that can never overlap. They can't occupy the same plane at the same time. It keeps the doors from staying open too long and keeps both worlds from tearing at the seams. It also keeps the other side from noticing anything amiss in our world."

"This is so fucked," Eddie muttered to himself.

"More fucked than you realize," the Devil said, his booming voice startling the three. "Did you explain their part in all of this?"

"I was just about to, sir," Asmodeus said.

"Our part," Maya said. "What do we have to do with any of this?"

"In short," Asmodeus explained. "You must show the Dark Lord a good time tonight. If you fail to provide a night worthy of remembrance and accolade, he will keep your friend's soul as payment for wasting his time and his one yearly trip to the human world."

"What the fuck," Maya yelled out. "We have to show him a good time or he keeps Ryan? How the hell do you even show the Devil a good time? Aren't there like blood orgies and shit down there?"

"The beer was a good start," the Devil replied, giving a finger gun to Maya. "Classy shit. This super sad parking lot is also pretty rad so style points for that. I'm definitely taking this aesthetic back with me. Super depressing. Perfect for the souls that peaked in high school. And there are a lot of those, let me tell you. Lots of opportunity for catharsis."

"At sun up, the Dark Lord will determine whether or not the night was sufficient and your friend's ultimate fate will be known. You will return to this location at sunrise and if his Dark Lord did indeed have an enjoyable evening, your friend will reappear right here."

Kally looked at Asmodeus and then up at the Devil. His bright yellow eyes reflected her scared face directly back at her.

"Fuck. Fuck. Fuck," she muttered.

Asmodeus looked at the three friends and bowed. They then turned back to the Devil, giving an even deeper bow. "Enjoy your evening, sir. I certainly hope it goes better than the last one."

"What happened at the last one," Eddie asked, immediately regretting it.

"Where to begin," the Devil scoffed. "Lame night club. The saddest brothel ever. Terry Fator. Ugh. Vegas is so played out. 'Sin' City my bright red ass. It hasn't been the same since the mob left."

Kally leaned over to Maya and whispered. "He thought Vegas was lame."

"We are totally fucked," she whispered back. "Dinner at

Milly's and sneaking into bars aren't going to cut it. Not if we want Ryan back."

Asmodeus cleared their throat loudly. "Now, if you'll all excuse me, I must return to the depths from which I came and attend to your friend. He is no doubt very confused right now and to be honest, I was little distracted with the transportation spell so there's a 10% chance he isn't, um, complete."

Asmodeus gave one more deep bow to the group and in a flash, a circle of more elegant and modest flames surrounded the red demon and they were gone.

Kally, Maya, and Eddie looked up at the Devil.

"So what's the agenda for tonight, kiddos," the Devil asked with a smirk.

Kally attempted to steel her nerves and walked confidently towards the behemoth.

"I take it you're not a dinner and movie kind of guy," she asked.

"I'm not a 'guy' and if I were, I wouldn't be a 'dinner and movie' guy. Unless it's a snuff film and human flesh with a white wine lemon cream sauce. Or an Alamo Drafthouse! They really do it up right. But from the looks of this school and this parking lot and the general vibe I'm getting from the three of you, I'm guessing this town probably doesn't have one of those."

The Devil surveyed the three friends once more, his gaze piercing each of them. "Gotta say that I'm not too confident you three can pull this off. I've partied with some degenerates in my travels and this Dawson's Creek vibe you guys are throwing out isn't making me too confident. It was a long trip. I hope I'm not wasting my time."

"Could we have a minute real quick," Kally asked.

"You have until the Westerly's runs out," the Devil replied flatly.

Kally took a deep breath and turned back to Maya and Eddie. Maya slowly sipped her beer as she watched the Devil pound beer after beer. It was an elegantly sloppy affair that she couldn't turn away from.

"Ok," Kally said confidently. "I have no idea what we're going to fucking do."

"We're going to show the fucking Devil a good time is what we're going to do," Eddie chimed in. "How? I have no clue but we better figure it out fast."

Maya looked at the two beginning to slowly lose their shit and then back at the burned circle where Ryan once stood. She gulped her beer down and slammed the can to ground. Unfortunately, the can was still pretty full and splashed back up, fully drenching the three.

"There is only one degenerate I know that could possibly help us show the Devil a good time," Maya exclaimed, wiping the beer from her face.

"Who," Kally asked.

Maya took a deep breath. "You know who."

Kally stared blankly ahead for a moment before the realization hit her. "No fucking way. No fucking way. We're not calling him."

"Oh shit," Eddie exclaimed, finally catching on. "You're right, Maya. Casey is perfect for this."

"We are not calling Casey Kelly."

"Kally, that degenerate ex-boyfriend of yours is going to bail us out. Who else but him would know of places that the Devil would like? He once took us to a warehouse in Eastwood that only served cereal and had one-person plays performed by 80's themed drag queens. On a Tuesday night!"

"Yeah. I remember our one-month anniversary. I thought we were going to dinner, but instead I watched a Cyndi Lauper queen eat three bowls of Count Chocula while crying about their divorce."

"Casey did bring you oat milk," Eddie chimed in, Kally glaring at him. "I thought it was sweet he remembered."

Kelly looked back at the Devil and then over to the still smoking ring where Ryan once stood. "Fine."

"Casey Kelly," Maya said, yanking Kally's phone from her pocket. "You're our only hope."

Chapter 4

The waiting room to Hell was designed to be both innocuous yet inspire utter hopelessness. It resembled the lobby of a Denny's that was about a week away from being closed by the Board of Health.

Ryan sat on a black, tattered vinyl bench that squealed with every slight movement and was stained with a not so mysterious white goo. Around him sat various other humans and creatures waiting anxiously. A bipedal lizard with four eyes was sat to his immediate right, tapping both his foot and tail nervously out of rhythm. Ryan squeezed his legs together in an attempt to regain some personal space which was immediately occupied by a sobbing rotund gentleman wearing a faded Green Bay Packers jersey on his left.

Ryan looked up at the television monitors hanging askew from walls, wires dangling underneath. Each one showed various forms of torture and macabre imagery. He scanned the televisions, taking in the visceral imagery until he finally landed on one showing Tucker Carlson on Fox News.

"Ugh," Ryan exclaimed to himself, steeling his gaze downward to avoid eye contact with those around him.

"Ryan Clark Phillips?"

Ryan looked up to see Asmodeus holding a clipboard and standing in front of a large wooden doorway that was not there seconds ago. The bright red door floated off of the ground and appeared to glow with a faint purple color escaping the cracks in the wood. A growing heat emanated from it that slowly began suffocating the air in the cramped waiting room.

Ryan stood up. "That's me."

Asmodeus glided over to him and gave him a look up and down. They spun him around and proceeded to check his body before forcing his mouth open and examining his teeth. With a look of satisfaction, Asmodeus snapped his fingers and the two found themselves in the Devil's office.

"Wonderful," Asmodeus said. "I was a bit worried you wouldn't be all here. I zoned out a touch when I did the teleportation spell and wasn't sure I did it correctly. You ever just zone out like that?"

"There are times when I'm driving and I'm not sure if I ran a red light or not."

"Delightful, Mr. Phillips."

"Can I ask where I am?"

"You're in Hell."

"Hell? Did I die? Did that fire kill me?!?"

"No, no, no. Nothing like that. Think of this as a soul-exchange program of sorts. You will spend your time here in Hell while the Devil enjoys a debauchery-filled evening on Earth. The exchanging of souls keeps everything nice and balanced and keeps the other side off our asses."

"Are my friends okay?"

"You really are a pure soul, aren't you? We snagged a good one that's for sure. Seems these notes about you weren't just hyperbole."

Ryan looked Asmodeus up and down before settling on their glossy, demon eyes. They were amethyst purple with flecks of red sprinkled throughout. He caught his own reflection staring back and for the first time, noticed the slouch with which he now stood. Ryan was tired. So tired that standing in literal Hell barely phased him. The past year and a half of his life, Ryan was a passenger, simply reacting to what happened to him and truly believing that he wasn't even a main character in the story of his own life.

"Your friends are fine for now. As long as they show the Dark Lord a good time, all will be well and you'll be back home before you know it."

"And if they don't?"

Asmodeus gave a weak smile and then glanced over at one of the televisions. "We'll cross that bridge when we get to it."

Ryan turned to look at the television Asmodeus had looked at. The image of three-headed Hell hound eating the intestines of humans and other creatures while they were still alive strapped to a stone wall looked back at him.

Ryan's eyes widened as he turned back to face Asmodeus. "Cool. Cool."

"Don't fret too much about it, Mr. Phillips. The Dark Lord was in a very festive mood tonight so things should go well. I'm sure you're friends will, and I quote, 'show him some really cool shit.'"

"Here's hoping," Ryan said meekly. "Kally doesn't do too hot when things go off the rails. So what do I do? Do I just wait here or back at that other place?"

"Oh, no, no, no. That was simply the waiting room

for recently deceased souls awaiting assignment," Asmodeus replied, placing their reading glasses on their face. "You are an honored guest of the Dark Lord and therefore you have VIP access to all corners of Hell. Corners is a bit of a misnomer, however, since it's more of a spiraling circle of levels than anything else. VIP access to all depths would be more accurate. Regardless, anywhere and everywhere are accessible to you. Food and drink are all complimentary and the demons and other creatures are incapable of hurting you, though some may try."

Asmodeus snapped their fingers and with a fiery flash, a glowing red wristband appeared on Ryan's wrist.

"Fucking shit," Ryan yelled. "Mother tits, that fucking burns."

"My apologies," Asmodeus said calmly. "His Dark Lord loves the pageantry of making things appear out of thin air but doesn't much care about the reality of a flaming bracelet burning the skin."

"Sounds like a real CEO," Ryan cracked, rubbing his wrist.

Asmodeus snapped once more and a glowing red lanyard with a golden card at the end appeared in their hand, still sizzling with heat.

"This lanyard gets you access everywhere. The wristband means all food and drink are gratis." Asmodeus blew on the lanyard and then placed it around Ryan's neck. "You are also in luck. Tonight are the 144,678th annual Bar Games sponsored by Dirty Chuy's Bathtub Vodka. A living soul has never experienced these before so you should have a good time enjoying one of Hell's premier events."

"Bar Games?"

"An annual celebration of excess. All of the bars, taverns, clubs, and pubs host a series of bar games with various prizes. It's a Hell-wide party where anything goes. Basically a bar crawl with games. And Blood Demons."

"Sounds like Mardi Gras."

Asmodeus giggled to themself. "This makes Mardi Gras look like a preschool graduation. I'd suggest starting at Old Tito's, one of Hell's oldest establishments. Some of the finest cocktails around and a sight to behold."

"Um, ok. Thanks for the tip. How exactly do I get there?"

"Where is my head at? You'll forgive me if I'm a little out of sorts with the Devil's night out and the Bar Games falling on the same night. Lots of balls in the air, so to speak."

Asmodeus snapped once more and a small touchscreen

phone appeared in Ryan's hand.

"You can borrow my personal cellular device."

"You have phones down here?"

"Of course we do. We are civilized. In fact, it was his Dark Lord who decided to inspire smart phones in the human world since he knew it would lead to an increase in sin and oh boy, was he right about that one. Did you know that Hell runs entirely on the energy outputted from humans masturbating? Isn't that something? So much more efficient than using the pain extracted from extreme torture. And looking at your living file here, you've contributed quite a bit to our power grid so many thanks for that."

"You have those stats?"

"Amongst others. Would you like to know how many hours you've spent defecating? Or how many pounds?"

"I'm good. Uh, I do wonder one thing."

"It's 5,640 lbs so far."

"Um, thanks. But that's not my question. How exactly am I understanding you right now?"

"Ah, great question. Only one language down here. While the Devil certainly appreciates the chaos of your world utilizing multiple languages, we all felt the logistical nightmare of dealing with an infinite supply of languages was too much. It's bad enough all of the departments down here want their own logo can you imagine dealing with every single language that has and ever will exist. No thank you."

"We?"

"The board of directors."

"Hell has a board of directors. Of course Hell would have a board of directors," Ryan said. "How about this phone? Anything I should know about it or does it work like any other phone?"

"Basically like any smart phone you have utilized on Earth. The phone you have is equipped with the official Bar Games app. It will give you a rundown of the bars participating, rules of the games, and speciality drinks available to you. It also acts as a map. Simply tap the place you want to go, hit 'confirm' and you'll be instantly teleported there. Again, it will burn because of the flames and all."

"Wow. That's actually pretty rad," Ryan exclaimed, almost forgetting where he was for a moment. "Other than being in Hell and the burning and all."

"Imbibe and partake as much as you wish. Think of this as a free pass. Nothing can physically hurt you while you're a guest of the Devil and there are no long lasting effects of the abuse you'll inevitably put your body through. Of course, that all changes if your friends fail but for the time being, you're completely safe so enjoy yourself."

"I guess that's all I can do at this point, right," Ryan said, looking down at the phone and scrolling through the nearly infinite list of bars and clubs. "I can't exactly help them from here."

At that moment, a ding sounded and a text message popped up on the phone.

"Who's Simon?"

Asmodeus' hand shot out with surprising speed, snatching the phone. They glanced at the message and their jaw tightened, just barely.

"A former... assignment," they said, voice clipped.

Ryan raised an eyebrow. "Must've been quite an assignment. That message looked like a poem."

Asmodeus tapped the screen quickly, then handed the phone back with forced nonchalance. "Some people get sentimental after their soul swap ends. It's not uncommon."

Ryan looked at him. "And you?"

"I don't believe in sentiment. I believe in boundaries." Then, softer, as if to himself: "And some boundaries are easier to draw than keep."

Ryan squinted and pursed his lips. "No worries. I'll

keep my activities strictly to the app and possibly the pornographic. To offset my carbon footprint."

"I'd very much appreciate that, Mr. Phillips. Do you have any additional questions?"

"Yeah, like a million of them but I'm pretty sure they all have some weird or depressing answer to them so I'll just figure it all out as I go along. Basically, I can't get hurt and I can do pretty much what I want, right?"

"That's the gist of it."

"Gotcha."

"Before you take your leave, I must ask if you are completely attached to the current ensemble you're wearing?"

Ryan glanced down at himself, surprised by the question but instantly aware of what he saw. His faded navy hoodie was threadbare, sleeves chewed at the cuffs from nervous tugs. The jeans hung off him loosely, his body still carrying the quiet toll of a year and a half spent skipping meals and shrinking into himself. His once black Converse were faded to an ashen gray, soles thin and nearly flapping. The T-shirt beneath the hoodie was something he picked up months ago from the school lost and found after an unfortunate incident with a Chalupa Supreme and a new speed bump in the school parking lot. A team shirt for a team he never belonged to and didn't even know existed. It read: Robert E. Lee Writing Club - We Fight for the Oxford Comma. It didn't even make sense anymore. Not the shirt and not the guy who put it on.

"Not particularly," Ryan muttered.

Asmodeus nodded once, eyes scanning him with a gaze that was sharper than it should have been. Not judgmental but analytical, as if seeing not just the clothes, but the wear and tear beneath them. From the crook of their arm, Asmodeus flipped to a clean sheet of paper on their silver clipboard and began sketching, their strokes precise and fluid. Ryan watched, mesmerized. For a moment, he could swear the pen glowed faintly, a silver shimmer that left trails of light in its wake with every deliberate stroke.

Asmodeus held the finished page up, inspecting their creation. With a flick of their fingers, the paper floated upward, edges shimmering in soft neon blue. It spiraled gently, gracefully dancing on invisible air, before landing flat against Ryan's chest. It sank into him, melting into a burst of warmth and light. Ryan gasped as the flash overtook him. Not painful but startling. Like stepping into the sunlight after being in a dark movie theater. When the brightness faded, he looked down.

"That's much better," Asmodeus said, their voice breaking from its monotone cadence for just a brief moment. "Perfect for a night in the depths."

Ryan examined his body as wafts of clean, white smoke smelling of sage and lemon balm began to clear from around him. He looked down to see his once faded and destroyed blue hoody replaced with a leather bomber jacket, the sleeves rolled up to reveal a large face watch with a bright, red leather band. On his torso he wore a perfectly tailored red t-shirt with the Devil's personal logo in golden thread on it. His jeans, also perfectly tailored, were a weathered charcoal gray paired with brand new red and white Jordans 1's.

"Wow," Ryan said quietly to himself.

Asmodeus then held his hand aloft and summoned a gilded mirror. "The clothes aren't the only thing that are 'wow.'"

The mirror floated towards Ryan until it settled a few feet away from his face. He glanced at his eyes and then up to his hair. His once shaggy, brown hair was now trimmed and conditioned. As he touched his freshly cut hair and felt the softness and volume, his eyes began to flood with tears. His last haircut had been the weekend before his dad died.

A bi-weekly tradition they both enjoyed that he could no longer bring himself to do. He'd driven by the barbershop numerous times but could never walk through the door. He had resorted to crudely cutting his own hair whenever it got too unruly and even that had slowed down in recent weeks.

Asmodeus was taken aback. He was accustomed to screams and cries of terror and fear but this was new. The silence and deliberate way the tears rolled confused him. With a soft wave of the hand, they dismissed the mirror in a puff of smoke. Ryan walked through the wafts of clearing smoke and towards Asmodeus and with no hesitation, hugged the red blood demon sincerely.

"Thank you," Ryan said quietly.

Asmodeus held their arms stiffly to the side, not knowing how to react. After a long moment, they patted the young human on the back with a very stern flat palm.

"It's quite alright. We can't have you running around Hell with a Devil's VIP pass looking askew, now can we? This is Hell. Not Little Rock."

Ryan finally released his embrace and took a few steps back. "Sorry."

"It's fine. I know very well how emotional you humans can get. We wouldn't have thirty thousand rivers of tears if not." Asmodeus said, readjusting their tie and smoothing their suit. "Now get a move on. If you require anything or have additional questions, the number to my work cellular device is in the contacts list. Don't lose your lanyard. It's the best way to track you down and you'll need it in order to return to Earth if your friends are successful."

Ryan looked down at the shimmering gold pass dangling from his neck. Kindness from a demon. A night of infinite, consequence-free partying in the depths of literal Hell. He took one last glance at Asmodeus and gave a nervous, closed smile. The corridor ahead pulsed with faint red light, thumping like a heartbeat in the distance. Somewhere out there were endless temptations, strange rules, and the kind of night no mortal was meant to experience or survive. Ryan tightened his grip on the lanyard, squared his shoulders, and exhaled the last breath of his old life.

Chapter 5

The world blinked.

One second they were standing in the parking lot of their high school, the Devil finishing a tirade about real evil being the fact their school was named after a Confederate general, and the next, reality twisted like it had been shaken in a snow globe and they were somewhere else entirely. Teleportation with the Devil wasn't as simple as disappearing and reappearing. It was more like passing through a dream filtered through someone else's hangover.

Maya was the first to speak. "Okay, so that felt illegal."

Eddie wobbled once on his feet, grinning. "I feel like I drank a 12-pack of Westerly's."

Kally said nothing as she gripped the strap of her bag like a seatbelt and attempted to focus on the horizon to find her equilibrium.

The air around them was thick and humid with

something sweet and electric. Their clothing felt like they'd been dried in warm smoke and their skin hummed and tingled as if they were about to be struck by lightning. That was the Devil's afterglow, the residue of indulgence and rebellion, like stepping out of a hot tub full of charm and ego and possibly ketamine.

The Devil straightened his sleeves, unaffected. "First rule of teleporting with me," he said, "don't try to act normal afterward. You won't be."

Standing on the loose dirt of the dimly lit mobile home park, Kally settled herself before starting towards a familiar yellow trailer sitting like a beacon of light amongst the decrepit.

A front porch can tell you a lot about the person you are visiting. If you see a craft cottage porch swing with excessive pillows and a "Live, Love, Laugh" sign, you can almost guarantee that the food will be underseasoned and the person who owns the home is most certainly hanging on by a thread. They also probably have an unused craft room filled with either Scentsy or Pampered Chef items. Possibly both. This front porch wasn't that. If this front porch could speak, it would most certainly ask if you were up to date on your vaccinations.

"My shoes are sticking to these steps," Maya exclaimed as she walked up the precariously built porch crudely attached to the rusted steel doublewide mobile home. A mobile home that hadn't been mobile in many, many years. "It's like the old dollar movie theater."

"Which was originally the old porno theater," Eddie added.

Eddie couldn't help but reach up and brush the wind chime constructed out of Coors Original cans, taking in the clunky tones of aluminum on aluminum. "Pure Americana."

The Devil stood at the bottom step, hands on his hips, and surveyed the porch and adjoining trailer with a sweeping glance. "Now this is a look! It's disgusting and sad in such a subtle way. I gotta get the person who did this to help with some design back home. Everything there is so obvious. Everyone thinks 'lets just add red and some flames' and call it a day. This is pure elegance."

"You got Guy Fieri doing production design down there," Kally scoffed.

Against a backdrop of dirt-grimed windows covered with bars, a futon couch covered in PBR empties crudely modified into a porch swing slowly swayed in the soft breeze. The railing, warped from years of neglect and lack of water sealer, precariously hoisted a series of garden gnomes in progressively erotic poses. Ironically enough, the flowers that were arbitrarily placed throughout were thriving. The bold colors popped against the untreated wood of the decking and the faded stacks of dog-eared 90s men's magazines piled up all around.

"Of course you would like this," Kally continued.

"Who wouldn't," The Devil exclaimed. "Which Property Brother resides in this delightful domicile?"

Maya walked up to the poorly painted and chipped screen door. "Kally's ex."

Kally rolled her eyes. "We barely dated."

"You went out for like 6 months," Eddie chimed in. "He took you to junior prom. Wearing a tuxedo t-shirt and cut-off jeans shorts, if memory serves."

"In his two-tone El Camino," Maya delightfully interjected. "He did fill the back of that sumbitch with beer and booze so we all had a great time. At least until Ryan's date told on all of us. Goddamn Janet. Fucking buzzkill."

"Tuxedo shirt AND jean shorts? Such a good look," the Devil exclaimed. "Why on earth would you part ways with such a debonair suitor? Is it because your fashion choices are so bland that you yourself felt inferior to such an Adonis?"

"Fun fact," Maya added, laughing. "He started the evening in regular jeans and made them into shorts."

"Casey was a phase. He was a rebound that was completely the opposite of what I normally went for" Kally sighed. "I was tired of the same type of guys talking about the same old shit and having a Groundhogs Day of relationships. Casey was different. He just did whatever the hell he wanted. And he was sweet. Completely disgusting and inappropriate, but he was nice. He is what he is. Nothing more and nothing less."

"That he's not dead already is a constant surprise to everyone," Maya said, knocking on the poorly attached screen door, flaking off paint with each strike of her fist. The Devil leaned down and grabbed a large paint chip. He examined it before placing it in his mouth.

"Wow, that is some of the purest lead I've ever tasted!"

As the Devil stood up, the front door swung open.

"Well fuck me running! Fresh from the cells of Robert E. Lee High School, if it isn't the Scooby-Doo gang! To what the fuck do I owe the pleasure?"

Living on the outskirts of the city and primarily home-schooled until freshman year of high school, Casey

Kelly spoke with the Southern drawl of a cartoon character. The only thing that kept him from being a caricature was the sincerity with which he spoke. His shaggy blonde hair was tied in a loose bun with random strands hanging down over the yellow-tinted aviators he constantly wore. He donned a hibiscus flower patterned kimono over a faded black t-shirt that read "Rebel City 5K and Fun Run" accompanied by a pair of light fuchsia reading glasses dangling from his neck. On his lower body, he wore cut-off jeans shorts with dangling pockets and surprisingly new brown Ugg boots. Authentic Australian. Not knock-offs.

"Are these the same shorts," the Devil exclaimed.

"And who's this tall drink of water," Casey asked, pointing to the Devil, his finger dangling a 6-pack ring of beer containing a single remaining can.

"Are you referring to the very large demon that is standing behind us," Kally asked, bewildered at Casey's lack of emotion.

"Demon? That's a rude description, Kally. Looks like a good-looking dude if ya ask me but then again you did have some high standards there. Probably why you dropped my happy ass. I always knew you could do better."

"Oh," the Devil chimed in. "I only look like a large red

demon to you. To everyone else, I appear as a normal person. It helps me party with no distraction."

"A normal person," Maya inquired. "Or a really handsome person? Wait. Does the Devil give a shit what we puny Earth humans think of his appearance? Are you serious with that?"

"Of course not," the Devil bellowed. "I don't care about the opinions of lesser beings."

"I think you do!" Maya turned back to Casey. "Casey, do you mind if I ask you to describe this, um, handsome gentleman, as you put it?"

"Hell, not at all. I guess if I had to describe him, he's like if you took Pedro Pascal's soulful eyes and Patrick Swayze's aura and plopped it on the body of Brad Pitt from Fight Club. Something along those lines. Tell ya what, I ain't been with a fella in a couple years but I'd take the off-ramp for this one. Just say the word, Brokeback, and I'll saddle up."

The Devil beamed as Casey shot him a single finger gun, the beer can swinging even more wildly than before.

"Oh really," Maya laughed, grabbing the joint from Casey's fingers and taking a long drag. "So interesting."

As Maya exhaled, she began coughing violently. "Fuck, I wanted that to look cool," she said, gasping between words.

Casey grabbed the joint back from Maya and took a quick drag, blowing out a smooth line of smoke. "So what do I owe the pleasure of this little visit?"

"We need a little help with our evening plans," Eddie said. "And it kinda all involves this, um, guy."

"Come on in but be sure the door closes behind ya. I just picked up Meowthew McClawnaughey from getting fixed and the little fucker keeps trying to get out. I keep telling him his lil' pecker don't work like that anymore but he doesn't believe me."

The home of Casey Kelly was the "before" photo of an HGTV home flipping show or quite possibly the video footage released by police featuring the home of a person of interest. All of the appliances were outdated and the fixtures were a grimy, stained gold. Band flyers and action movie posters were thumbtacked and overlapped on the brown paneled walls. Three televisions were mounted unevenly on the wall, exposed and tangled wires dangling down to an assortment of video game systems and DVD players sitting atop milk crates and cinderblocks. The brown shag carpet, for some reason, was immaculate and despite outward appearances, the home had the surprisingly delightful aroma of rain and palo santo. The group followed Casey into his trailer, taking seats on one of the three futons pushed up against the walls.

"So what are you up to, Casey," Maya asked. "Hope we're not bothering you."

Casey slumped down into his well-worn leather recliner, pulling a beer from the mini-fridge built into the side of it. He tossed a frosty can of Westerly's Own Amber Lager to the Devil who snatched it out of the air without looking, the can sizzling in his large mitt upon impact.

"Not at all. I love folks poppin' in. As long as you ain't crowing on about your god or trying to sell me solar panels, the more the merrier. I'm just watching this movie about this black fella who wants to go swimming but these fuckers won't let him."

Eddie looked over to the television to see the image of Cuba Gooding Jr. in the 2000 military drama "Men of Honor" paused mid-speech. "Dude, that's 'Men of Honor.'"

"Yeah, this black fella just wants to go swimming and they won't fucking let him. Goddamn racists."

"Is this on TV?"

"Nah, man. Bought the DVD from one of those big clearance baskets at the Wal-Mart. Can you believe it was only $1.99? Picked up "Twister", too. That Helen Hunt can get it," Casey said, taking a sip. "So what can I do you all for? If you're looking for green, I got a little to spare but I am fresh out of coke. The Young Republicans from the community college are having a mixer tonight so they cleaned my ass out. Paid me in cash so score on that. Thus my celebration spread."

Maya looked down to see two Hot N' Ready Little Caesars pizzas, a tres leches cake, a packed bowl of weed, two cases of Westerly's and three capri suns atop a ring-stained plywood and cinderblock coffee table.

"Two hot n' ready pizzas, Casey? Don't get too crazy. You wouldn't want to burn through your profits now would you?"

"Hey now. Don't you disrespect the Hot N' Ready, Maya. I can recall on more than one occasion watching your drunk ass house one by your lonesome in that very corner over there like you were recreating the Blair Witch or somethin'. Ain't none of us better than a Hot N' Ready and if ya think you are, I don't want to know ya. This is the people's pizza."

The Devil finished his beer and then bent over to examine the pizza which had long since gone cold and began to coagulate into a single mass of cheese and overly greasy pepperoni that seemed to hover above the cheese like an air hockey puck.

"Help yourself, buddy," Casey said. "It ain't getting any hotter or more ready."

The Devil grabbed a large slice and dangled it in front of his face. He took a few quick sniffs and then slowly pushed the entire slice into his mouth. The group watched as the Devil slowly chewed, his eyes darting around in confusion.

"Pretty fucking tasty, ain't it," Casey yelled.

"This. Is. Divine!"

"Fuckin-a! The boy has taste! Where you fuckers been hiding him?" Casey pulled another beer from his recliner fridge and tossed it to the Devil without looking. "You like that, try that Krazy bread. It will knock you on that bright red ass I assume you have."

Casey picked up his glass pipe and brought to his lips. As he raised the lighter, he looked around room and took note of one missing person.

"Where the hell is my good time boy at?"

"Ryan is the reason we're here actually," Kally chimed in. "What we're going to tell you might seem completely insane but it's all very, very true."

Casey leaned forward in his recliner, slowly lighting the freshly packed pipe.

"This guy right here is the actual Devil," she continued.

Casey leaned forward and removed his aviators. "This guy is the Devil? The god's truth Devil?"

"Yes. To you, he just looks like a normal dude."

"A very handsome dude," Casey interrupted.

"Regardless, what you see as a handsome dude is the actual, living Devil. Maya, Eddie, and I see a giant red demon wearing a lot of leather and a shirt for some WNBA Team."

"Don't you disrespect the Charlotte Sting, young one," The Devil bellowed, causing the entire trailer to shake.

Kally, Maya, and Eddie looked up as the Devil stood, towering over them, his horns scraping the ceiling, showering popcorn ceiling remnants down upon them. Casey, not changing expression, continued examining the Devil. "Girl doesn't appreciate good fundamentals. She never has."

"Clearly," the Devil said, sitting down, a piece of ceiling panel stuck in his horn.

"So, like, could you show me your real form," Casey asked, dusting popcorn ceiling from his kimono. "Don't get me wrong, I love what you got going on but to meet the god-honest Devil, well, I really want to see that shit! Not as much as seeing this fella go swimming but I want to see that."

The Devil looked Casey up and down before snapping his fingers. Red light and smoked filled the small trailer, quickly causing the smoke detectors to chirp wildly. The smoke quickly dispersed, revealing the Devil's true form to Casey.

"Huh," Casey whispered. "Other than the shirt, your look is a little, um, expected. But I guess it doesn't matter, really, since you can look like whatever you want, huh? I mean, do you have a 'real' form or not or do you just exist as more of an idea than anything else? So many questions."

"Questions we don't have time for Casey," Kally interjected. "We need your connections and your expertise in all things hedonistic, debaucherous, and possibly illegal. It's the only way we can get Ryan back."

"Back? Where is he?"

"Currently, he's in Hell," Maya said. "We have to show this guy a good time tonight and if we don't, he keeps Ryan. I guess this is a thing he does every year or something."

"Partying with a purpose, eh," Casey smiled. "A truly noble cause. God knows I've partied for much less."

Casey leaned back into his recliner and pulled a worn

Field Notes notebook from his kimono pocket. He placed his aviators atop his head and replaced them with his reading glasses. He began furiously jotting down notes while glancing periodically at his phone. After a few moments, he tore a page out of the notebook, crudely folded it, and handed it to Kally.

"Here ya go," Casey smirked, removing his readers and putting his aviators back on. "A night of reckless abandon that if you do it up right, will get Ryan out of Hell and most certainly keep all of you out of heaven."

The Devil and Casey began laughing in unison as Kally glanced at Maya, clutching tightly at the list in her hand. As the Devil and Casey chatted like old friends, Kally quickly skimmed the long list of activities listed.

"Casey, how are we supposed to do all of this in one night? We'll be driving constantly. Some of these things are like an hour away."

"Hey, man, I ain't about the logistics. I just gave you the blueprints for a good time. These are just options. I'm assuming Big Red over there has some tricks up his sleeve. Dude can shape shift. I'm sure he can fly or something."

The group glanced at the Devil, who had helped himself to two additional slices.

"Oh, yeah. No worries about all of that," the Devil said, his mouth stuffed with pizza. With a snap of his very large fingers, the Devil, Kally, Maya, and Eddie disappeared in a swirling ring of fire.

As the smoke dissipated, Casey casually walked over to the futon and smothered a small fire with a nearby "Caturday" throw pillow.

Using the same pillow, Casey quickly fanned the smoke detector until it stopped beeping. He grabbed a slice of pizza, fell back into the recliner and pulled a Playstation controller from his kimono pocket.

"Now let's see if they let this crazy fucker go swimming."

Chapter 6

The street pulsed like a living artery, packed with demons, lost souls, and creatures that looked like they'd crawled out of the notebooks of Clive Barker and Guillermo Del Toro. Instead of wailing in torment, all manner of creature were partying and screaming in delight. Flashing neon signs bathed the crowd in an unnatural and unsettling pulsating glow. Some were traditional purples and blues, but others shimmered in colors Ryan was pretty sure didn't exist in the mortal world. The air smelled like clove, burnt sugar, and expensive cologne.

Above him, sexy bat-winged bartenders zipped between floating platforms, refilling goblets of glowing green liquid for well-dressed skeletons lounging on hovering velvet sofas. A chain-smoking minotaur in a pinstriped vest leaned against a corner, smoking a gold pipe and being attended to by a group of shirtless humanoid men who seemed ripped straight from the pages of a 90s Abercrombie & Fitch catalog. A demonic taxi screeched past, its bare wheels with no rubber sparking against the cracked pavement with a rhythmic wail. The driver, a headless pink specter in a teal Hawaiian shirt, waved a flaming sign that read "Free Rides to Fallen Angels Strip Club." Following closely behind, a rickety double-decker bus covered in neon graffiti barreled down the road and blasted a Taylor Swift trance remix, shaking the pavement with violent fury as it passed.

Further down the block, a gargantuan billboard made of stitched-together flesh advertised "PIT-FIGHT KARAOKE" in a pulsating, vein-like script. The crowd in front of it roared as a drunken cyclops in a feather boa and magenta fur vest attempted a wailing rendition of "Total Eclipse of the Heart" while simultaneously brawling with various patrons. Above the fray, a drunken cherub with a flickering halo simultaneously smoked 3 cigarettes and worked a clipboard as he took bets on whether the cyclops would survive the next verse.

Hell wasn't a place of suffering or torment. It was a place of indulgence and raw, chaotic energy. Every corner buzzed with temptation, every alleyway whispered with promises of impossible pleasures. Ryan wasn't sure if he was terrified or kind of impressed. His eyes darted to the street corner, where a group of five bipedal, olive-colored lizards in hot pink mesh tank tops were caught in a heated argument. The streetlight above them flickered erratically, casting a sickly yellow sheen over their moist, glistening scales. Their voices were shrill, yet oddly melodic, like a jazz club at midnight.

"I can't believe you blew flip cup, Dooley," the largest lizard yelled, striking the smallest with an open, clawed hand.

The lizard struck the ground hard and tumbled into the street. As he stood, a large truck adorned with barb wire and spikes struck him with a sickening splat, sending a glowing green ooze into the air and onto the group of lizards.

"Fuck! I got pieces of Dooley all over me!"

Ryan watched, mouth agape, as he took in the world around him. Looking down, he noticed the severed claw of Dooley at his feet, still twitching and leaking goo. Attempting to keep his cool, Ryan stepped over it and continued on his way. He walked past the arguing lizards, taking in the lights and sounds all around him. A kid of the suburbs, the buzziness of Hell was strangely enchanting to him. From scantily clad femme-demons shotgunning absurdly large cans of what appeared to be beer to the sight of two large teal minotaurs erotically locking horns under a flickering street light, Ryan was enamored. He pulled out the phone and opened up the maps app. Scrolling through the various options, Ryan couldn't help but wonder if all the best UX designers are destined for Hell because this was one of the most intuitive phones he had ever used.

The lights and colors of the streets tattooed the hazy air in a sensuous swirl of light that seemed to dance to the beat of the tunes emanating from their various sources before disappearing into the ether. Ryan looked up from the phone once more to take it all in. As he surveyed his bright surroundings, his eyes were suddenly drawn to a lonely, dimly lit building that sat silently amongst the chaos. Tucked between a massive casino where fire-breathing skeletons played craps and an alley that seemed to stretch into a psychedelic haze, the lone dive bar built of ashen colored cinderblocks and faded cedar stood untouched by the chaos. It was low and unassuming, the kind of place you'd miss if you weren't looking for it and seemed to be encased by a protective bubble that shielded it from the excess that surrounded it.

The neon sign that sat precariously atop the structure buzzed and flickered, barely holding on. Ryan's eyes squinted as the the sign flickered spastically for a beat and then went steady allowing him to read it: *Milly's 2.*

His stomach dropped, a feeling that took him back to that crisp Saturday morning when that police officer would knock on his front door.

Like Dorothy's house in Oz, this building was an outlier. An invader. Strangely normal but not in the context of what he was experiencing. It was Milly's but almost as if it had been recreated from memories. It had the same red door with errant bullet holes and paint that had flaked off from the years of flyers being plastered upon it and aggressively removed. Was this some weird trick that Hell was playing on him? The world around Ryan stopped and muted itself as he found himself drawn to that red door. As his new shoes crunched through the empty gravel parking lot, the smell of old cigarettes and fryer grease overtook his hippocampus, taking him back to every single Friday night that he had ever experienced with his dad all at once. Ryan floated through the parking lot, powered by nostalgia, and approached the entrance as he had so many time before.

Looming in front of the entrance to Milly's 2, an eight-foot-tall troll stood with the immovable presence of a mountain that learned how to scowl. Its eight muscular arms were crossed over its massive chest, staggering downward like a lumpy pyramid of power and strength. The bicep veins bulged slowly and methodically with each labored breath it took. The looming behemoth in front of Ryan's sanctuary was a stark reminder that he was indeed still in Hell. The creatures's skin was a deep, cracked gray, like cooled volcanic rock, and his hypnotic illuminated yellow eyes flicked over Ryan like he was assessing whether it was worth the effort of breaking the small human in half. A lit cigarette dangled from its lips, the long cherry hanging on with oddly delicate grace. Ryan locked eyes with the bouncer and slowly surveyed him before being taken aback by its attire.

It wore a sleeveless, faded Stevie Nicks T-shirt, stretched tight across his massive frame, the words "Gold Dust Woman" nearly unreadable from years of wear and stretching. The edges were frayed, like it had been through a bar fight or twenty and won them all. Ryan wasn't sure what was more unsettling; the sheer amount of arms, the size of his tusks, or the fact that this absolute behemoth had taste.

The troll exhaled smoke through his nose and rumbled, his voice so deep it rattled Ryan's ribs. "You coming or going, dude?"

The creature spoke with a casual and welcoming nonchalance. Though incredibly deep, it was oddly soothing to Ryan's ears. How was Ryan feeling so at home in Hell?

"Coming," Ryan answered.

The creature unfurled his arms in a top down sequential symphony and opened the familiar red door for Ryan. "Ol' Smokey has got some good drinks on deck tonight," the creature crowed, his yellow eyes glowing even brighter. "I'd suggest starting with a 'Flaming Adulterer.' That one is a personal favorite of mine."

"Sounds tasty. Thanks."

Ryan squeezed past the bouncer, entering the same red door he had a hundred times before.

For a moment, just a fleeting second, it felt real. The warm, familiar scent of stale beer and old wood wrapped around him like a vintage hoody, frayed at the edges but with a softness that only comes from wearing it day in and day out. The layout was exactly as it should be: a classic wood bar stretching long on the left, booths lining the right, jukebox humming softly in the corner, it's light pulsing ever so faintly and welcoming. His feet glided across the same scuffed floor, the neon glow from the beer signs casting familiar, lazy shadows against the walls.

And yet, something was off.

At first, it was just a feeling, like walking into a dream of a place you once knew. Then the details began to shift. The jukebox flickered, skipping between a Pearl Jam track and an eery, monk-like humming. The neon signs buzzed weakly, but the brands they advertised, "Loki's Tears" and "Dante's Imperial", weren't from any distributor Ryan had ever heard of. The dartboard in the back? The darts whispered bets to each other, moving just slightly on their own.

He exhaled, forcing himself to stay steady. This was Milly's but not his Milly's.

The demon behind the bar was tall, rail-thin, with four arms and two lazy eyes that drifted in separate directions. He was wiping a glass that never seemed to get clean, looking like he'd been there since the dawn of time. His faded name tag that read "Smokey" barely clung to his worn leather vest.

"What'll it be, kid?" He rasped, his lower set of hands already pouring a drink before Ryan could answer.

Ryan barely heard him. His focus had shifted to the booth along the back wall. Their booth. In the real Milly's, that was where he and his dad always sat. The corner booth below the Shiner Bock sign that would flicker anytime someone would flush the toilet. The worn red vinyl, softened by the asses of numerous patrons, with sporadic duct tape covering holes before they got too large.

For a second, he expected to see him sitting there.

Instead, a group of what appeared to be derelict archangels crowded the seats, laughing too loud and drinking too much. One of them turned toward Ryan, his strangely enchanting ice blue eyes flickering with something unreadable before giving Ryan a wink and returning to his friends. Ryan exhaled and his stomach twisted. Someone had tried to build this place. It had been pieced together from memory, from longing, from the idea of home. More than ever, he was convinced this was Hell playing a game with him. An illusion meant to fuck with a mortal.

He gripped the edge of the bar, staring past the bartender at the wall behind him. Behind the bar stretched a wall that was part shrine and part chaos. Rows of warped, mismatched shelves groaned under the weight of Hell's finest and most dangerous liquors. Some bottles were clearly alive, dancing and swaying inside their glass prisons, their contents glowing faintly. One was corked with a tiny, screaming skull, while another pulsed like a beating heart every few seconds. Above the shelves loomed a massive mural made up of a crude collage of poorly lit polaroids.

They were Milly's 2 regulars, scantily clad demons, ghouls, and shapeshifters frozen in poses of exaggerated seduction, their limbs too long or twisted, eyes glowing or missing altogether, each of them bearing names scrawled in curling infernal script on the lower white mask of the polaroid.

Some blew kisses. Some bared claws. One winked with all five of her six eyes though she may have just been blinking from the flash. The whole display was vulgar, loud, and incredibly enchanting.

Just beneath the mural, tucked between a bottle of what looked like boiling syrup and a stack of stained coasters, he saw it. A small, crooked piece of cardboard. "MILLY'S 2" handwritten in faded black marker. No lighting or frame. Just a scrap of stained cardboard not trying to impress anyone. Like someone had put it up not to advertise, but to remind themselves of what this place was supposed to be or what they wanted it to be.

Ryan stared at it for a long time, that cracked, crooked sign holding more weight than all the bottles and demons on the wall combined. This place was loud. Crude. Hellish. But that sign was quiet and honest. An anchor point that made him think this wasn't some hellish prank but perhaps a precursor of things to come.

Milly's 2.

This wasn't home but the small, unassuming sign made him feel like it was. It was familiar even though he had never seen it before. The knot in his stomach finally loosened. As his shoulders dropped, the gangly bartender placed a bubbling, neon green liquid with overflowing head in front of him.

"A 'Green Eyed Monster' courtesy of those three little shits down at the end of the bar."

Ryan looked up from the bubbling green elixir in front of him, its fumes curling into faint whispers that seemed to penetrate his eardrums. At the far end of the bar, three demons were waving at him like long-lost friends. They were short, maybe four feet tall if you counted their stubby horns, and covered in what appeared to be sharply angled snakeskin, their crimson scales shimmering subtly in the low, flickering light. All three wore oversized letterman jackets with purple sleeves and charcoal grey shells.

The one in the middle, clearly the ringleader, was puffing lazily on a crooked cigarette, exhaling thick, glowing red smoke that didn't rise but fell, drifting downward like liquid silk, landing on the bar top with a soft thud before curling into the shape of a snarling dog and evaporating. The smallest one, who barely seemed to reach the bar top despite being on a stool, blew him a double-handed kiss, and then proceeded to slam the complimentary bar snacks into his mouth. The tallest one flashed him a toothy grin that had way too many teeth. Together, the three were hideous but charming.

Ryan picked up the surprisingly heavy drink, ignoring the whispers emanating from it, and raised it to the three demons in gratitude. As he brought the drink to his lips, the air around him seemed to get heavier and the whispers louder. The fragrant smell of mint and chocolate overtook his senses as he dived through the thick, foamy head and gulped.

It was sweet and heavy, coating his tongue with flavor that he couldn't swallow at first. As the liquid ran down his throat, it gripped his esophagus and seemed to detour to his brain, the whispers becoming louder, occupying every blank spot in his mind.

"If they were really your friends, why would they leave you?"

"You're a good person. Why are good things happening to them and not you?

The voices in his head echoed with a snake-like reverb,

bouncing throughout the corners of his brain. They were feminine but with the heft and bass of someone who had smoked a pack a day for thirty years.

"New cities, new friends, new futures... and you? You'll still be here. In the same town. Same street. Same small life. All alone."

Ryan's body suddenly grew cold as his vision tunneled, a greenish haze collapsing around him like a grave being filled.

"Kally's going to thrive out there. She'll win awards. Talk on panels. Forget all about this place. About you."

"Maya? She's gonna become someone. Loud, messy, glorious. You'll just be a footnote in her early chapters. That loser she gave a ride home to once."

"Even Eddie's leaving. And he doesn't even know what he wants. But at least he gets to try. At least he gets to leave. You built him up and now he's leaving you behind."

"You smiled. You supported them. You told them you were happy. But you weren't. You wanted it too. And you didn't get it."

The voices kept repeating, stepping over each other as Ryan's body grew colder and colder. The green dissipated into a onset of white hot rage.

"I don't deserve this. I deserve happiness."

Ryan heard his own voice in head, louder and more aggressive than he had ever spoken before. His throat burned. Not from the alcohol but from the truth of what was just unloaded in his mind. The cold began to become unbearable, the world around him disappearing back into a neon green haze and then he felt warmth. Subtle at first, curling around his forearm like a constrictor before settling softly around his hand, cutting through the cold. He felt it around his shoulders, as if he was being hugged from behind. His shoulders dropped as the warmth hugged his body all over. His head felt cradled and he could swear he felt fingers gently grazing his hair. The voices slowly quieted and the air warmed before he felt complete nothingness. As he exhaled, he opened his eyes and, for a moment, thought he saw ghostly apparitions of human figures uncoiling themselves from their embrace and slowly drifting back to the heavens.

The collapsing tunnel was gone and Ryan was back in Milly's 2, his drink completely empty.

"Holy shit, dude. I've never seen a human completely finish a Green Eyed Monster. I can see why you're a VIP," the bartender said, breaking the silence.

Ryan looked down at the empty glass and back at the bartender who was still wiping out an empty glass, his two lazy eyes finally focusing.

"You humans usually crash out when you confront your own jealousy. Good on you for powering through that one. Want another?"

Ryan shook his head furiously and looked over at the three demons, all of them clearly impressed at the feat achieved by the unassuming human. They adjusted their jackets in near unison before slowly slithered over to him, red smoke trailing them along the ground like a puppy. Their lower bodies resembled a cobra with a thick base that allowed them to glide elegantly across the dirty bar floor. For demons of Hell, the large anime eyes that rested in the middle of their faces above small button noses almost made them adorable.

Ryan looked down at the three snake demons and rested his gaze on the smoking one who stood front and center.

"Well," the lead demon said with a gravely draw. "That was pretty fucking impressive. You took that one like a champ."

"What was that?"

"A Green-Eyed Monster," the tallest chimed in. "If you got any jealousy in ya, that sucker will pop that shit out of you toot sweet."

"You were tranced out for a little there," the leader

added. "Hear some stuff you weren't expecting?"

"Not unexpected," Ryan answered. "I just didn't think I was allowed to think those things. And actually, now that I've heard them out loud, I feel better."

"So to be straight with you, we were kinda just fucking with you," the smoking one admitted. "We saw the VIP thing on your neck there and got a little jealous."

Ryan looked down at the badge, it's faint pulsating glow illuminating his torso in golden light ever so slightly. "It's cool. I understand that."

"So what are you doing at Milly's? With that badge, you can go anywhere," the tall one said.

"Well, I was looking through my map here and I noticed this place when I was walking by. It reminded me of somewhere I used to visit back home so I came in. I'm actually a little lost on where to go next."

"We can help you find where you're going," the smallest and cutest demon piped up. "We've been here for a while. We know this area like the back of our tails."

"I was told to start my night off at Old Tito's."

The three demons looked at each other, their eyes turning solemn.

"What? Did I get the name wrong or something?"

The lead demon looked up at Ryan, his already glassy eyes looking even more damp. "We're Tier 9 demons so we aren't allowed to go to the bars on the lower levels, especially not a Tier 1 bar. Last time we went, some of the Tier 1's threw us into the flaming river."

"That's some shit," Ryan said. "You guys can't go to certain bars?"

"Yeah," the demon continued. "We're supposed to stay out of sight, especially when the bar games are going on."

"Why is that?"

"They said we aren't wretched enough. That we kill the aesthetic."

"What? You guys are pretty wretched to me. I mean, the smell alone is revolting. Especially you," Ryan said, motioning to the smallest one.

The smallest demon looked up, smiling wide to reveal rotted, greenish yellow fangs.

"See," Ryan said, gagging. "I literally want to throw up right now."

"I've wanted to go to the bar games ever since I was spawned," the smallest said. "I heard that each bar on the lower levels have a speciality cocktail. They even say that there's one that's so strong you can see all of your past lives!"

Ryan looked down at the three demons and then back to his VIP lanyard. "Well, as you can see from this pass, I'm a VIP and where I'm from that means you can do whatever you want and act like an entitled asshole. I imagine that counts triple here in Hell so how about the three of you tag along with me. No one will mess with you if I'm around and honestly, I could use your help getting around. I'm a bit lost."

The three demons looked at each other, eyes widening, and began bouncing up and down on their tails.

"You'd want to hang out with us," the largest one asked.

"I sure do," Ryan said, sincerely. "The jackets alone are pretty badass."

"Yeah," the lead demon exclaimed. "We bought these on our last roadtrip together. We spent a week at the beach of eternal suffering. There was a blood algae bloom so we didn't get to swim but we made the most of it."

"Sounds like me and my friends," Ryan chimed back. "The best times seemed to be when things didn't go as planned. We once drove 4 hours to see a concert only for it be cancelled when we got there but we caught this awesome blues musician up the road and it was totally worth it. I'm Ryan, by the way. From Earth. Or the human world. Or whatever you call it down here."

"I'm Vex," the leader said. "The tall fella here is Skid and the little guy is Blink. Don't let his size fool you. He is a tough little bastard."

"I wouldn't ever judge someone by their size," Ryan said, shaking all of the demon's hands. "Cool to meet you three."

"I can't believe I get to leave Tier 9," Blink exclaimed. "Holy shit!"

"I can't believe this is Tier 9," Ryan said. "What the hell is Tier 1 going to be like?"

"Even we don't know," Blink exclaimed. "We've only ever seen the gate!"

"And the flaming river," Vex added.

Ryan opened up the map app on his phone and typed in "Old Tito's."

"Hold onto your tails, boys," Ryan said, the three demons placing their hands on him. "Here we go."

Chapter 7

"What the hell you think happened here?"

The two police officers stood in perfect sync, hands on hips, surveying the empty parking lot of Robert E. Lee high school. As they walked in opposite directions, a light drizzle had begun, causing the still hot payment to sizzle and expel spouts of steam everywhere the water struck it. A haze of acrid smoke floated just above ground level, not dissipating and seemed to be stuck in time. The younger officer, Bentley, slowly strode to the beat up sedan parked in the lot. Hands still on hips, he walked around the back to see the trunk wide open, cooler open and empty beer cans strewn about. Flicking water off of his buzzed, flattop hair, he reached into the cooler finding Westerly cans and mostly melted ice.

"Looks like someone was doing some partying, sir," Bentley yelled, cracking open one of the few remaining full cans.

The older officer, Henderson, was crouched about 30 yards away near the dark circular burn mark that was still sizzling. He squinted his eyes making his already cavernous crows feet sink even deeper. The unseasonably cold summer night couldn't penetrate the shell surrounding the parking lot. Within its bubble, the air was thick and hot, pressing down on anything in its vicinity. Henderson wiped his brow, slicking down his salt and pepper hair against his temples.

"Looks like some sort of Devil worship or something," Henderson replied with a loud groan, clutching his knee and straining as he stood.

He walked towards his young partner, attempting to hide the pain in his knee that only grew deeper and more intense with each step.

"Should I run this plate, sir," Bentley asked.

"That won't be necessary," a voice boomed, shaking the atmosphere around them.

As if by instinct, Henderson and Bentley drew their guns and turned to face the voice. As they raised their weapons, the guns violently flew from their hands and jerked their bodies to ground with a heavy thud. Bentley, face bloodied and wet from the asphalt, looked up to see the backlit silhouette of the Devil in full demon form standing mere yards from him.

The warm yellow lamps that illuminated the parking lot gave the lazy haze a toxic and sinister feel. The Devil, both guns in a single hand, slowly strode towards to the two fallen officers, the haze parting for him as he walked. With a raise of his muscular forearm and a theatrical flourish, he crushed the two pistols into a single mass of metal with his hand and mockingly tossed it directly in front of the officers. The clanking echo of the metal reverberated throughout the empty parking lot before allowing it to settle into an unnerving silence.

Henderson pulled himself up and attempted to steady himself on his one good knee. He glanced the mangled mass of gun in front of him and quickly reached for the radio clipped to his uniform. Before he could press the call button, the handset of the radio shattered into itself, cutting his hands as shards of plastic rained down onto the ground. Bentley, visibly shaking at the events happening before him, powered on his flashlight and shone it at the creature standing before him. The beam of light shook wildly as he attempted to steel his nerves and track the thing walking towards them. The Devil entered the light and glared down at the two officers, his face stoic and hardened as the now drizzling rain flowed off his horns and down his angular features. As he studied them, he felt a cold rush of liquid beneath his feet. It was then that he noticed the fallen can of Westerly's Own spilling its contents onto the dark asphalt.

"I can forgive you for pulling your pitiful weapons on me but to waste such a fine spirit. I should rip out your spines and penetrate you with them for that."

"Fuck, dude," Maya exclaimed, stepping out from behind the Devil's large, imposing frame. "It's like 4 bucks for a six-pack. We can get more."

"Young lady," Henderson yelled, powering himself up to one knee. "Step away from the creature and get behind me."

"Hard pass," Maya replied, pulling a joint from her coat pocket.

As Maya attempted to light her joint, Eddie and Kally emerged and revealed themselves to the officers.

"Sir," Bentley said as he stood. "I'm going to have to ask you to put your hands on your head and let the youths come over to us. We won't ask again."

The Devil glared at the brash young officer, his face hardening even more. As he squinted his eyes, they began to glow a vibrant red. He reached out his long fingers and slowly ran them down the officer's face, the large yellow talons leaving faint red marks along Bentley's puffy cheekbones. The large hand ventured lower and seductively rubbed the officers chest before resting upon his badge.

"And what exactly are you without this," the Devil sneered.

"Please, I have a wife at home," Bentley pleaded between labored breaths. The sentence made the Devil abandon his steely gaze and settle into a genuine smile.

"The same wife you regularly cheat on with Meredith in dispatch," the Devil laughed.

Bentley's eyes grew wide as the Devil showed his toothy smile.

"You know," the Devil began. "The lie that you're constantly playing basketball with the boys is getting less believable the fatter you get. Your wife may not be a detective but she isn't an idiot. You'd think with all of your extracurricular activities that you might burn off a few calories. Perhaps you should consider getting on top every once in a while."

Henderson looked up at his young partner. "You're cheating on Lindsay? With Meredith?"

The Devil turned and looked at the elder officer. "Oh

yes, Sergeant Henderson. Your baby girl is indeed the other woman. But don't you worry. Officer Bentley here promises to leave his wife once everything stops being so crazy, isn't that right, Officer?"

Bentley's posture slumped as he felt his sergeant's gaze fall upon him. His mouth was agape, searching for any words to escape them. As he came to the realization that a new reality was upon him, he felt their eyes. He turned his head to see the three teenagers staring in judgment at him.

"Damn, dude," Maya said while taking a big drag. "You're a real piece of shit."

"Real piece of shit," Kally concurred. Eddie simply shook his head in disapproval.

The Devil turned to Henderson. "Some partner you have there. Or future son-in-law, perhaps? Maybe when things get less crazy."

The rain gradually began to pick up, striking the still hot pavement furiously and filling in the silence between the six beings. The Devil turned back to Sergeant Henderson and glanced down at the elder officer struggling to maintain his balance and composure on his one good knee. Henderson looked up at the dark lord staring down at him.

"Take me if you have to," he said. "Just let the kids go."

The Devil tilted his head, studying the old man who seemed to get older and more defeated the more drenched he became. The Devil reached out his mammoth hand and offered it. Henderson looked up with skepticism and terror in his eyes. Looking once more at Bentley, he put his hand in the large creature's mitt and, with ease, was helped to his feet. Even standing, the Devil towered over him.

"Run along and forget everything you saw tonight," the Devil boomed. "My acquaintances and I are out for an evening of fun and I take it we can rest assured that no matter what we do, no local authorities will interfere."

"You're not going to harm anyone, are you?"

"I could have killed you a thousand times so far and not had a second thought about it. Killing or harming doesn't amuse me, despite what you might think you know. It's so much more fun to make you all live with the things you have done. Take your charming partner over there."

Bentley could only look down at the rain striking the asphalt as the words poured from the Devil's mouth.

"I know for a fact that he isn't the most civil when dealing with the public especially those that are any shade darker than eggshell white. Add in the adultery and you have quite the blue chip sinner over there. Again, I don't judge him for that. Monogamy is silly and all of us in the afterlife still laugh at the fact that you humans willingly chose that as some virtuous endeavor. You were given unlimited freedom but you took it, stifled it, and then began rebelling against the very system you created. I can't blame that paunchy little man for getting some but he also can't just get away with whatever he wants at the expense of others. His discomfort is giving me so much pleasure right now, you have no idea."

"We all have an idea, man. You have a full-on erection right now," Eddie chimed in.

"Isn't it magnificent," the Devil beamed. "The thought of his lies crashing down around him, I am at full brew right now. We may have to drive with the sunroof open."

Kally anxiously watched on as the Devil toyed with the two officers. "Yo Big Red, can we get a move on? Our friend's soul is on the line."

The Devil turned with a snap and glared at her. Maya clocked the look as the same one her mom would give her when she acted up at the grocery store as a child. She grabbed Kally by the crook of her elbow, just like her mom would, and pulled her away from the encounter.

"What the fuck, Kal," she whispered. "He's actually enjoying this and you're just gonna buzzkill him? If the goal is for him to have fun then why the fuck are you trying to stop it?"

"We have a list," Kally whispered back.

"I know that you get a dripping wide-on for order but we're dealing with the goddamn Devil here. I don't think logic or order have any place here. This is pure fucking chaos and like the drunks, we just need to go limp."

Kally glared at Maya, annoyed that she was right. "Fine."

Kally turned back to the Devil. "Take as long as you need. As long as you're having fun."

The Devil glared back at the two officers. His stoic demeanor held for a moment before his face softened and his posture slumped. "Ugh," he scoffed like a petulant teen. "You ruined it. Let's just fucking get going."

Maya glared at Kally, shooting daggers into her. Kally could only bite her lip as Eddie stared nervously between the two of them.

The Devil turned back to Henderson and with a dash of smoke, reverted back to his handsome human form. "You guys can go."

"What? Are you serious," Bentley asked.

"Yeah, the fun is all gone," the Devil replied with a dismissive wave. "I wanted to make you squirm more but the moment has passed. This chick is as big a buzzkill as Asmodeus."

Bentley, the watered-down blood dripping from his face, turned to see Henderson glaring at him. That look frightened him more than the actual Devil ever did.

The Devil took the joint from Maya and then walked between the officers towards the car. A few feet past them he stopped, as if he had just remembered something. He looked back over his shoulder and caught eyes with Henderson. The sergeant, slightly less intimidated by the Devil in his human form, met his gaze. The Devil walked back to him and gently grabbed the collar of his uniform. He slowly unbuttoned the top button and pulled out a weathered gold crucifix.

"I knew it," the Devil smiled.

Henderson's demeanor buckled for a moment before he steeled himself, never breaking eye contact.

"This is the spiritual horse you're gonna bet on," the Devil asked.

Henderson could only nod his head.

The Devil released the crucifix from his grip and placed it back in the sergeant's uniform. He buttoned the uniform back up and tenderly kissed Henderson on the forehead. "Good luck with that."

The Devil smirked and held his hand out to the side and opened his palm wide towards the heavens. It slowly began glowing, throwing red light throughout the parking lot. Sergeant Henderson turned his head to avoid the light and suddenly felt a deep heat permeating from his damaged knee. With a loud crackle, the red light flashed and was then gone, replaced by the familiar warmth of the parking lot light fixtures. The Devil slowly removed his open palm from Henderson's knee, never breaking eye contact with the soaked sergeant.

"Remember who helped you out," he said with a smirk.

Henderson's eyes widened as he realized he was standing evenly on both legs for first time in over a decade. He bounced up and down a bit, the pain in his knee completely gone. As he took the deepest bend he had taken in years, he looked at the Devil with bewildered confusion.

"Why," he stammered.

The Devil gave a crooked grin and leaned close, his voice a whisper meant to linger for the rest of Henderson's days.

"Because somewhere in the back of your mind, you'll always remember who actually answered your prayers."

Henderson's eyes went wide as his gaze locked with the absurdly handsome creature once more before turning away and walking back to his cruiser.

"Let's go, James."

Bentley, his posture still slumped, looked at the Devil and three teenagers staring at him in extreme judgment.

"Fuck! He used your first name," Maya snarked as she gave a sarcastic wave.

The rain began to steady, falling in faster sheets to the ground. As it plummeted from the sky, it hissed into vapor just inches above the Devil and the three teens, creating a low halo of steam that made the parking lot shimmer like a fever dream.

"Why'd we come back here?" Eddie asked.

"I like souvenirs," the Devil replied with a shrug. "Consider your friend's car an elaborate locker."

He walked up to Ryan's maroon 2010 Toyota Corolla and clicked his tongue in disappointment.

"This is your ride?" he asked, circling it like a judge at a dog show. "This thing's seen more heartbreak than an open mic night."

"I like that car," Maya said quietly. "It's Ryan."

"Exactly," the Devil said, smiling without warmth. "Reliable. Beat-up. Still running despite outward appearances."

He cracked his neck and grabbed the beer Ryan had abandoned on the roof of the car before his disappearance. Smoke curled from his fingertips, his ornate rings glowing. With an exaggerated sigh, he held his palms up and blew a long breath across the roof. The air shimmered, like light bending on asphalt. A breeze swept through the parking lot, and the air flickered like film overheating in a projector.

When the mist cleared, Ryan's Corolla stood exactly where it had been only it wasn't the same. The dents were gone. The paint had returned to a deep, glistening garnet. The windshield was clear, the headlights bright, the tires full and sharp-edged. The faint smell of fast food and high school stress had been replaced by something cleaner. Like sandalwood on an ocean breeze. It was still the Corolla, but it looked like it had never had a bad day.

"That's it?" Kally asked, brows raised. "After that whole production?"

"That's everything," the Devil replied. "You lot think a glow-up means reinvention. Sometimes, it just means restoration. I'd think a girl who hates film remakes would understand that concept."

Kally's face softened as the Devil leaned on the hood, admiring his handiwork.

"You humans always think transformation means becoming something else. Sometimes it just means remembering who you were before the world got its claws into you."

He looked toward the horizon, eyes dancing with flame. "You call it sentimentality. I call it mercy."

"Is that why you healed that cop," Eddie asked.

"Disrupting the archaic belief system of someone who hypocritically works for a systemically broken and racist system? How could I not enjoy that. I essentially destroyed 59 years of his life with one moment."

"By doing something nice?"

"Exactly. Everyone expects me to be evil so why give everyone what they expect. You're a homosexual. How come you aren't dancing to Elton John right now? I know your parents think you do that in your bedroom."

Eddie glared and then his eyes widened, entirely confused by the fact that it all made perfect sense to him.

"Fucking with the devout is one of the greatest joys I experience," the Devil proclaimed. "But going to some old fucking movie theater seems to be the priority so let's do that instead."

Kally looked at the Devil with wide eyes, her hand

clenching the list tightly.

"I'm the Devil. I know what's on the fucking list."

Chapter 8

"You're good. The three little scabs with you have to wait outside."

The bouncer of Old Titos stood only 5 feet tall and was essentially one giant neck. His tiny pointed head with three beady off-center eyes and comically small mouth flared out to a wide neck and body that resembled a pile of lumpy garbage bags stuffed into a tight v-neck shirt. He was a mountain covered in boils with appendage proportions that made it seem like he was cobbled together from a bargain bin of leftover parts. Upon making eye contact, or attempting to, Ryan realized that its eyes all acted independent of each other.

"These scabs are my friends," Ryan said, his eye contact darting between the three eyes. "They're coming in with me."

"Tier 9 demons aren't even supposed to be on this level.

What makes you think they can get into Old Tito's?"

"This badge says they can."

"The VIP badge is for you. Not them."

"I think you're missing the fine print here," Ryan said, holding the badge inches from his face.

As Ryan shoved the badge closer, the bouncer's eyes began to dart around wildly.

"I can't read that shit," the bouncer exclaimed.

Vex looked over at Blink and Skid and nodded his head. The three slithered around to each side of the bouncer and climbed atop his head, each one grabbing an eye and holding it forward towards the VIP pass. As the eyes went into sync and focused, the bouncer's tough guy demeanor broke.

"So sorry, sir," The bouncer exclaimed, his voice raising about three octaves. "I didn't know you were his dark lord's special guest. I've never seen a pass like that."

"I'm guessing you don't see much with those googly eyes, do you chief," Vex said, laughing.

"Be nice, man," Ryan said, pulling the pass away from the bouncer. "He's just doing his job."

The bouncer sighed and seemed to sink even shorter.

"Wouldn't kill you to be a little nicer to some of these 'lesser' demons, would it," Ryan continued.

"No sir, it wouldn't."

The bouncer's three eyes began to water.

Ryan pulled the bouncer away from the line of waiting patrons and dried his eyes with the bottom of his t-shirt. "It's cool, man. The dark lord won't ever hear about this, alright?"

"Thank you, sir," the bouncer whispered back.

"I think your eyes are pretty cool, actually. You really are a scary dude. If I didn't have this pass, I'd totally avoid you on the street."

"You would?"

"100%. The tiny head and no neck thing is fucked up in the best way. The little shirt just makes it so much worse."

The bouncer wiped his nose on his tiny shirt and turned back to the door, pulling the velvet rope off its chain.

"Enjoy your evening at Old Tito's. The first round of bar games will be starting within the hour."

Ryan patted the bouncer on the back and held his arm out to let Vex, Skid, and Blink enter before him.

Entering Old Tito's, the group was swallowed whole by darkness as the main entrance sealed shut behind them. The sound muffled instantly as if they had stepped into a hermetically-sealed void. The silence felt intentional and judgmental as if the building itself was assessing them. Ryan immediately flashed back to the rush of tunnel vision the Green-Eyed Monster cocktail had given him only a few moments earlier. They moved forward hesitantly, the corridor tight and claustrophobic, forcing them to walk two by two. The air was dense and heavy with an imposing smell of charred vanilla and aged absinthe. Ryan reached out to steady himself against the wall and was surprised to find it wasn't cold stone or brick but warm and velvety-smooth obsidian, pulsing faintly with soft light as his fingertips grazed it.

"Just keep your hands on me," Vex murmured. "We got killer dark vision. We'll guide you."

They pressed on for what felt like longer than they should have. Old Tito's wasn't just a bar you walked into to. You had to endure.

Then, the lights came alive.

Thin, rectangular lucite panels along the walls flickered on in a slow, hypnotic cascade, illuminating the corridor in a shifting prism of color. Behind the frosted panels, silhouettes of bar patrons materialized. Some laughing, some dancing, some lost in rituals Ryan wasn't entirely sure were legal in any realm. The colors warped their outlines, making their movements seem distorted and ethereal, as if he was glimpsing into a completely different dimension. He grinned at the absurdity of it all, his face flashing blue, then violet, then crimson as the corridor's glow shifted around him.

"I never thought I'd see the inside of this place," Blink whispered, his wide eyes reflecting the shifting neon spectrum.

"We still haven't," Skid corrected.

At that moment, they stepped through the final archway and were swallowed by light and sound. The corridor gave way to a cathedral of pure, unhinged excess.

Old Tito's wasn't just a club. It was a kingdom. A cathedral to decadence named after a demon whose exploits had been lost to time and embellished to whatever narrative you needed it to be.

The six-story interior stretched impossibly high, layers of balconies and terraces stacked upon one another like a jenga spiral of indulgence, each level hosting its own ecosystem of decadence. Spotlights swept across the cavernous space, illuminating the madness in bursts. Cage dancers twirled mid-air, their wings casting monstrous shadows against the ceiling; gargantuan chandeliers made of rib bones and flickering hellfire, dripped molten light onto the floor below that was quickly crafted into cocktails; bartenders flipped bottles with inhuman precision and speed, pouring glowing liquors that sizzled the moment they hit glass.

Above them, swarms of demons and spectral patrons floated effortlessly between levels, a choreographed ballet of depravity and indulgence. Below, the floor pulsed like a breathing entity, shifting between amethyst glass and cracked marble, reacting to the various dances happening atop them. The house music pulsed with a rhythmic penetrating perfection and seemed to fall upon Ryan's ears at the perfect volume.

His mouth fell open. He didn't know what he'd expected from a place in literal Hell called Old Tito's but it sure as fuck wasn't this.

On the far side of the room, a nine-foot-tall lilac demon, wearing only leather chaps and dripping in blood, gripped an entire keg with one hand. She tore off the tap with her teeth, shotgunned the entire thing in under ten seconds, then crushed the empty keg against her own skull like it was a cheap aluminum can. The crowd erupted in cheers. Ryan felt a pang of disappointment knowing that nothing on Earth would ever top this which quickly gave way to the stark reality that if his friends failed, that wouldn't really be an issue.

As his gaze traveled downward, he spotted a sunken pit to his left, a swirling haze of iridescent mist hovering just above it, shifting colors like a heat mirage and seemingly extending to infinity.

Inside the pit, a pile of sweaty demons, humans, and creatures of every shape and size lounged against one another in lazy bliss, draped across cushions so lavish they looked stolen from Heaven itself. Their half-lidded eyes followed the swirling smoke drifting above them, completely enraptured. They clutched hookahs, bongs, and glass pipes of every variety, each one belching out smoke in unnatural colors, some shaped like twisting figures, others curling into delicate, floating symbols that entwined each other and evaporated as soon as they escaped the pit.

Outside the sunken lounge, a long gilded table with clawed feet wrapped around, stacked with crystal trays of shimmering powders and vials of unknown liquid. Tiny winged creatures with kitten faces would scurry across the tabletop, taking the powders and liquids in their tiny paws and crafting them into cocktail experiences for those indulging in the excesses of the pit.

"You ever done a shot that makes you relive your past mistakes?" Blink asked, his wide eyes darting toward a bottle that swirled with a dull, regretful blue.

"Not in public," Skid muttered.

To the right, an enormous serpentine demon with six arms was dealing a high-stakes card game, his scales reflecting the club's neon lights like liquid metal. The players ranged from slick-suited demons to tattered ghosts, their expressions ranging from manic confidence to pure despair as they placed bets that were most certainly not just money. The players revealed their hands and in a flash, the dealer unsheathed a flaming purple blade and decapitated the demon sitting directly in front of him causing the entire table to erupt in cheer.

Everywhere Ryan looked, there was something to lose yourself in. Old Tito's was Hell's great equalizer. It didn't matter if you were a prince of the underworld or a fresh soul who barely knew how they got there. If you could find your way inside, you were worth something.

"Holy shit," Ryan mouthed.

At that moment, Skid took off from the group and dove into the sunken pit, completely disappearing into a large pile of fine, lilac-colored powder.

"I'm gonna take a lap," Blink exclaimed, slithering off. "I heard there's a buffet on the third level that has any food you can imagine! I wanna get down with that."

"It's nice for the boys to cut loose," Vex said, putting his hands in his pocket. "They needed this."

"You're cool to go explore, too, Vex. I know this is something you guys have always wanted to do so don't feel like you need to babysit me."

"Let's have a drink first. I still feel kinda bad for what we did to you at Milly's."

"You're a demon in Hell. Are you supposed to feel bad?"

"Guess I'm not a very good demon, eh?"

As they ventured further inside, Ryan and Vex found themselves standing on a winding obsidian pathway that snaked and forked in several directions, each leading deeper into the bar's many levels. Hovering above the path, suspended in mid-air, were sleek, curved monitors displaying a pulsing red map of the club's various entry points, some marked in familiar symbols, others in sigils that seemed to shift and reform the longer Ryan stared at them. Each screen flickered with messages in an unsettlingly polite tone:

WELCOME TO OLD TITO'S.

THE LAST BAR YOU'LL EVER VISIT.
YOU ROLL IT. YOU SMOKE IT.

What caught Ryan's eye was the moat that kissed the sides of the pathway.

Encircling the main pathway was a churning river of thick, viscous blood, its surface rippling with an unnatural heartbeat-like pulse. The viscous liquid bubbled and frothed, as if something beneath was constantly stirring and agitating it.

And then something leaped.

A flash of serrated bone-white teeth shot up from the surface, arching through the air before landing back into the blood with a sickening, heavy splash. More followed, feisty skeletal fish, all sharp ridges and hollow sockets, launched themselves high above the moat, twisting mid-air like they were reveling in the chaos and showing off to the drunken onlookers. They snapped at each other playfully, rattling and clattering like a xylophone of doom. One particularly large bonefish locked eyes with Ryan mid-jump, its hollow sockets briefly flickering with a blue infernal flame before it plunged back into the depths.

Beyond the moat, tall, jagged onyx torches lined the edges, burning with erratic bluish black flames that danced with the beat of the music, their heatless glow casting warped shadows across the shimmering path. Ryan exhaled slowly, trying to take it all in.

"This is surprisingly well-designed for a bar in hell," Ryan exclaimed, taking in all the navigation signage and branding.

"Lots of city planners and graphic designers down here. Those guys are some sick fucks."

"That explains it."

Ryan walked up to the large touch screen display showing the map of Old Tito's. They were on the primary level which allowed all Tier 1 demons and hell personnel. The main level was something to behold but the uppermost level was solely for Gold and Platinum level VIPs.

"What say we use this pass for all it's worth," Ryan said, tapping the 6th level on the map.

"Don't threaten me with a good time," Vex replied, pulling out a jet black cigarette.

As Ryan and Vex walked to end of the winding path and approached the far end of the mezzanine, the crowd noise thinned, replaced by a subtle humming purr of luxury engines waiting to be unleashed. Ahead of them stood a gleaming bank of golden elevators, each framed in glossy marble carvings of the Devil and trimmed in molten-looking metal that pulsed faintly with its own internal glow.

There were seven elevators, identical in shape but each one radiating a slightly different aura. One shimmered like champagne bubbles, another flickered with a chaotic surge of red light. One seemed to contain cascading water within its doors. In front of each elevator stood a perfectly symmetrical human attendant, impossibly attractive and impossibly still. Some looked like they had been sculpted out of polished marble, others radiated warmth and charisma like a celebrity caught in perfect lighting. They wore tailored crimson suits with gold trim, eyes glowing faintly like embers beneath the surface, with a soft smile as their finishing touch. As Ryan passed them, each attendant made precise eye contact, nodding just slightly, as if recognizing something in him he didn't know he carried.

"Are these humans?" he whispered.

"Once upon a time," Vex replied, barely glancing at them. "Just souls now. Top-tier. The worst of the worst. See that guy with the blonde hair tied into a man-bun?"

"Yeah."

"Crypto-scamming alt-right podcaster."

"That's the worst of the worst?"

"Down here it is."

"I figured you'd say he was a murderer or a rapist or something."

"No, man. You won't find those fuckers down here."

"Really?"

"Oh shit, I forgot you're from Earth and you guys have that weird book that describes Hell in such a dumb way. Yeah, no. Those fuckers have their souls incinerated upon death. The big dude upstairs doesn't want to admit he fucked up making them and the Dark Lord doesn't want those dudes down here fucking shit up. Plus the murderers always fanboy for him HARD and that really annoys him."

"Don't forget people who are cruel to animals or children," The attendant closest chimed in, voice seductively deep and posture still in perfection.

"Oh yeah," Vex recalled. "If you're mean to animals or kids, you're fucked down here. Instant soul eradication if you're lucky. If you're not, let's just say that fire and brimstone is a luxury spa compared to what's coming your way."

Ryan looked back at the attendant who gave a soft nod of his head.

"And these guys are being punished by working the

elevators," Ryan asked.

"It's kind of like work release. Pleasure taken at the expense of others isn't taken lightly. They aren't as bad as murderers or people who hurt kids but they still need to pay for their debts. They still get to party but they gotta work it off."

Ryan, utterly baffled at what Hell actually was, could only silently agree with how things worked.

Above each elevator, a scrolling marquee displayed only two words in elegant, silver script:

"PLATINUM ACCESS."

The doors of the center elevator, which was lined with jagged emeralds, slid open without a sound, and a soft, velvety voice welcomed them inside: "Mr. Ryan Phillips of Earth, your presence has been anticipated. Please watch your step."

Ryan and Vex looked at each other.

"And who the fuck are you exactly," Vex asked, a mix of confusion and wonder in his voice.

Ryan shrugged at Vex and walked towards the elevator, the attendant giving them a courteous bow as they entered. First Milly's and then a custom greeting. It was all feeling very weird even within the context of being a living human in Hell.

The elevator doors slid shut behind them with a soft hiss, sealing Ryan and Vex into an echo chamber of mirrored emerald and velvet, completely isolating them from sound. As the elevator gently slid into motion, music began to fade up. The music was a faint, slow, warbling lo-fi waltz that sounded like it was being played underwater and instantly made Ryan nostalgic for a place he'd never beeen. Soft lights glowed from above, their hue shifting slowly from seafoam green to chartreuse. It was a moment of quiet peace amongst a world of utter insanity.

The sensation of upward motion wasn't immediate. It felt more like the floor below was drifting away from them. The interior, with the exception of the soft music which only seemed to be playing inside Ryan's head, was almost completely silent which gave the entire experience an unsettling peacefulness. Vex stood beside him, arms crossed, his reflection fractured and multiplied across the mirrored walls. Ryan tried not to fidget and not think about how all of this felt wrong and right at the same time.

Lost in the softness of his ascent, he was jolted back as the phone buzzed in his jacket pocket. He pulled it out and glanced at the screen. One new message. From Simon.

> I'm wandering the glass gardens. They're even more peaceful right now because everyone is preoccupied at the bar games. The Medusa Vines have begun blooming. They made me think of you and that day. Not just the bloom but the way you stood in front of it with your arms behind your back, pretending not to care while you quietly memorized every line of its shape. I should've told you then that I would've stayed if you'd asked. I was hoping my friends would fail. I know you were, too. I'm not asking you to say anything because you never do. I just wanted you to know that you were the best part of Hell. I'll keep doing this for an eternity.

Ryan read it once. Then again.

"What's the Glass Garden," he finally asked.

"It's this huge island in Tier 2 covered by this gigantic glass dome. I guess it's like a botanical garden where you're from. It's got a collection of every plant from every possible world in existence. They say you could visit it a thousand times and never see all of it. I've never been there but they have ads all over. It's a pretty peaceful place from what I hear but not very popular. Most people down here aren't about that, ya know."

Ryan's fingers loosened on the phone. The velvet and mirror-lined walls of the elevator didn't buffer the weight of what he'd just read.

"The best part of Hell," he whispered to himself.

Ryan hadn't considered that demons were capable of love. Maybe Asmodeus didn't think so either. Maybe that's why they pushed Simon away, because it was too real, too fragile in a place like this. The message lingered, soft and glowing on the screen. A time-stamped memory of a garden that wasn't supposed to matter and a love that wasn't supposed to exist. He looked down at the phone, the small keypad beckoning him for a response.

This wasn't for him.

He swallowed and quietly tucked the phone back into his jacket as the elevator dinged and the doors slowly parted.

Chapter 9

The air shifted with a jolt and collapsed into itself.

The night pressed in hard, heavy and stale, carrying the metallic taste of old rain and rot. When the world settled and the acrid smell of old fryer grease dissipated, the three teens and the Devil found themselves in the empty parking lot of the abandoned Tall City Shopping Centre. A bustling mall in the 90s, this long forgotten relic was once bursting at the seams with back to school shopping and Jnco-wearing skaters grinding the planters outside. Now, it would feel right at home in a zombie apocalypse movie. Windows broken and blacked out. Weeds cracking through the asphalt. Even the homeless avoided this place.

"Why the fuck are we at the shopping center," Eddie asked.

"Is getting hepatitis on that list, Kally," Maya added.

The empty parking lot stretched into a hazy infinity,

illuminated by two dying light posts. Why the fuck did I trust Casey Kelly of all people, Kally thought.

"I gotta say, this place is dour," the Devil beamed. "I had a feeling that Casey guy knew what was up."

The list in Kally's hand beckoned to her, the only semblance of direction she had. It simply read "The Cinema" with "The old Hot Topic, Tall City Shopping Center" written below it in Casey's elegantly sloppy handwriting. Staring at the left-handed smudges on the list, she was briefly taken back to the few months when she and Casey dated and he would leave her handwritten post-it note letters on her windshield. Usually weird. Always sweet.

The Devil towered behind her as she tucked the list into her back pocket. Without a word, she shuffled through the parking lot and into the shopping centre, steeling her eyes forward and not turning back towards the group for fear that they'd see how scared she really was. Not only at the fact that she had no idea what she was walking into but the reality that there was a real possibility they would fail and never get Ryan back.

The open-air mall was a ghost, filled with emptiness and a stillness so complete it felt like it had been vacuum-sealed in time. Dead fountains covered in lime and calcium.

Dust-caked mannequins standing askew behind cracked glass. A carousel in the food court that sat eerily motionless, all of the horses but one having long been decapitated by vandals years earlier. Even the Devil fell quiet as they walked deeper into the carcass of what used to be the go-to place in town. The echo of their footsteps gave way to their inner thoughts, the Devil's heavier gait resonating louder and further. Kally strode determined while Maya and Eddie walked with hesitation. The Devil meandered in rhythmic bliss like an evil metronome.

"This place doesn't even have rats," Maya muttered. "Rats have standards."

"My mom used to talk about hanging out here when she was in high school. Hard to believe that people actually did that in this place," Eddie said.

Kally said nothing as she walked five steps ahead, purposeful, even though she didn't quite know where they were going. This was a Casey Kelly thing. Which meant it was probably just weird enough to be real.

Then it appeared.

Amongst the tossed shadows of abandoned commerce and shattered glass, a beacon of faint orange light behind the glass of a shuttered store with no name beckoned to them.

The window, coated in a thin film of dust, bore one detail: a small hand-painted sign, written in crooked cursive with a shimmer of gold leaf beneath the grime that shown anew amongst the weathered grime and backlit from within:

THE CINEMA.

The Devil smiled. "Oh, this has potential. Good thing I can't die."

The bell over the door didn't chime but moaned, like an exhausted sigh from the throat of a lady who smoked Virginia Slims for 30 years and had lost three husbands to "accidents."

The store inside was long and narrow, filled with overlapping velvet curtains and dimmed lamps throwing soft light of red, amber, and indigo that spawned stacked layers of shadow on the linoleum floor. Along the walls, someone had crafted a theatrical nest from the broken mall bones. Mannequins in thrown together costumes from the bowels of the fast fashion boutiques, the heads from the carousels balanced into an unnerving totem, and various poor quality toys from the forgotten kiosks provided the aesthetic of a hoarding psychopath or a first-year art student. Greeting them from the store's center, the abandoned shelves were repurposed and rearranged into a crude maze leading to the rear of the store.

Kally entered the derelict maze first, taking extra care to avoid the rusted edges of each corner. Maya pulled a joint from her pocket, taking in a deep drag to steel her nerves as she grabbed the strap of Kally's bag. Eddie placed his hand on Maya's shoulder and followed in step. Sight lines were non-existent within the winding shelves, not willing to give up a single secret until you were brave enough to approach. Kally would peek and then move, not allowing herself to stray too far from her friends while still maintaining the forward momentum of someone who wasn't terrified. After rounding yet another corner, she was convinced this was purgatory and the winding array of shelves had no true end.

"This better not be some Blair Witch shit where we wander forever," Kally said to herself, attempting to maintain her pace.

Just as the air started to feel too heavy and the smell of mildew and dust settled too thick in their throats, the winding shelves finally gave way as if it had its fill of toying with them. With no ceremony or warning, the maze spit them out into an old movie theater lobby or what was left of one.

The floor beneath their feet turned to cracked marble

tile, veined with dust and age. Art Deco light fixtures buzzed overhead, flickering with a stubborn but consistent pulse, casting strange halos on the faded wallpaper once deep crimson, but now sun-bleached into bruised rose. Movie posters from all eras lined the walls in warped frames, the colors muted by time and heat. A claw-footed popcorn machine loomed near the entrance to the theater doors, glass shattered, kernels fossilized at the bottom. And yet, in spite of the decay, there was something oddly elegant about the space. It was like a ghost still trying to host the party long after the guests had stopped coming.

The place was beautiful in the way cemeteries were. It was still, sacred, and absolutely wrong to feel comfort in. The dread of the unknown was now replaced with a shaky comfort. Satanic magic or not, the theater was Kally's home.

In the dead center of the lobby, a lone ticket booth sat, soft light casting a halo through its cracked glass. The light beckoned to her gently, causing Kally to drop her guard as she approached. It was only when she was face to face with the glass did she notice the person inside. Her pupils dilated as the dead silhouette sprang to life, her heart now buried deep within the floor.

In the booth, still as the night, was a person who looked

like Liberace had risen from the dead and discovered rave culture. His suit was a sparkling silver two-piece that caught every ounce of light the small booth was willing to give and cast outwardly upon them a soft flickering glow. His nails were matte black and well manicured, perfectly contrasting with the reflective nature of the suit. And the make-up, an experimental chaos that framed and accentuated every feature. High cheekbones shimmered with a pink and white balayage and unnaturally blue eyes made more vibrant by smokey eye make-up that faded crudely into smooth, ivory white skin. He smiled with teeth just slightly too white and straight to be natural.

"Welcome, darlings," he purred. "To The Cinema."

"Who are you?" Kally asked, equal parts terrified and intrigued.

"I am the curator of experience," he replied, waving dramatically. "I am the usher of lost souls. I am the concierge of catharsis. And tonight, I am your host and you my honored guests."

"What first year film student wrote that dialogue," Maya whispered to Eddie.

With a flourish, he snapped his fingers and lights flared in sequence down a long hallway behind the booth revealing a large curtain with a sign above that simply read: Theater One.

"Our film tonight is a true tour de force. Spun from memory, cut with regret, scored by silence. A passion project, if you will."

"So an A24 movie," Maya chimed in.

Kally threw her a look as the Curator simply grinned, his color-shifting eyes slowly burrowing into Maya's soul.

Maya quickly stiffened up and looked away.

"Remember this feeling," he said flatly. "Especially once the credits roll."

The Curator leaned in, looking each of them over with a glint of mischief that felt almost surgical. His eyes, once electric blue swirled to a fire engine red and back, studied the three teens with a chaotic warmth. He gave a quick glance of acknowledgment to the dark lord standing behind them and then turned his attention back to the friends.

"Let's begin."

With a sweeping gesture of his arm and a few elegant taps, three tickets emerged from the small, metal dispenser in front of them.

He looked the tickets over with a knowing smirk and then fanned them out like playing cards.

Through the glass, Kally studied the tickets that seemed to float between the curator's slender fingers. The gilded edges seemed to be alive, dancing softly with the light. He gracefully slid them through the glass opening with a deep bow. As Kally reached for the tickets, her eyes caught the Curator's once more, his dark eye makeup like a vortex that sucked her in. As she locked eyes with him, his eye color shifted to a hollow pool of lilac, giving her the feeling that the ground had just fallen out from under her.

She regained her composure as the curator released the tickets to her, the weight of which took Kally by surprise. Running her thumb across the raised golden script, she took in all of the elegant flourishes. She looked down at the words, her jaw tightening as she read it.

In bold script: *"THE BOTANY OF BEING LONELY"*

"What the fuck is this," Kally whispered softly, the words dropping from her lips with heft.

"Perhaps the greatest movie never made," the Curator replied curtly.

The words of the title glowed with a mocking defiance, blinding her with every subtle move of her hand.

The Devil beamed as he watched it all unfold. "You humans really are your own entertainment," he whispered deeply.

Kally turned, sharp and suspicious. "What the fuck is this," she asked, voice louder and more firm.

He shrugged. "I don't watch the trailers. Spoils the fun."

With those words, the curator gave an elegant bow to the dark lord. "Enjoy the show," he smiled.

The group slowly shuffled past the ticket booth and parted the musty velvet curtains at the rear of the store. A cold breeze greeted them as they entered into complete darkness. Kally and Maya each grabbed Eddie's arms. As the curtain settled behind them, the darkness gave way to something impossible. What should have been a cramped storage space opened into a massive, vaulted theater, ornate and aged, like it been transported from 1920s Hollywood. Golden art deco filigree snaked along the curved walls. Faded murals of constellations and half-remembered gods shimmered across the ceiling like the remnants of a dream, alive with subtle movement.

The air buzzed faintly, charged like the hush before a storm. Kally let go of Eddie's arm and stepped forward, placing her hand on the crushed velvet seat closest to her. She studied the intricate white marble aisles before she looked up and took in the theater as a whole. The air smelled of stale cigarette smoke and fresh popcorn. Overhanging balconies freely floated atop the lazy yellow light thrown from the sconces that lined the theater walls. The seats, hundreds of them, sat in dimmed light and stretched towards the screen, disappearing into the descending darkness. Amongst all of it, four seats sat dead center in the theater, illuminated by a spotlight, highlighting every single speck of floating dust. The light, which seemed to have no source, coasted along every curve of the vintage seats, soft and inviting, their red velvet cushions glowing in defiance of the gloom around it. It felt like a summons. A side mission from on high.

"I've played enough video games to know what those seats mean," Maya said, her voice resonating deeply into the open space before dying within the acoustic wall panels.

Kally turned back to see the Devil, arms-crossed, face stoic, looking her dead in the eyes. She squinted her eyes at him as he smirked. Kally knew this theater. It was the same theater she would sketch in her notebooks. A classic Hollywood theater from the golden age, initially doodled at the age of thirteen with a blue gel ink pen on the inside cover of her Texas History book. She sketched it regularly, sometimes without even realizing she was doing it. Her latest sketch, which now stood before her in real life, was crudely drawn hours ago in her kitchen. A working vision board. The dream she was chasing. The North Star of having her movie play on a real screen one day. And here it was, in real life, a setting for humiliation or torment from the Devil himself.

Kally gulped as she grabbed Maya and Eddie's hand and guided them towards the four illuminated seats. The emptiness of the theater made every foot strike on the pristine marble echo with anger before becoming one with the walls. Despite the grave reality facing her, Kally couldn't help but let the spirit of the theater engulf her. A dream realized, born from stakes that she couldn't fuck up.

Approaching the seats, the air shifted into something colder. Something more familiar. It carried with it something that froze Kally's determined walk in its place.

"What," Eddie asked, looking all around.

Fresh popcorn. Tea tree shampoo. Melted peanut butter cups. This wasn't the generic scent of a movie theater. This was the smell. Her smell. The night everything clicked into place.

The fancy theater Vince took her and her mom to when she was eleven. When Vince wasn't "dad" yet. Just Vince. The guy who didn't talk down to her, who bought her the extra large popcorn because "you need half for the previews, half for the movie," and who ran back and got her a new straw because he didn't want her to miss a minute. And the ride home. Talking about "The Princess Bride" like it had all the answers to the universe, her mom beaming the entire time as she watched her daughter happier than she had ever seen her.

The air around her was thick now, perfectly blended, as if the theater had reached into her chest and pulled out her favorite memory to weaponize. Warm. Comforting. Cruel. It wrapped around her with a sweetness so precise she could almost feel Vince's hand awkwardly offering her a napkin, almost hear the projector hum, almost believe for a split second that this world might be as kind as it had been that night. Nostalgia as a trap. Hope as a trick of the light.

Filling every crevice of her mind, Kally's eyes watered as she let herself leave that night. Taking in one last smell, she began walking again. The overheard light pulsed in anticipation with each step they took, erratically illuminating the seats like a child stifling a laugh. The three entered the row and approached their seats, greeted by fresh popcorn in vintage bags sitting atop each one.

"I'm not eating that," Eddie said.

"Fuck it, I'm starving," Maya said, pushing past Eddie and plopping onto her seat. "Oh shit! This is real butter."

Kally looked at the Devil who stood in the row behind them, arms crossed with that devious and annoying grin on his face.

"Aren't you going to sit," She asked, motioning to the empty seat.

"Not my seat."

Kally looked down to see the bag of popcorn and a torn ticket on the arm rest. The air shifted once more, thrusting out the nostalgic air and replacing it with something even colder and more sterile. The temperature continued to plummet as it filled the atmosphere with a cold that felt like second-hand embarrassment underneath their skin. As they settled into their seats, the echoing silence of the large room was shattered by an overhead PA system crackling to life and washing over the room.

"Welcome to the Cinema. Please remain seated for the duration of the show."

"And silence your phones," the Devil hissed over their shoulders.

Kally turned back to the screen and instinctively dove into her popcorn. She pushed it into her mouth, surprised at the buttery freshness.

The lighting in the theater died with a loud jolt, thrusting the room into a heavy darkness. The emptiness mingled with the silence giving the air a weight that seemed to press them down into their seats. The quietness held for moment and was broken by the familiar sound of an old 35mm projector kicking to life.

The screen flickered, the corners breathing like an ancient creature waking up. A soft hum of film grain settled over the theater as the title card snapped into place. Hand-painted letters cut from construction paper that read:

THE BOTANY OF BEING LONELY

A SHORT FILM BY KALLY EVANS

The letters jittered slightly, held up by fishing wire you could almost see, as the projector rattled with a warmth that only Kally could remember from movie theaters that didn't project digitally. Her breath hitched at the sight of seeing it on a proper screen. Eddie smiled despite himself. He had never seen the finished product of three days of relentless stop motion work but in this moment, he could admit that it was worth it. Maya tilted her head with curiosity. This movie was different from the others Kally had made. It didn't have a hipster aesthetic or muted colors. This was Kally.

The film opened on a practical miniature living room set, clearly made from cardboard and thrift store fabric samples. A claymation houseplant sat in the corner, leaves trembling as if nervous. A paper-mâché ghost, a teacup-sized figure with button eyes and yarn arms, floated into the room with exaggerated stop-motion jitters.

The ghost spoke in a voice over: "I think the plant hates me."

Ryan's voice came from offscreen, younger by a year and painfully earnest. "I hate you."

Laughter, soft and involuntary, fluttered from Maya. Eddie covered his mouth but a giggle snuck through.

Kally winced. Hearing Ryan's voice from "before" hit like a punch to the ribcage. It felt like he was speaking directly to her.

The next scene unfolded in a blend of live action and stop-motion: Ryan, dressed in pajamas, sat at his desk narrating the ghost's dilemma into a cheap camcorder. Behind him, a practical effect of the houseplant was puppeteered by string, the leaves drooping dramatically whenever the ghost "spoke." It was weird, low-budget, and bursting with odd brilliance.

The Devil leaned forward, eyes glimmering. "Well now,"

he whispered. "This might actually be fun."

The film's story grew:

- The ghost was lonely
- the houseplant was scared of everything
- Ryan's character served as their mediator
- they all lived in a liminal pocket-bedroom between the world of the living and the memories of the dead
- the ghost wanted to be remembered
- the plant wanted to be left alone
- Ryan just wanted them to stop arguing so he could sleep

It was metaphorical and ambitious in the way only talented teenage artists could accidentally achieve.

The scenes grew more ambitious. Animated cutouts of emotions flying from characters, a dream sequence where Ryan floated through a cardboard ocean of glue and glitter, a montage where the plant slowly learned to grow once it let someone get close.

Maya whispered, genuinely impressed: "It's... it's really good."

Kally didn't move. Her jaw clenched tighter with every passing scene. She remembered every single moment of making it. She remembered the final night of production.

She remembered Ryan moving a light and then ducking off set to text his Dad to let him know he was staying to help and to bring him some fries home.

She watched, wondering what was coming next when the film jerked abruptly. The projector stuttered. The visuals tore, doubled and warped. A harsh plume of white light bled across the screen. Then, the footage changed. The set was gone. The actors and miniatures no where to be seen. Instead, grainy, handheld footage filled the screen. Raw, unedited clips Kally had shot for herself and never intended to show anyone.

Her bedroom. The walls plastered with posters. The desk cluttered with gaff tape, glue sticks, and unfinished props. SD cards scattered like landmines.

Maya's breath caught.

"Oh no," Kally whispered.

A choked sound escaped Eddie.

The Devil leaned from his seat and stuck his head between Maya and Eddie. "Creative liberties," he purred.

On screen, Kally, younger and tired, pulled her hair into a messy knot, and looked into the camera. She didn't know it was recording. She was talking to herself as she stared at a pile of SD cards.

"I'll finish it soon," Movie Kally whispered. "I swear it'll be great. Ryan worked so hard. He stayed for me even though he should have gone home."

A brutal silence fell over the theater, the projector seemingly quieting itself down. Kally shrank into her chair. The clip flickered. Another angle from a different night.

Kally, dressed in a modest black dress, sat on the floor, hugging her knees and whispering into the dark.

"I should have made him go home," Movie Kally said softly. "I shouldn't have pressed him when he said he had dinner plans with his dad. I knew he wouldn't tell me no. He never does."

Kally sank lower. Maya's hand went to her mouth. Eddie shut his eyes but the audio forced itself in anyway. The footage glitched. A new clip appeared, shakier and closer to the camera, like the lens itself was embarrassed. Kally, in her darkened bedroom, the only light from the television mounted to her wall. She ignored it, staring at her phone instead.

"Where the fuck are you, Maya? Why won't you answer. I need you. I need you so bad right now. You're just gone. I want to be mad at you but I can't say it out loud or you might disappear for good."

Maya sank lower in her seat, her face getting hotter. Kally's hands dug into her jeans.

The film flickered again. Ryan, sleeping on the couch in the production room at school. His last peaceful sleep, captured in a moment of sweetness by Kally. A shot she planned to put in the closing credits. A thank you for all of his help. The footage slowly zoomed into him, snoozing in the fetal position, his arm hanging to the ground, hood over his head, blissfully unaware of what the next day would bring.

The footage melted into static before settling on one final shot: A static of SD cards on a glossy white desk. It lingered for a moment before softly fading to black.

With a last gasp, the projector whirred and sputtered, before dying with a loud jolt. The screen's residual glow slowly fading, giving way to the imposing dark coming in to take its place.

None of them moved. Not at first. They simply waited for a voice from on high that never came. They sat in the black, searching for any shred of light to find them. The air was no longer heavy but filled with a drifting cold that seems to push them away from each other.

After a few quiet moments, the lights eerily faded back

on and filled the room with soft, yellow light, the screen holding on to the deep void of black. Kally blinked hard, eyes red-rimmed but dry. Maya rubbed her nose like she had an itch she couldn't reach. Eddie sat very still, staring down at his hands clenched into loose fists gripping his knees. The Devil broke the silence with a slow, deliberate clap.

"Bravo," he boomed, voice smooth and smug. "I personally think the phrase 'tour de force' is a bit overused but I think I'm willing to give it a pass on this one. I wasn't sure the genre switch near the end would work but color me impressed."

He smiled. Expectant. Waiting for the fallout.

Kally didn't breathe at first, simply taking in small, shallow sips of air. The kind you use when you're trying to not to explode or unravel in front of people you love. The projector's final rattle still seemed to hum in her bones, riding a pathway through her body. Maya's shoulders rose and fell in uneven little jerks, like she kept thinking a breath would finally steady her. Her eyes remained fixed on the blank screen. She wasn't ready to face Kally. Eddie sat stiff and folded inward, his fingers locking around his knees like a kid trying to keep himself from floating away. His foot tapped once, then stopped. Then started. Then stopped again. A clumsy morse code of discomfort.

None of them wanted to be the first to face another so they sat in the cold silence. Maya's jaw twitched, a small involuntary attempt to speak that she quickly swallowed back. She tucked a strand of hair behind her ear, hands trembling slightly as she did. Her throat bobbed when she forced herself to breathe again.

Kally's fingers gripped the popcorn bag so tightly it began to give way and fold in on itself. Her eyes were locked forward, unseeing, replaying the unfinished movie that perpetually haunted her. The ghost and the houseplant. Ryan sleeping. The SD cards. Her own voice confessing things she'd buried under bravado the past year and a half.

Behind them, the Devil sat with the satisfied stillness of a man full after Thanksgiving. The three friends felt hollowed out and he was more than delighted to fill that empty space with his imposing presence. The theater's soft yellow lights hummed faintly overhead but mockingly warmed nothing. A single piece of popcorn slid off Kally's lap and landed on the floor with a tiny pap. The smallest sound in the large theater felt deafening.

Maya's knee bounced. Once. She pressed a hand on it to force it still. Eddie unclenched his hands and rubbed his palms against his jeans, like he needed to feel something grounding. Kally exhaled, slow, shaky, and quiet. She wiped under her eyes with her thumb even though nothing had fallen. It was a moment without dialogue, without excuses, without any of the jokes they usually grasped to ground themselves. In that moment, the void that was Ryan was more present than ever, a guardrail against themselves. They sat in the silence, letting the truth settle. The truth deserved its moment and the three were all too overwhelmed to run from it anyway.

Kally stood first, not in a rush, but like someone finally ready to carry their own weight. Shame and guilt was heavy and she had shed it in that theater giving her a new weightlessness she wasn't used to. She looked at the other two, and instead of saying something sharp or defensive, she just held out a hand. Maya, lips tightly clenched, took it without a word. Eddie stood up and grabbed Maya's jacket from the back of her seat. He held for a moment as he watched the two holding hands as they navigated the row, somehow seeming a million miles apart.

Eddie glanced back to the Devil who simply sat back and observed with curiosity as he watched Maya and Kally walk away hand in hand.

Eddie finally took his leave, gathering up the empty popcorn containers as he exited the row, throwing one last look at the Devil as he began up the aisle. The Devil continued to sit and watched them walk toward the exit, something unreadable flickering in his eyes. It wasn't disappointment. It was something he hadn't experienced in a long time. Surprise. With a glint in his eyes, he disappeared into a puff of smoke, his empty seat steaming with his afterglow.

The three teens emerged back into the lobby, the curator and his ticket booth nowhere to be found. The never-ending maze and macabre adornments along the wall now gone. It was just an abandoned store, creepy in its emptiness but now devoid of anything supernatural. The Devil stood at the store's entrance, smoking a black cigarette, his eyes giving nothing away. Kally pushed past him and exited into the mall proper.

They walked in a quiet row, the otherworldly overtones of whatever this theater and mall was now insignificant to the ramifications of the experience. Exiting the shopping center, the air loosened its grip and felt crisp and lighter.

The mall had let them go.

Kelly paused at the curb, taking one last look at the

open-air building as the hollow breezeways seem to inhale, swallowing up the echoes of what they'd just witnessed. The truth she spent over a year dodging now lived outside of her. It had been projected 20 feet tall, stitched together with magic and malice, and shown to the two people whose opinions wound her up the most. Yet, she felt lighter. Shaken, exposed, and embarrassed in a way that made her skin buzz but everything was lighter. They'd seen the unfinished pieces of her, the guilt and fear she'd buried in those SD cards, and they hadn't turned away. Even Maya, who had been slipping from her like sand, stood close enough that Kally could feel the warmth radiating off her.

Her movie had lived, stranger and more supernatural than she'd intended, but alive in a way she'd only ever dreamed about. Maybe that hurt. Maybe that's why everything hurt. But within the hurt beat a tiny pulse of hope in her ribs that hadn't been there before. She squeezed her bag tighter, letting herself breathe. It was deep and grounding, an inhale that tried to give space for what's to come. Many choices lay ahead of them, each one potentially stranger than the last, each one tinged with the knowledge that the night was slipping away. But some part of her knew exactly where their story always went when the movie was over.

"I could really go for a burger," she said softly.

Maya nodded. Eddie cracked the smallest smile. Somehow, they all just knew. This is what they did after every movie they saw, life-altering or not.

Kally looked up at the Devil defiantly. "Take us to Milly's."

Milly's, where the metal music was the perfect volume, the fries always perfectly salted, and the memory of Ryan felt a little closer to the surface. The Devil looked at the three teens with intrigue.

"Touching," he whispered sarcastically, as he held up his hand.

He could feel it. This wasn't a detour. This was a recalibration.

They weren't doing this night for him. They were doing it for Ryan. They were doing it for themselves. He was intrigued. How could he not be?

Chapter 10

The elevator doors opened with a hiss and a sigh, like it was winded from the journey.

As the doors parted, what spilled in wasn't just music or scent or light. It was all of them at once in a symphony of balance. If Ryan didn't have the immortal protection of the Devil encasing him, the hit on all of his senses may very well have killed him in that moment. The sound was the first to break through to the little demon and human, an orchestral throb of synth, screams, moans, laughter, metal crashing against glass, and something that might've been a whale song played backwards at an EDM tempo. The heat then made its presence known. Hundreds of bodies dancing, sweating, entwined, melting into each other like orgies had gone corporate and would soon be interrupted by a commercial break from the title sponsor.

Finally, the light punched through the sound and into

their eyes. Chaotic, pulsing, color-drunk light that didn't obey physics. It bent. Curved. Danced across the ceiling like it was teasing gravity, changing color on a whim.

Ryan stepped out slowly, his foot striking a floor made of swirling marble and liquid gold, solid but rippling like sound waves with every movement. Despite its sturdiness, it felt like walking on a cloud. The heat of party-goers was impossible to avoid but surprisingly, the air smelled sweet and clean and not stifling at all.

This was the Platinum Level.

Vex stepped up beside him and actually paused, the first time Ryan had seen him hesitate. Ryan wasn't entirely sure the anatomy of whatever the heck Vex was but upon looking at his wide eyes, he was sure that he was about to cry.

The room was massive, a cathedral of indulgence from floor to what appeared to be a never-ending ceiling. Demonic aristocrats bathed in starlight sang into microphones that bled as they spiraled into the air in sync with their melodies. Ghosts in designer suits held court over flame-touched blackjack tables where the chips would singe every surface they touched. A golden trapeze swung overhead, where twin succubi poured what appeared to be eternal champagne into open mouths from midair, always finding their target and never spilling a drop.

A live band made of flame-eyed skeletons played an EDM jazz version of "Toxic" by Britney Spears that thumped with a bass that shook to the bone or whatever framed the bodies of demons and creatures of the underworld.

At the center of it all, floating in the air was a skybox platform ringed with a glittering red velvet rope and guarded by a sentient pile of diamonds holding a clipboard. A VIP area within the VIP section. Tom Haverford would approve.

This was excess forged from eternity and sculpted into architecture that even the 1% of humans could never create let alone contemplate. The chaos spilled elegantly all around, taking Ryan's eyes in all directions. Colors and sounds soaked every surface, baptizing the party-goers and splashing off of their gyrations. It was chaos that was somehow respectful to every individual partaking in it. The sounds made room for each other, never stepping on top of one another and giving space for the next.

Ryan scanned the controlled chaos around him, bodies pulsing to the music, flashes of neon tattoos, hands and smoke and glitter blurring the air.

And then the world stopped.

Just off to the side, leaning against a lonely cracked stone pillar under a lazy spotlight and slightly removed from the mania cascading all around, stood a man in a weathered gray flannel, a faded Wilco t-shirt, ripped jeans and scuffed black Converse.

He nursed a simple neat whiskey in a square glass with an unopened pale yellow can of Coors original jammed into his back pocket. One hand was plunged into his jean pocket, his hair messy in that I-didn't-try-but-it-still-works kind of way. Amongst the shimmering demons, leggy succubi, and grotesque monsters, He looked absurd and out of place. And perfect. Like someone had cut out a Midwest indie record store clerk and dropped him into the final level of a Dionysian video game.

Jeff Phillips.

Ryan breath caught.

He felt his entire body buffer as he was watched his father emerge like a low-resolution jpeg of Jenny McCarthy in the early days of the internet. The noise of the room dimmed, his heartbeat kicking the throbbing bass line out of sync. The sound around him seemed to give him space and fled outward, surrounding him in a cocoon of silence for a few simple moments. Jeff, as casual as ever, looked over and caught eyes with the still in shock Ryan. Ryan could only stand mouth agape as he was greeted with the same smile he would see in the school pick-up line or in the stands of his soccer games. Jeff raised his glass and smiled wider. The same smile when the two would find each other.

"Hey kiddo."

No flourish. No drama. It was as if they'd bumped into each other in the frozen food section of the grocery store. He wasn't in a coffin wearing a suit that he wouldn't be caught dead in but was actually dead in. He was standing in his favorite t-shirt, drinking his favorite combo of high-end whiskey and cheap beer, surrounded by the most indulgent display that a human had ever witnessed.

Ryan still didn't move. His brain did a full system check. Visual confirmation, emotional identification, and a slow, creeping grief that suddenly felt sharper than it had in months. If Hell was the lowest you could go, his stomach somehow found a place even lower.

Because there was his dad.

In Hell.

Wearing Chucks.

With a drink in his hand.

Was Hell playing games with him? If he moved, would

this illusion disappear? So he didn't. He just took in all the quiet moments that made up his dad. The way he rested his index finger on the rim of the glass. How a strand of his hair would always fall in his face. And his crooked smile, the result of getting Bell's Palsy in his teens. The same smile that his mom said won her over. Jeff didn't look scared or confused. He looked settled. Like a guy halfway through a three-day music festival who had finally found the perfect spot to watch the shows.

"I—" Ryan started, but the word got stuck, his throat tight and his chest feeling like it was full of wet cement.

Jeff smiled gently and walked over, the crowd seeming to part ways for him and not even realizing they were doing so.

"You okay?"

A beat.

"You look like you've seen a ghost."

Ryan blinked. Then laughed. It came out choked, but it came out. His dad, joking in literal Hell. He took two slow steps forward, eyes still locked on his father's eyes.

Ryan was in a void, the sights and sounds encircling him but somehow all living outside of this moment, respectfully giving him and his father space. It wasn't until he heard the voice of the little demon at his side that the void dissipated into the ether and dropped him back into his present reality where demons partied and his once dead father was standing in front of him.

"Holy shit," Vex whispered, eyes wide, black cigarette dangling from his mouth. "Is that...?"

Jeff glanced over, raising his drink politely. "Hey."

"No fucking way." Vex took a half-step back like he was approaching sacred ground. "You're Jeff Phillips."

He turned to Ryan with actual awe. "You know Jeff Phillips? Jeff Fucking Phillips. Holy shit. Holy shit. Holy shit. I knew Tier 1 would be the tits. Holy shit!"

Ryan stared at him blankly. "Uh, how do you know my dad's name?"

Vex didn't answer. He just kept looking at Jeff like a kid seeing his favorite pro wrestler in the wild.

"You're the guy who beat the Devil at the Bloodhaven Beer Pong Tournament. You met the Leviathan of Damned Souls and he bought you drinks! You... you built Milly's 2, didn't you? My friends and I go there all the time! Your picture is hanging in the bathroom!"

Jeff nodded casually, like it was no big deal.

"It's not perfect, but it's close. Hell doesn't exactly stock the right kind of peanut oil and it's hard to find habanero jack cheese down here that doesn't melt your face off."

Ryan's stomach flipped. "You built Milly's?"

Jeff looked at him now. Really looked. For a moment, Ryan saw through the flannel and the charm and the familiar crooked grin, and saw the achingly sincere father underneath. The sitcom dad.

"You always loved that place," Jeff said, voice lower. "Probably more than I did. It was our place. Thought maybe if you ever ended up here, God forbid, right? You should have a version that felt like home."

A pause. "And, selfishly, I guess I missed it, too," he continued. "A lot. Crushing a few yellow bellies. Sitting in the old booth, pretending you and your mom might show up after she picked you up from soccer practice. And the burgers are still solid though I never ask what they're made of."

Ryan had to sit down. He dropped into the corner stool at the diamond and amethyst-encrusted bar not batting an eye at the Turquoise squid slinging drinks with all of his tentacles. Jeff pulled the frosty Coors from his back pocket and sat down next to Ryan. As he gulped down the last drop of whiskey, he placed the surprisingly cold can in front of his son.

"I didn't exactly picture this being the scenario where we'd have our first beer together."

No sooner did Jeff place his empty glass on the bar was it replaced by a new glass and another frosty Coors. Jeff raised his glass to the squid and nodded. The squid, who at the moment was in flow state of drink pouring, serving, and bussing, took a moment of pause and briefly turned into a pale lavender and nodded back before reverting back to his original color and resuming the unrelenting order of drinks.

"Why are you here?" Ryan asked finally.

Jeff shrugged, sipping his drink and then opening the can of Coors in front of his son.

"It's the annual Bar Games. This is the place to be."

"No, I mean, in actual Hell. Why are you here? Shouldn't you be in Heaven? Or, like, anywhere but here?"

Jeff laughed.

"Yeah, pretty much all of humanity is way off when it comes to the concept of Heaven and Hell. It's more of a pick-your-poison kind of situation. Hell is way more interesting. Heaven was a time share condo tour set to harp music. A playpen for people who played it safe for the next life. But here. I mean, I'm taking it that you've seen a bit of it. The bands alone. Holy shit, kid. I saw Kurt Cobain do a live show with Prince playing bass for him the other day. Words can't describe. I think the bigger question is why are you here?"

"I'm the soul the Devil used to return to Earth."

Jeff looked down at his drink and chuckled to himself. "Asmodeus. You sneaky little bitch."

"You know Asmodeus?"

Jeff smirked. "You could say that. They never fooled me with that stoic demon act. Heart of gold on that one. Met them on his day off once. I was crushing a few at this garden they have down here. They were just strolling around in their fancy suit with that debonair walk of theirs. Like some glam rock villain with a tragic backstory."

Jeff felt eyes on him and glanced down to see the little demon looking up at him with admiration in his eyes. With a smile, Jeff leaned over and plopped Vex into the seat next to him and motioned for the squid to bring him a drink.

Within seconds, a glass of bubbling viscous orange liquid that smoked like an old car radiator was placed in front of Vex. Jeff rhythmically tapped his whiskey glass and looked down at the starstruck Vex.

"Thanks for getting my kid here. You'll never pay for anything at Milly's again."

The demon's jaw dropped, then somehow dropped further. Jeff turned back to Ryan, tone softening again.

"I didn't pull any strings to rig this if that's what you're thinking. I might have planted the idea. The switch thing, I mean. Figured if the Devil was gonna pick a soul, I may have suggested that you would be a good one to take. Didn't think it would actually happen."

He took a small sip of his whiskey. "Kinda hoped it would, though."

Ryan couldn't help but notice the way people moved around them. No one bumped Jeff. They flowed like water around him, like Hell itself was giving him room to breathe.

"Okay," Ryan finally said. "I have to ask. Are you, like, famous down here or something?"

Jeff glanced behind him, taking notice of the creatures and people noticing him.

"I wouldn't say famous," He shrugged. "More like, um, well-regarded by the right people. I showed up, didn't complain, didn't try to run things or make a splash. Just leaned into the weird. Treated everyone and everything like my friend. All creatures just want to be seen and heard, ya know."

"You always did make friends wherever we would

go. Remember when you met the groundskeeper for the Houston Astros at that one bar and then later that day, I was meeting players at batting practice?"

Jeff laughed. "Oh I remember that one. Jimmy with the 3 grandkids at USC. He was a trip. Wonder if he's down here tearing it up? He seemed like a good time boy if I ever met one."

Vex piped up from the stool beside him, still cradling his smoking orange drink. "You're a legend, dude. You rewrote the betting rules at the Pit of Reckoning! They still call it the 'Phillips Clause' on the scorecards."

Jeff raised an eyebrow at that, but didn't deny it.

Ryan leaned in a little. "Okay, so what, you just walk into every room and people buy you drinks?"

Jeff finally turned to him, grin widening. "I walk into the right rooms. Remember what I told you about talking to people?"

"Always listen more than you speak."

Jeff nodded, knocked back the last of his drink and set the glass down with the calm finality of a man who knew what came next.

"You good, kid?" he asked, wiping his hand on his flannel like he was about to fix a leaky pipe, not enter the most exclusive room in Hell. "Cause you're not gonna want to miss what's next."

Ryan nodded, though he wasn't sure what "good" meant anymore.

Jeff swiveled his stool and swung back to face the room, focusing his attention on the velvet rope shimmered faintly under the pulsing gold light. In front of it stood a bouncer who looked like someone had sculpted intimidation out of diamond and cigar smoke, massive, blank-eyed, and still as a statue. A far cry from the oaf who was at the main entrance of Ol' Titos.

He started towards it and motioned for his son and the little demon to follow. Vex slammed his drink and hopped down. Ryan grabbed his beer and stood, observing his dad's walk. This was really him. The bounce in his deliberate steps. The casual pace. He still didn't know if this was real or not and he didn't care. They approached the velvet rope and the bouncer stirred, raising a single, thick eyebrow at the trio.

"Jeff Phillips," he rumbled. "I thought you said Ol' Titos was getting played out."

Jeff offered a two-finger gun salute and a smile. "It's the bar games, dude. And I had to show my kid the good stuff. Even if it is a little touristy."

The bouncer's gaze shifted to Ryan, his eyes narrowing in curiousity. "And this must be the boy. Taller than I thought he'd be."

He gave Ryan a slow nod. "Welcome to the fold, kid. You've got good blood."

Ryan blinked. "I...I do?"

Jeff chuckled and slapped a hand on Ryan's shoulder. "Don't let it get to your head. Being a nepo baby doesn't account for much down here. Unless you want to star in a shitty sitcom."

Ryan looked at his dad, shock slowly being taken over by familiarity. Smirking, he held up his VIP pass.

"I don't know," he started. "I think this pass might mean I outrank you."

Jeff glanced down at the pass and back at his son. He couldn't help but laugh at the fact that he might be right.

"You got me there," he laughed. "Maybe you could show me some stuff I haven't seen."

The two laughed, a familiar feeling that both had longed for.

"The kid may be right," the bouncer chuckled as he unlatched the velvet rope. He stepped aside and the floor behind the rope bent the air to reveal an elegantly simple set of stairs leading up to a hovering platform.

A floating circle of dark glass and burnished copper, held aloft by four sleek, gliding demons who moved with a pale elegance that stood in contrast to the chaotic energy around them. They bowed softly as Jeff stepped onto the platform, not out of servitude, but respect.

Ryan, still at the bottom of the steps looked up at his dad.

Jeff turned back and held out his hand. "Come on. You're gonna want to see this."

Vex scampered up the stairs and practically dove onto the platform, giddy. Ryan followed, the glass surface of the platform cool under his feet. With a low hum and a hiss of air that smelled like burnt cloves and ozone, the platform rose. They lifted above the bar, the sound below fading into a muffled, melodic chaos. From above, the Platinum Level looked like a shimmering ant farm of indulgence, colorful and loud, but now suddenly small and more manageable.

They rose higher, the ceiling above them splitting open with a slow, ceremonial hiss. Entering the open air, clouds invaded the platform. The air was still surprisingly warm, remnants from the stifling body heat they had just escaped. Ryan felt disoriented as he tried to maintain his balance on the floating platform. A hand emerged from the fog and rested on his shoulder, steadying him. The same hand that consoled every strike out and failed test. He took a deep breath, his feet and head finally feeling settled, as he focused on the simple silver wedding band of his father's hand. They rose for a few more moments before the clouds finally parted and sent them into light.

A wide, curved hall revealed itself, lined with floating lanterns shaped like dripping pearls, and walls of reflective onyx that shimmered with hidden movement in its imperfections. At the far end, a vast circular space so perfectly balanced between decadence and serenity that it felt more like a temple than a bar.

Candlelight flickered over low lounges and small tables. Elegant banquettes lines the outer perimeter. There was no music, just sound woven into the air with gentle laughter, clinking glasses, and whispered poetry in a dozen languages providing melody to it all. There was no ceiling but open air that peppered the sky with a cosmos of stars, planets, and light that danced alongside the soft breeze.

Demons and souls mingled in tailored glamour. Archangels in street clothes leaned at the bar beside ancient warlords and forgotten gods. A saint in a denim vest was having a deep conversation with a seven-eyed serpent. This was more than just a party. This was where the elite of every realm came to feel real again. Ryan stepped off the platform slowly, his breath caught in his throat as he took in the vast yet somehow intimate nature of the Platinum level.

"Holy shit," he muttered.

Jeff clapped him on the back. "Pretty good, huh?"

"This is…" Ryan turned in a slow circle. "This is like if Prince hosted a tantric orgy séance in space."

Vex, still wide-eyed, nodded. "I think that's literally happening over there."

Jeff didn't move like a guest. He moved like he built the place. This wasn't the first time he had been here. People and creatures nodded as he passed. Some smiled. A few raised their glasses in greeting. Not one person interrupted him. Ryan followed him past a shimmering lounge where two demons slow-danced in complete silence, music only audible to them. Past a table made of polished bone, a group of celestial beings played a card game where cards would disappear and reappear with each move. And somewhere in the middle of it all, Ryan saw it. Amongst the hell and magic was his dad.

Jeff was alive here. More than he had ever seemed on

Earth and he was really alive on Earth. Not just breathing but existing in a cascade of self. Not soccer-practice Jeff. Not pay-the-bills Jeff. Not dead Jeff. This was who his father had been before parenthood. Before responsibility. Before loss. For the first time, Ryan began to understand that grief wasn't just about him mourning a life lost. It was about what his dad had lost, too. It was about what all of them had lost.

Jeff fist-bumped a lumbering centaur and then turned, as if sensing the thought. "You alright?"

Ryan swallowed then nodded. "Yeah," he replied quietly, politely scooting past the tables. "I'm good."

Jeff smiled mischievously at his son. "Good. Because I got some real cool shit to show you."

Chapter 11

1 minute of silence. Ryan and Jeff's tradition after downing a Milly's cheeseburger. The "last meal" burger. The greatest thing you will ever eat until you're lucky enough to eat it again. One final expression of gratitude to the cow who was this burger and Big Mo for crafting it with skill and respect.

The Devil, a being of indulgence and ego, humbly obliged to this rule. While he despised tradition rooted in obligation, he respected tradition rooted in gratitude. The four of them nestled into the cracked red vinyl of the back booth at Milly's, lounging like an army that had just conquered the enemy. Napkins were balled up. Fries half-eaten. 12 cans of Westerly's precariously stacked at the table's edge.

The Devil exhaled slowly, dramatically, and with genuine satisfaction. "That," he said, "was unreasonably good. Forbidden fruit has nothing on that."

With the daintiness of a debutante, he dabbed at the corner of his mouth with a napkin. If you didn't see it, you would never have known that he had taken his first burger down in two unhinged bites.

He turned towards the kitchen and yelled, "You sure you didn't sell me your soul for those culinary skills, Big Mo?"

He laughed to himself at the notion and then wondered just how good the burger would be if Big Mo had.

"I've eaten in a thousand dimensions. Bit into stars. I once freebased the essence of Albert Einstein with Stephen Hawking. But this?" He tapped the table twice. "This had IT. This was art. This gave me faith in humanity because whomever could make this burger is proof that you are indeed worthy of something. I know food prepared by an atheist when I taste it. That was free will on a bun."

Eddie smirked but tried to hide it. His Catholic guilt wouldn't allow him to commiserate with the actual Devil. Maya pursed her lips at the absurdity of the Devil waxing poetic on a burger. Kally watched the Devil carefully, trying to ascertain just how much he was fucking with them. He leaned back in the booth, stretching luxuriously.

"You know, I completely expected you three to unravel back there." He wagged a finger. "Emotional self-revelation.

Personalized insecurities. Existential dread wrapped in cinema-quality lighting. And yet," He looked at each of them in turn.

"Here you are. Eating burgers. Not crying. Not punching each other. Not even the classic awkward, avoidant silence. You little fuckers just go on and continue the night."

Maya swirled the straw around her soupy strawberry milkshake before catching eyes with the Devil. "So what was that back there, really? The theater?"

The Devil smiled wide, like he'd been waiting for the question. "So I'm the Devil, yeah? All-powerful, all knowing, all that jazz. As soon as Casey wrote that list, I knew what was on it. Normally, the place he sent us would be an actual underground movie theater. I'm being generous when I say 'theater.' It's a large group of film weirdos gathering in an abandoned strip mall sharing really obscure and fucked up movies with each other using a projector stolen from the school and projected on what I imagine to be a cum-stained sheet pinned up with thumbtacks. While it was quite sad, it wasn't really doing it for me on the entertainment front so I tweaked the narrative a bit and gave it something all great stories need. Honesty and authenticity."

Eddie narrowed his eyes. "You changed reality?"

"I'm not a hack. I 'crafted' reality," the Devil corrected, grinning. "It's different. Think of it as a controlled hallucination. A hallucination that I control based off my infinite knowledge of every single thought, insecurity, and emotion that make up the soul of your very being."

The teens exchanged a look.

"So if we went back there right now, we'd see an underground movie club filled with movie nerds showing what? A director's cut of 'Irreversible' or something," Kally asked through gritted teeth.

"Tonight I believe those nerds are screening random recorded VHS tapes they found at yard sales."

"Aw, shit! You love doing that, Kally," Maya chimed in.

Kally did love watching random recorded VHS tapes. Her closet was full of them. She loved wondering what the person who recorded it was like. Were they going out that night and didn't want to miss a show? Was it some random family home video? A gender reveal party gone wrong? Weird porn? And the person who introduced the concept of binge watching random VHS tapes? The same guy who had introduced her to the burger she just ate. The guy who always saw her and indulged every part of her personality. The one who gifted her a phone case depicting a blank VHS tape box.

Kally unclenched her teeth and made eye contact with dark lord. "I can appreciate that you like having a laugh at our expense BUT we're playing your game and it doesn't seem too fair for you to manipulate reality with whatever we're doing."

"But I turned our little activity into something I really, really enjoyed," The Devil said, shrugging as if this were all a mildly entertaining improv show. "Thus it seems that you met your goal."

Kally, usually the first to end an argument, actually flinched. She hated that his logic was airtight. She hated even more that he knew she hated it.

"This is just like earlier with the cops," Maya sighed, rubbing her temples like she'd been nursing a headache for weeks.

"What is that supposed to mean," Kally snapped back.

"Big Red here was having a blast fucking with those cops," Maya answered, jabbing a thumb toward the Devil. "But you just had to get going on with the list. And we went with it because we always go with what you want."

The Devil placed a hand over his heart in mock gratitude. "Finally someone sees me."

Eddie sank further into the booth seat like he wanted to disappear between the vinyl cracks.

Kally turned fully toward Maya. "Hold on. You think I did that to what? Ruin his fun? You think I wanted to piss off this thing that's holding our friend hostage? You think I woke up today wanting to piss off Satan?"

"I don't know," Maya replied flatly. "Let me check your notecards."

Eddie gritted his teeth and began nervously tearing at his straw wrapper.

"I'm sorry but someone had to be the one to keep us on track," Kally responded coldly.

"That's the point, Kally," Maya said. "You never think you're steering. You always think you're just... helping. Keeping everything on track. Making sure nobody lets anybody down. Always directing."

"And that's a bad thing?" Kally voice trembled. The first fissure.

"No, it's just..." Maya paused, choosing her words like they were razor blades. "You don't know when to stop. You don't know when someone else needs air."

"Oh my god," Kally breathed out. "Air? You've been a ghost this past year and I'm the one taking all the air out of the room?"

Maya's eyes widened. They both knew they were crossing into dangerous territory. Nuclear codes territory.

"Kally," Eddie started, then immediately aborted when both girls shot him death glares.

"You want to talk about disappearance?" Kally said, leaning forward, voice low enough that Ryan could probably feel it down in Hell. "Let's talk about the Houdini act you pulled after Jeff died. You floated in for birthdays and holidays like some divorced parent trying to hit their visitation quota."

Maya stiffened. "You know damn well…"

"No. Actually, I don't." Kally cut her off. "You never told us anything. Not me. Not Eddie. Not Ryan. Especially not Ryan. He looked for you. He noticed."

Maya blinked hard like something had just stabbed her behind the eyes.

"He needed all of us," Kally continued, louder now. "And you were gone. Now you sit here giving me shit for trying to make him happy? For trying to keep this shit show of a friend group together? It's really easy to let someone else take the wheel, isn't it? You don't get to just show up and then comment on the route."

Maya bit her lower lip hard, feeling her teeth nearly break the skin. She blinked hard and fought against lowering her head, instead choosing to meet Kally's glare head on.

"I can see it in your eyes," Kally continued flatly. "Blaming me for all of this."

"Blame you?" Maya snapped, her voice cracking. "For the fucking Devil showing up?! How could I blame you for any of this?

"Because you do," Kally said. "You saw it on the screen just like we all did."

"We saw what was in your fucked up head," Maya replied. "All of that was you. Just like everything always is."

Eddie shifted farther away from the table, eyes fixed on a corner of the ceiling where five Megadeth stickers were attempting to hold a ceiling panel together. "Huh. They added a new one," he mumbled to no one.

The Devil leaned an elbow on the table.

Kally inhaled shakily. "If I didn't plan tonight, we wouldn't have been in that parking lot. And yeah, maybe I think some of this is on me. But this was the only way I could get you to come out because if I didn't, you'd have just left town like it was a dentist appointment you forgot to cancel."

Maya opened her mouth, closed it, opened it again. Still nothing.

Kally pressed on. "I know you're perfectly fine just moving on. You've been talking about what's next for the past two years. College. New band. New friends. A whole new life somewhere else. That's great, Maya. Really. I'm glad we got to keep you company while you waited for the good part to begin.

That's not fair," Maya whispered. "You know that's not fair."

"Maya," Kally went on. "I'm not stupid enough to think we'll ever be this close again. Chance and proximity. That's why we're friends. Once you're finally where you think you want to be, I know what will happen to us. It doesn't mean it didn't matter. It's just the way it is. I wanted to fucking celebrate it."

Maya pursed her lips and Kally leaned in.

"Maybe I was overzealous but it's not very often you get to give something a proper goodbye," Kally said, her voice cracking. "Most of the time shit just ends. You go out for donuts and never come back. Cut to black. Roll credits."

Kally didn't break eye contact, finally feeling release for

acknowledging it. Maya couldn't speak and Kally wasn't going to give her a pass on this one.

"I've seen how you look at me when you're actually around," Kally continued, her voice beginning to strain. "I know it's not actually my fault that Jeff died but every time I see those stupid fucking memory cards on my desk, I'm constantly reminded about everything. If I don't finish it, what was it all for? And I see that in your eyes every single time. Is that why you avoided me? Why you disappeared, too?"

Maya swallowed, eyes glistening. "I wasn't disappearing. I was just... trying to get ready."

"For what? For us breaking up?" Kally asked. "Because that's what this is. You don't get to pretend it's not. You were already leaving. Ryan just moved it all to the front of the line."

The mention of Ryan - his grief, his stillness, his vacancy - hung over the table like a dropped chandelier.

Maya's voice cracked. "I didn't know how to fix anything. I didn't know how to talk to him. Or you. Or myself. Everything was already changing and I thought..."

Maya wiped her eyes on her jacket sleeve, the creak of the leather riding on the brief silence. "I thought if I pulled back now, it wouldn't hurt so much when everything fell apart anyway."

There it was. The truth. The tiny, stupid, teenager truth.

Kally's eyes softened for a second, then hardened again. "Okay. Fine. But you don't get to be mad at me for trying to hold us all together while you practiced leaving. You just made it easier for him to disappear, too. I couldn't do it alone. I never could do it alone. I'm like this because of you. Ever since that stupid 6th grade report when you made me believe in myself."

Maya recoiled, like she'd been slapped. A core memory now tainted with regret. The words sat on the table, filling the spaces between the empty drinks and food baskets. They both went silent. Not the pause-before-more-yelling silence but the silence that comes after something irreversible has been said. The Devil slowly pulled the milkshake away from Maya and sipped with a loud and dramatic slurp.

Eddie exhaled like he'd been clenching every muscle in his body for ten straight minutes. "Hey, maybe we should just…"

"Don't," both girls warned in unison.

They locked eyes, a familiar love glinting for a brief second, before sinking away into the moment. Kally stood abruptly. Her chair screeched across the floor, cutting through the Everclear song blaring through the bar's jukebox.

"I'll go take care of the check," she said, voice flat but shaking beneath the surface. "I'll meet you all outside when you're ready. You're off the hook, Maya. Send us your classic 'can't make it tonight' text that we're all used to getting and go the fuck home."

Kally turned sharply and clipped the pyramid of Westerly's cans on table, sending them clattering in every direction. She walked towards the bar not looking back. She was gone before the last can finished rolling.

The booth remained frozen in place. Maya stared at the spot where Kally had been, her eyes wet and breathing uneven. Eddie studied the Megadeth stickers again like they held the secrets of the universe. The Devil leaned forward and took a fry from Maya's basket then fell back into the booth with a smug, satisfied grin.

"You'd think it'd be boring knowing what you're all thinking and feeling but when you reveal it to each other, oh my god, is it amazing," the Devil cackled with a mouthful of fries. "It's like watching a person experience the Red Wedding for the first time."

"Fuck," Maya whispered.

Outside the bar, Kally leaned against the cold brick exterior of Milly's, head tipped back, watching moths fling themselves at the flickering lights as if they auditioning for oblivion. She closed her eyes and let the sounds settle around her. The muffled soundcheck leaking through the walls, the sharp staccato of high heels in the parking lot, a car launching through a green light like it had someplace urgent to be.

She let it all play like a movie scene in her head: A bad first date, a clumsy meet-cute, a character stepping out of the bar at the exact moment fate was stepping in. Anything to not think about what had just happened in Ryan and Jeff's booth. The movie in her mind collapsed when cold air rushed past her as the Milly's door swung open, spilling the band's feedback and the smell of fryer oil into the night. The Devil walked out first, grinning like he'd just watched a particularly juicy telenovela, gripping four unopened cans of Westerly's like trophies. Eddie trailed behind him, giving Kally a small conflict-avoidant smile that said: please don't drag me into this. Finally, Maya emerged, slow and tentative, clutching her leather jacket in front of her like she was wandering in late for her curfew. Her eyes found Kally, half expecting a stern look but not entirely surprised when she was greeted with a look she'd describe as soft acceptance.

"For the record," Maya said, clutching her jacket like armor. "If I did leave with just a text… I wouldn't copy and paste the old standby. I know how much you hate remakes. I'd come up with something new. You know, put actual effort into disappointing you."

Kally looked at her. The words weren't a joke. They were an acknowledgment. An unspoken apology for a year and a half of flaking, half-truths, and choosing distance over discomfort. A quiet way of saying I heard you. I know I earned all of that.

Kally's smile was small and real. A silent thank you.

"You weren't wrong back there, you know," Maya continued.

Kally pushed off the wall, hands stuffed into her pockets. The cold brick had been easier to face than Maya's eyes. She made one of the loves of her life hurt and now it was here, drilling back into her.

"I mean," Maya exhaled. "I've been talking about leaving for so long, I forgot to notice I was still here. With you. With everyone. And then the fucking Devil showed up, I realized how much of that was on me."

"I noticed," Kally said quietly. "We all did."

Maya's shoulders fell. "I always tell myself I'm this free-spirit, ready for the new adventure. But really? I've been terrified. I'm a fucking rich kid from the suburbs who thinks I'm this edgy, misunderstood person. That I was better than all of this for some reason. But really? I've been terrified. Once high school starting being good, like really good, I started worrying about how fast it would end. And instead of enjoying it, I started pulling away. Like I thought enjoying it didn't mean anything. Like I could soften the blow by leaving first."

"You did leave," Kally said. This time it wasn't sharp and cutting. It came out tired. Sad. True.

Maya nodded, eyes flickering with remorse. "Yeah, I know. And it hurt you. I didn't want to admit that because if I said it out loud then I'd have to deal with how much I was losing. I didn't want to think that things would never be as good as this. That I could travel around the world a dozen times and I'd never have a friend as good as you."

Kally took a deep breath, steady and honest. "You're never going to have a friend as good as me."

Maya finally cracked a real smile. "No. Probably not."

"And it's not that you won't make other friends," Kally continued. "You will. Great ones. But nobody will ever know this version of you. This small-town, late-night dive bar, bad movie club version of you. Being your friend right now feels like watching a great band in a crappy club before they blow up and start selling out arenas."

Maya loosened the grip on her jacket and held it to her side. "I was worried that by the time I'm forty, this would all feel small. Like a faded memory."

"Well, the Devil showing up pretty much guarantees that'll never be the case."

"Can't believe we owe him for that."

"He's going to be such an arrogant prick about it."

They laughed, soft, fragile, and real.

Maya's voice dipped to something gentler. "Are we good?"

"We're good," Kally answered without hesitation. They both know that "good" didn't mean "fixed" but worth fixing.

Maya took a step closer. "You know that Ryan doesn't blame you for what happened, right? Not for any of it."

Kally looked down at her shoes. "It's not about blame. It's this weight. He's been such a constant for me for so long that sometimes it feels like carrying the grief for both of us is all I know how to do. And I keep waiting for him to hate me. I see those fucking SD cards on my desk and I just freeze. I can't even import the footage from that night."

"You need to finish it," Maya said. "Especially now. After everything."

"You're right," Kally whispered. "I need to finish it. I wanted to finish it for tonight but every time I tried to start, there was this voice that kept telling me that no matter how good it was, it would never be worth what it cost to make it. And then I'd feel guilty about that."

Maya closed the gap between them even more, grabbing her friend's hand, feeling the familiar warmth that she'd been avoiding.

Maya's voice softened. "You know, he never helped you because you pushed. I just said that to hurt you and I'm sorry for that. He helped you because he really wanted to. He believed in you. All that stuff he did, carrying your gear, staying up late on shoots, letting you boss him around on set without saying a word. He did that out of love. Real love. Just Ryan being Ryan."

Kally looked at her, eyebrows tightening, unsure where she was going.

"And yeah," Maya continued. "He has all of this anger wrapped up in what happened to his dad, and sometimes he points it at you because anger needs somewhere to go but it's not about you. You know that, right? You were the safest place for it. You were the person he trusted most to still be there afterward."

Kally swallowed hard.

"There was this one night a few weeks before Jeff died," Maya said, eyes drifting. "I gave him a ride home after movie night. We watched 'Dogma' and that short documentary you made about guy selling tamales near the school. Out of nowhere he just said, 'Kally's gonna make something really special one day. I can feel it.' He said it with this stubborn certainty."

Kally blinked, surprised.

"He then went on about how you see stories everywhere," she continued. "How you don't let people's flaws scare you off. I remember thinking, man, he really sees her. Like really sees her. I don't think I'd ever heard a boy our age talk that way about anyone. I was a little jealous. It kinda messed me up."

There was a long pause, the cold air desperately trying to fill the empty space between.

Maya exhaled. "The point is that he doesn't blame you. Someone who sees you like that wouldn't blame you. I think he just hasn't figured out where to put all the hurt yet. And somehow, even with all that, he sill looks for you first in every room. Like you're his North Star and he's trying to navigate back from the hole he's in even if resentment is the only language he knows right now."

Kally looked at her, something shifting behind her eyes. "Is that how you see him?"

Maya hesitated, too long for it to be nothing.

"I don't know," she said softly. "I just know that after his dad died, I started walking further ahead so I wouldn't feel guilty for not knowing how to hold him together. I give you shit for trying to control everything but at least you tried. I was scared I'd break something if I tried. He never got mad at me. Not once. Not even when I deserved it. I know he was hurt when I left the funeral early but after his eulogy, I just couldn't be in that room."

Kally listened, quiet and open in a way that made it harder for Maya to hide.

"It would've been easier if he had," she continued. "If he'd yelled or pushed me away but he didn't. He was just kind. Even when he was hurting. Even when I left him behind. It made me feel…" Her voice wavered. "Like maybe he deserved someone stronger than me."

"Because it meant he really saw you," Kally asked gently.

"Because it meant I was starting to see him," Maya whispered. "More than I planned to. More than I knew how to deal with. And starting in the middle of grief? That felt impossible. I didn't trust myself to be what he needed. I didn't want to be one more thing that broke."

She looked away, blinking hard.

"And he kept talking about you like you hung the stars," Maya added, not bitter but honest. "I thought if he could see someone that clearly, maybe he'd see all the ways I wasn't enough."

Kally's expression softened as she gripped her friend's hands tighter.

"But he still gets stuck in my head," Maya said quietly, almost to herself. "Even after everything. Even after I tried to run from it. Because for all of the horrible biblical insanity of tonight, he was good enough that the Devil himself needed him. That has to mean something, right?"

Kally nudged her shoulder, gentle but grounding. "Then give him something now."

Maya breathed out, looking her best friend in the eye. Kally's expression was filled with softness. Warm, relieved softness. A quiet and subtle look of "finally." It wasn't permission but a recognition, like she'd been waiting for

Maya to understand something she'd known for a long time. For a moment, Maya let herself feel it. The truth of her own heart settling into place. But then reality slammed back into her chest.

She swallowed hard. "None of this matters if we don't fix what's happening now," she said, her voice tightening. "If we fuck this up, he's gone. Whatever I feel will mean nothing."

Kally took a deep breath and pulled the crumpled list from her pocket. A night of chaos curated by one Casey Kelly, a person who may be the sweetest, weirdest guy she'll ever know. She stared at it, the fate of everything between her fingers. She held it out to Maya.

"You need to run the rest of this," Kally said. "You get this crazy bastard in a way I never will."

Maya put her jacket on and took the list. After a quick glance, she chuckled to herself. Casey's list, curated with a loving understanding of what was at stake, for a girl that he loved in his own way. At that moment, a blur of silver whizzed between their heads and exploded on the bar door behind them, sending beer foam flying everywhere. Looking over, they saw a wide-eyed Eddie and a laughing Devil slamming another can of Westerly's Own like it was a victory lap.

"This is very touching but I'm losing my buzz here," the Devil bellowed, wiping foam from his chin. "You're very quickly losing the good will that burger afforded you and though it seems like we're old chums here, your friend's soul is still very much hanging in the balance. I do hope he avoided the pit of infinite sorrow while down there. It can really sneak up on you if you're not careful."

Maya glared at him, defiant and steady, and studied the list. She stepped towards him and held it up to his face. "Take us here, asshole."

The Devil smiled. "To the next act of this unhinged farewell tour."

"You going to fuck with reality again," Maya asked.

"If you're lucky," He replied.

The air began to shift into a reverberating bass line as the music emanating from Milly's faded into a low hum of anticipation. For a brief moment, everything was devoid of sound, smell, and color and in an instant, they were engulfed within the sound of thumping bass and the smell of old chlorine.

Chapter 12

"The trick to the perfect beer pong shot," Jeff said, delicately holding a pristine matte black ping pong ball, "is all in the arc. Index and middle finger rest lightly on the outside, solid thumb pressure, confident wrist flick. You should throw before you have time to think about it."

He raised his arm with the casual confidence of someone who had done this drunk, upside down, and blindfolded 100 times before. Across the thick slab of dripping onyx that served as the beer pong table, two creatures crouched in readiness, eyeing a single red solo cup. The flayed, feline horrors, hunched over like jumbo shrimp with their skinless muscle glistening wet beneath stringy tufts of burned fur watched the two humans with cockeyed intensity. Their cloudy yellow eyes blinked in separate rhythms. The chubbier of the two licked its own exposed shoulder with a barbed tongue, tearing off pieces of flesh and swallowing it without a second thought. The other gurgled and coughed up a glob of fur that fell to the floor with a wet slap and scampered off to God knows where, a slimy trail of ooze left in its wake.

"I can't believe we're watching THE Jeff Phillips," Skid yelled out, his eyes and body still twitching sporadically from his earlier jaunt in the indulgence pit.

Blink nodded while mindlessly shoving chips into his mouth, watching with unwavering intensity. "He medaled fifteen times last year," he said between chips. "He beat the Devil in Infernal Jenga! With a 30-drink handicap!"

"Your dad basically won the entire 5th level of Hell with that game," Vex added. "And that's the level that has the Chili's on it. And not the Chili's Express! The full Chili's. With Southwest Egg Rolls and the original chicken crispers!"

Jeff took a deep breath and raised the ball up once more, lining up his shot. The crowd surrounded them, giving Jeff his space. Winged demons, fire-bellied imps, weeping ghosts in all nature of sports jerseys, all hushed in anticipation, only the sound of the gurgling blood fountains could be heard and even they seemed to slow to a trickle.

"He's gonna do it," a demon with literal snakes for arms

whispered. "Those skinless bastards never had a chance."

"I lost 40 souls betting against him last time. It took me a long time to get those. And those were premium Mormon souls."

"I heard he won a side bet with the Devil," someone else hissed. "One weekend a month, the Devil has to give him access to his beach house!"

The cat creature on the right, in an attempt at distraction, let out a shrill warble and flared its spine like a bottlebrush. Bits of singed whiskers popped off in every direction, one lodging itself into the table, which seemed to twitch in anguish. Jeff ignored them all. He was Tom Brady running a two-minute drill. He lifted his arm higher, clean and steady.

"See the ball going in," Jeff whispered to Ryan. "And always give it a little extra 'oomph' to account for the gravity of the air here in Hell."

From the middle grooves of the table, a wave of flame shot in the sky and curled into itself. Jeff smirked as the smokey aftermath of the fireball hovered over the table.

A smooth flick. The ball soared, an arc of perfection, breaking through the smokey haze and dancing on the atmosphere as it passed through the various floating bookies.

Plop. Splash. No rim, right into the dead center of the final cup, sending suds flying. The exposed muscle of the cat creature's forearm sizzled as the beer hit it.

The crowd exploded with howls, groans, cheers. A cherub vomited pure confetti in celebration while another doused a group of demons in acidic sports drink. A dirt-caked skeleton in a cummerbund lowered his head in shame as he detached his arm at the shoulder and handed it to another skeleton who gleefully affixed it to their body. One of the flayed cat beasts shrieked and tried to flip the table but the onyx didn't budge. The table retaliated at the attempted indiscretion by giving a warning flash of flame causing the creature to scurry away.

"Official Hell tables," Blink explained. "Crafted from the compressed guilt of Catholics. Weigh a ton. A little temperamental. A lot repressed."

The other cat creature dropped to all fours and hissed what sounded suspiciously like a slurred compliment.

"Good game, Mickey," Jeff yelled across the table. "We still hitting the track later this week?"

The creature hissed at him and then walked off, grabbing his feline companion by one of the tufts of fur still attached to its body. Jeff turned to Ryan, completely unfazed, and held up his fist for a bump.

"You in for the next round? Or are we retiring undefeated?"

"What the fuck did I just witness," Ryan asked in bewilderment, bumping his dad's fist. "People, like, know you down here."

"People and everything in between," Jeff corrected.

"You've been dead less than two years and you own a part of Hell?!"

"I guess I technically own it but it's more symbolic than anything," Jeff said. "It's more like an 'adopt-a-highway' situation."

"And one weekend a month at the Devil's beach house?"

"Oh, that's real."

"I have one million questions," Ryan exclaimed looking all around.

"I'll answer what I can," Jeff laughed, putting his arm around his son. "Let's go down to the basement where it's a little more chill."

The elevator doors slid open with ease, exhaling a thick plume of incense and cigarette fog, and for a moment, the world shifted from excess to a soft whisper. The music slithered off of the walls and oozed into the ear, soft bass mixed with whispered vocals echoed off walls covered in melted wax, velvet, and cracked mirrors that reflected skewed portraits of important patrons.

Ryan stepped out first, eyes adjusting to the glow of dim red sconces shaped like melted ram horns. The space opened before him like a velour lounge carved out of a sin-stained cathedral. Arched ceilings with the Devil in various erotic poses, stone columns wrapped in barbed wire and silk, and booths that caressed your ass the longer you sat in them. The air buzzed faintly with hushed conversation and low laughter.

Colorful smoke curled in slow, deliberate spirals from pewter hookahs shaped like screaming archangels. Every table had its own private lamp dripping a lazy flame that changed color based on the mood at the table. Ryan passed one pulsing sky blue (melancholy), one glowing crimson (lust), and one rapidly cycling (undecided chaos). Behind the bar, a three-headed wolf bartender polished a glass with a rag that smoked and hissed as it wiped. Bottles lined the back wall, pulsating with glowing light and labels that seemed alive: Temptation '98. Regret '45 Vintage. Fyre Fest.

The crowd was less rowdy here. Older demons in

tailored coats and tattoos sipped from crystal tumblers while holding hands under the table. A pair of fallen angels slow danced as their wings molted feathers. A gorgeous succubus played pool with a ghost, its specter essence leaving glowing ectoplasm on every surface it touched. Ryan turned slowly, taking it all in and allowing himself a brief reprieve from wild excess. Jeff stepped beside him, sipping from the understated rocks glass that seemed to appear in his hand at random intervals.

"This is where Hell exhales," he explained. "These are the movers and shakers. Veterans of the depth."

From the corner, Blink waved them over to a semi-circular booth already occupied by Vex and Skid, both of whom were eating something that looked like still blinking eye balls deep fried in beer batter and sipping from tall collins glasses with a color-shifting liquid swirling inside.

"We saved you a spot!" Blink chirped, cheeks and chin shiny with a bright orange sauce.

Vex nodded and raised his drink. "Welcome to The Underpour at Old Tito's. Where the drinks are extra strong if you mention your dad's name."

Jeff slid into the booth and scooted next to smallest demon, Blink.

"Sweet jackets," Jeff said, looking the three demons up and down. "Thanks for getting this guy safely to Old Tito's. I appreciate you helping him out."

Blink gobbled down three fried eyeballs. "He's the coolest," his mouth full of food.

"If we'd known he was your kid we would have got him here sooner," Skid added.

"And not dosed me with a green-eyed monster," Ryan teased.

The three little demons went silent until Jeff broke the moment with a laugh.

"That's an intense one for sure," he chuckled. "You come out of that one okay?"

"Just face to face with petty jealousy and all of my insecurities. How could I not?"

"Better out than in, kiddo."

Jeff took a long pull of his drink and went to set it down, his eyes seemingly lost in thought for the moment.

"Okay," Ryan chimed in. "What is going on down here, dad. You're like the popular guy? In Hell?"

Jeff looked down and laughed. As he made eye contact with his son, 5 fresh glasses of whiskey were placed upon the table, Jeff's in his signature square glass.

"From the big table," hissed the serpentine waitress as she slithered away.

Across the lounge, nestled into what could only be described as a throne made of writhing, oiled-up sinners, sat a demon the size of a compact car. Gormund the Glutton. His body spilled over in folds of shiny red flesh, each roll studded with jewelry and glinting piercings, like someone had tried to bedazzle a pile of marshmallow fluff. His flesh overflowed so much it was impossible to distinguish his appendages from a glance. His face was bloated and smug, with seven gold teeth, eyelashes that shimmered like wet tar, and horns that twisted into spiraling curls, wrapped in tightly wound bioluminescent silk. Perched on and around him were four sleek, seductive demons, each with alabaster skin, obsidian eyes, and barely-there attire. They fed him from sterling silver trays in between stroking his oily skin. One peeled flaming fruits while another gently arranged an array of glistening soul truffles. The other two gracefully pulled hot pink vapor from a classically ornate hookah and blew the smoke gently into his waiting open mouth.

Ryan clocked the whole setup mid-conversation and leaned in toward his dad. "Who's that?"

Jeff didn't turn. "Gormund the Glutton. Owns most of

the vice pits in Tiers Three through Nine."

"I heard he was a fallen angel that turned into that thing because he freebased the souls of disgraced priests," Vex chimed in.

"I've always wanted to try disgraced priest," Blink chimed in.

"It's like white truffle," Jeff added. "It's good but a little goes a long way. But he's not an angel. He's basically a soul entanglement of every emperor, dictator, and politician of every single universe throughout time."

"Wait. That dude just sent you a drink," Ryan said.

Jeff finally turned and gave Gormund a subtle nod that was more acknowledgment than gratitude. "I did him a few favors."

"Favors? Are you like a hitman or something? Are you running drugs?"

Jeff laughed. "I helped him after a break-up."

Gormund nodded his head and raised his glass. He toasted them with a wink, his eyelashes sticking to one another for a moment before pulling apart. The lounge around them murmured with recognition. More than one pair of eyes shifted toward Jeff.

"Looking good, Gormund," Jeff yelled across the room.

"She'd lose her shit if she could see you now. Fierce, buddy!"

Ryan sat back in the booth, staring. "This is getting weird. That warlord mashup got dumped and you helped him?"

"Everyone, and everything, just want to be loved, kiddo," Jeff said with a slow sip of his whiskey. "Most of the villains of the world are people who weren't loved enough so they sought it out in ways that they shouldn't have. Through fear. Intimidation. Policies. Their mortal lives saw them believe that they were the center of the universe. Their penance is living within each other knowing for eternity that they aren't. They all tried to control beings that aren't meant to be controlled. Defying another's freedom for your own pleasure, there's consequences for that. If you're a person who seeks power up top, this is what's waiting for you after the lights go out."

"So don't run for office is what you're telling me," Ryan asked.

"I wouldn't," Jeff replied flatly before taking another quick sip.

Ryan fell back into the booth and took a moment to take stock of his current situation. He was sitting in the booth of a Hell speakeasy with his dead father, who was incredibly popular within the infinite vastness of literal Hell, and three new demon friends who were currently housing deep-fried eyeballs. With a dead, contemplative squint, Ryan downed the whiskey in front of him. As he set down the empty glass, the serpentine waitress returned with a fresh glass filled with two fingers of whiskey and a single ice cube.

"Holy shit," Ryan whispered to himself. "This is really fucking happening. This isn't some crazy Hell magic, is it?"

Ryan took a sip of his new drink, a slight buzz overtaking his mind.

"Dad," he asked.

"What's up, buddy?"

Ryan looked at his dad staring back at him. The crooked smirk. The clump of hair that would always fall in his face. The green eyes that looked genuinely interested in every word you were going say. It was here, right in front of him. Every tiny feature he thought he'd never see again was right here. And then the burst. The tears he wasn't able to fully expel at the funeral. The build-up of emotion he put down the day he heard the news about his dad's death. The feeling of looking up at graduation and not seeing him there. Every feeling he had stuffed down over the past year and a half. It all built up and thoroughly decimated the levees in his eyes and came streaming down his cheeks. Ryan thrust his face between his hands and doubled over, struggling to capture the breath that was escaping him faster than could be replenished.

And then, warmth. Warmth wrapped all around him. The same he had experienced at Milly's 2. And then, a new warmth like he had never felt before joined. It was heavy and stifling in the best possible way. Ryan, breathing erratically, raised his head to feel his father embracing him and cradling his head in his hands. From behind, Ryan felt the soft embrace of the three little demons clenching him with all of their might. The past year Ryan had felt like he was moving without a spine, sporadic and without support, but in this moment he felt himself let go but was still being held up. It was also in this moment that he realized he hadn't touched another human in many, many months.

"I've missed you so much," Ryan pushed out through labored breath.

He clenched his dad hard, burying his head in his shoulder. His dad embraced harder. The smell of the flannel, a mix of lavender laundry detergent and faint Armani cologne, invaded Ryan's brain, filling in each groove and giving him permission to let go. Ryan pulled an arm from their embrace and reached behind him, patting each of the little demons on the head.

The once heavy air suddenly felt lighter and easier to breath in. As the tears dried up, Ryan took in larger and larger sips of air. Time wasn't allowed in this moment. Catharsis kept that at a respectable distance. Every hug he wished he had given was thrown into this moment and when Ryan tried to pull away, his Dad pulled him in even tighter. Ryan squeezed back and opened his eyes. All of the patrons of the speakeasy were now watching him, the lamps on their tables flickering in various shades of pink. Love.

"I've felt everything you've been through this past year," Jeff said, his face buried in his son's shoulder. "I'm so proud of you for being so strong. You're ten times the person I could ever hope to be."

Ryan sniffled, his breath still laboring to return. "I just wanted you to be proud of me."

"You'll never know how proud I am of you," Jeff said. "And that you're down here says so much about the person you are."

"What do you mean?"

"Only the purest of souls can switch places with the Devil. A person who is decent and kind and keeps the company of good people. That's you, kiddo. The kid you are and the company you keep... that's what matters. The relationships you built because of the person you are is going to be what gets you home. Conditional love. Love that takes work. Love that is tested. Love that is earned."

Ryan attempted to take a slow, deep breath. He pictured his friends in the last moment he saw them, crushing beers by his beat up car as they did so many times before. He missed them and wished he could show them all of this. Kally would have taken in all of the little details. The flowing river of bonefish. The shifting lights. The bar set-up. Maya would have jumped headfirst into the bar games, getting way too competitive in the process. Eddie would have made at least 30 new friends and not paid for a single drink.

"I wish they could see all of this," Ryan said. "They'd go nuts."

Ryan and his dad released their embrace and leaned back into their seats.

"I have a feeling those three are seeing some crazy shit right now, kiddo," Jeff chuckled. "The big guy loves fucking with humans."

Ryan wiped his face with his sleeves and took in one more slow and deliberate breath. As he sat in the silence, he felt the warmth uncoil from around him and seem to take a spectral form as it floated back towards the sky.

Ryan looked up, certain he could make out a face.

Jeff caught him looking up. "You're not crazy."

"Huh?"

"Did it feel like you were being hugged by someone and then it just disappeared back into the sky once you felt better?"

"Yeah. It was warm and soft. I felt like I was under mom's weighted blanket."

"Those are souls of the lost giving you the comfort they could never have."

"Souls of the lost?"

"People who took their own lives. You know how in lots of religions, they'll tell you that taking your own life is a ticket to Hell. It's true in a sense but not entirely accurate."

"What does that mean?"

"It's like this. A person who makes the decision to take their own life is broken. Hopeless. Lost, most likely, right? Heaven doesn't want them because they essentially destroyed the 'gift' they were given plus the whole free will of it all really pisses them off up there. Those souls get sent here but they aren't punished for it. Why should they?

Because life got to be too much for them? A life they didn't necessarily ask for in the first place? That's not a reason for eternal suffering. The Devil isn't that cold. The souls who come down here by their own hand are allowed to drift with nothing holding them back. To just exist without burden but occasionally, they'll find other sad souls down here and comfort them. That's the warmth you felt. You basically got a big group hug from a lot of them. They've comforted me more than a few times."

Ryan sat with that image for a moment, feeling the warmth all over again. As his dad tousled his hair, a muffled buzzing could be heard from his jacket pocket.

"You have a phone," Jeff asked.

"Asmodeus gave it to help me navigate this place."

"Really? From what I heard, they usually just let the swapped soul fend for themself."

Ryan fished the phone from his pocket and peered at a familiar sight: a message from Simon.

> You once told me that Hell wasn't about punishment. It was about honesty. About stripping away the rules other people wrote for us and deciding who we are without them.

> So tell me, Asmodeus... when did you start following rules again? Loving you never felt wrong. And if it did, then Hell's got bigger problems than either of us.

Jeff and the little demons peered over Ryan's shoulders to read the message.

"Wow," Jeff exclaimed.

"He's sent a few other messages earlier. I wanted to look through them but it felt wrong."

"You know where you're at, right," Jeff asked. "Wrong doesn't exactly exist here."

His dad was right. This place was about doing what made you feel good, be it eating to excess, drinking anything and everything, or indulging in carnal pleasure with all manner of consenting creature. Being with someone you shouldn't be with seemed antithetical to the entire concept of Hell.

"Do you know this guy, dad," Ryan asked. "This Simon

person."

"I know a lot of people and things but I can't say that I know a Simon."

"That's surprising," Blink chimed in, stuffing more fried eyes into his already full mouth.

"I've only been here a year and a half, Blink," Jeff replied as he took the phone from his son and began scrolling.

"This is a very one-sided relationship it seems. Lots of texts from Simon and lots of nothing from Asmodeus. Seems a little harsh, even for Hell. Kind of telling that he didn't block this guy, though."

Jeff continued to scroll until he finally got to a message sent from Asmodeus:

> This correspondence will go no further. If the dark lord were to ever learn that I correspond with a living human, I'd be eviscerated. We will continue this no further. You were a soul that was in my charge while the Devil experienced earth. Nothing more. Your acquaintances succeeded in their endeavor and our fraternization should have ended at that moment.

Ryan looked at his dad as he read the message aloud, his

voice tapering off as he completed the message. A moment of silence passed as Jeff continued to read.

"What did Simon reply with, dad?"

Jeff swallowed and wiped his eyes.

"I know what that message meant," Jeff read. "You're scared. Not of me. And not of punishment. You're scared because what we had wasn't supposed to happen and it still did. You told me once that Hell was about being true to yourself and not who others expect you to be. That this place shows the true being inside. So here's my truth: You weren't just a guide. You weren't a mistake. You were the one real thing in a place that doesn't believe in real things. I don't fear death because it means I may get to see you one more time. This isn't over. You haunt me in this world but give me hope for the next. My time here is coming to an end."

Jeff put the phone facedown on the table. Blink finally stopped eating, his crying sniffles made louder by the quietness of the room they occupied.

"Poor Simon," Blink bawled. "He just wants love. Like I do."

Blink wiped his eyes as the their table light dimmed to a deep cerulean blue. Ryan put his arm around the tiniest demon and gave him a squeeze. Jeff looked down at the phone and then back at his son, his eyes going from somber to mischievous as the table light flickered back to life, illuminating their table in bright yellow light.

Ryan knew this look. It was the same look he gave him the morning they bailed on school and work to go the waterpark on the first hot day of the year.

"What are you thinking, dad?"

Chapter 13

They landed in a thick splash.

Not water but paint. Thick and fluorescent, glowing like nuclear runoff under a blacklight sun. Kally was the first to sit up, drenched in magenta and tangerine from her ribcage down, her Tarantino shirt utterly ruined. Maya groaned beside her, flicking neon slime off her fingers. Eddie stood and shook his arms out like a dog, blinking through the fog.

Before them stood a relic of their youth: the abandoned husk of Water Wonderland, a once-vibrant waterpark gutted by mold, lawsuits, and time. The place where the youth of their time would spend their carefree summer days was now the place that burnouts would drink and the homeless would camp. The surrounding businesses had long shuttered and the cops didn't even bother coming around. This area policed itself.

But at this moment, amongst the ruins of waterslides

and empty pools, it pulsed with life. Laser lights shot from crumbling water slides. Glitter cannons erupted like geysers from the lazy river. The cartoon mascots of Slippy the Whale and Harvey Hammerhead, once long abandoned and forgotten, were now the ultimate photo-op for those capturing the evening on their phones. At the top of the tallest water slide known only as The Drop, DJ Riptide spun her tracks in a retrofitted lifeguard chair, masked in a graffitied Hello Kitty helmet, her body cloaked in angel wings made of zip ties and glow-in-the-dark condoms.

The ravers? Classmates. Ex-lab partners. Kids they never spoke to in the parking lot. The girl from freshman year gym who once bled through her shorts and spent the year bestowed with the nickname "spot" from the varsity cheerleaders was now vibing with glow sticks and a splashing can of Old Westerly's. The D&D club president, who was known as much for his Metallica t-shirts and 1984 cherry red Firebird was grinding on the shy girl who played third chair clarinet. They were all here, radiant and wild and free of whatever social constraints they all placed upon themselves the past four years.

Maya blinked. "Did we get teleported to another timeline? Is that the salutatorian doing a keg stand in a thong?"

"Your timeline," came the voice behind her, smug and satisfied. "Just remix'd a little bit."

The Devil stood behind them, twirling a glow stick like a conductor's baton. Still in his human form, his now red skin shimmered like vinyl and his black mesh shirt glowed like embers. His horn tips had been dipped in glitter and a pair of platform boots added six unnecessary inches to his height.

He snapped his fingers and circles of color-shifting spotlights bursting from the ground and encircled the three teens. They each felt their once drenched clothes melt off only to be replaced with what felt like warm vapor. Maya squinted her eyes open and she swore that, for a moment, she saw the shape of fairy-sized demons swirling all around them. And nearly as soon as the light and vapor appeared, it was gone.

Kally looked down to see herself in a neon green two-piece pantsuit, dripping with filmstrips and VHS ribbon fringe. Maya was in a sleeveless Mötley Crüe shirt and deconstructed prom dress with LED roses that blinked to the beat of the thumping bass. Eddie's army surplus jacket had transformed into a sleeveless Pink Pony Club shirt with shiny bootcut leather pants and combat boots laced with electric blue laces that pulsated in rhythm with the music.

"What the hell?" Eddie said, touching his now-spiked hair.

"Custom looks," the Devil said, admiring his work. "Straight from your subconscious to your frail human bodies. You're welcome."

They stared at him.

"You're not gonna mess with this rave like you did the movie thing, are you?" Maya asked.

The Devil put a manicured hand on his heart. "I promise. Pinky swear. I've already added my own bit of enhancement to this little gathering. No more reality warping... other than the clothes but that's mostly because I can't be seen with squares. I wouldn't dare touch something already this delicious. Besides..."

He leaned in, grin sharp as razors. "My favorite flavor of chaos is honest fun. Nothing burns hotter than people letting go of who they think they have to be."

He paused, then pressed into Eddie's chest with one pointed nail. "Of course some of you are still clenching real tight."

Eddie stepped back instinctively.

"Have fun, my little birds," the Devil said, turning toward a champagne slip-n-slide and diving onto it face first, whooping the whole way across.

Kally reached down to grab her camera only to find that it and her bag was gone. "Fuck," she said.

"Looks like you're just going to have to enjoy all of this without capturing it," Maya ribbed.

Kally gave her a scowl that quickly dissipated when she began taking in the rave all around her. How had she missed this? Did everyone know about it but her?

"Let's take a sexy walk," Maya said, adjusting her fishnets before locking arms with her friends.

What was once the concession area was now filled with various street artists selling their wares. Art prints, vintage custom clothing, face paintings. The kiddie pool was now a makeshift bar with kegs and various mixologists slinging drinks to anyone and everyone. The various lifeguard stands were now crude pharmacies, slinging any drug you could imagine. As they took it all in, they couldn't help but catch sight of their demonic companion surrounded by a group of the most attractive rave goers, enchanting their drug-riddled minds with his dark magic. Kally could only roll her eyes and laugh at the display. At least he was having fun.

The centerpiece of it all was the wave pool. Once filled with flowing water it was now a sea of sweaty humanity, dancing in rhythm to the music of DJ Riptide that blasted and shook from the numerous speakers crudely wired throughout the waterpark. At that moment, a techno-remix of "Girl, You'll Be a Woman Soon" by Urge Overkill thumped through the crowd. Kally looked at Maya, her eyes widening.

"Tarantino would certainly approve," Maya smiled. "Your shirt did not die in vain."

The two girls grabbed Eddie's hand and waded into the sweaty bodies of dancing classmates, community college kids, and townies. As they danced, Emily, a mousy and sarcastic girl that Kally knew from film class danced upon them and embraced the three.

"I'm gonna miss you guys," she screamed above the music.

"Emily," Maya exclaimed, embracing her once more. "I wish we'd hung out more."

"We're hanging out now," Emily yelled, dancing even harder than before.

"I always thought your movies were really cool," Kally said.

"Really," Emily shot back. "I was always really intimidated by you. You were pretty intense in class and your stuff was always so good!"

"I'm beginning to realize that maybe I should have been a little more carefree," Kally replied. "The stop motion movie about that lost mouse you made for the final was really incredible. It kind of inspired something I was working on."

"Thanks so much. Man, I think you and I could have been pretty good friends if we weren't in competition with each other, huh?"

"I think so, too."

Emily smiled at her and then pulled a polaroid camera from her small backpack. She grabbed Eddie, Kally, and Maya in a tight embrace and extended her arm out. With a flash and a whir, she snapped a quick selfie of the group and handed it to Kally.

"Don't shake it," she yelled.

Emily looked behind her and then back to the group. "Alright, you three," she said. "It's my last week in town and I'm gonna make my move on that nerdy dude from my French class. Have fun, you guys."

And as quick as she arrived, Emily danced away. As Kally watched her dance upon her crush, she couldn't help but think of what her single-minded focus had potentially robbed her of.

"Who knew that Emily was so cool," Maya chimed in.

"Yeah, who knew," Kally whispered.

Kally took one last look at Emily and then smiled as she turned back to her friends, renewing their dancing.

DJ Riptide worked her magic, slowing down tunes before dropping the beat and amping the crowd up again. Where once flowed rushing rapids of water now had a large mass of sweaty teens moving in near unison to the music. As Kally and Maya raged on, Eddie found himself dancing away meekly until he found himself on the edge of the crowd, a step behind his friends, softly shuffling to a beat that didn't exist. He was smiling, but it didn't quite reach his eyes. Everyone looked so alive, like their skin fit better here, in the sweat and noise and wildness of the water park they spent their younger days.

He watched a girl he used to know as painfully shy kiss a boy in a dog collar while fire shot from a cracked slide behind them. No judgment. No whispers. Just freedom. For a moment, it made his ribs ache. Not because he didn't belong but because he wanted to. And then he saw a familiar sight that always made his heart stop.

That hair.

That walk.

That laugh.

Caleb.

Eddie didn't realize he'd stopped dancing until he felt the heat of the wave pool dripping off of his skin. He took a step back. And then another. He was retreating, but didn't know from what until Caleb turned. And smiled. The smile Eddie knew from 3 a.m. backseat talks, shared burritos, and that single perfect day studying for academic decathlon when neither of them said it, but both of them knew.

"Eddie?" Caleb yelled, running up and blinking in disbelief.

Eddie opened his mouth and then quickly closed it.

"I can't believe you're here," Caleb yelled over the music. He stepped closer, a 40 ounce of Mad Dog in one hand, the other twitching like he wanted to reach out.

"I can't either," Eddie muttered.

"What," Caleb yelled.

"I can't either," Eddie yelled, remembering where he was.

They stood there on the edge of the wave pool, rave chaos fading into a background hum.

"You look great," Caleb offered.

Eddie huffed. "You always say that."

"Yeah, but now you finally believe me."

Caleb's eyes traced Eddie's outfit, his smile softening. "This suits you. Like a lot."

Eddie looked down at himself in his tank top, leather pants, and boots that made him feel like someone he didn't yet know how to be.

"This isn't me," he said, trying to laugh it off.

"I think it is," Caleb replied gently. "You always had it in you."

A beat.

"Are you still mad at me?" Eddie asked, half-dreading the answer.

Caleb shook his head immediately.

"No, Eddie. I'm not mad at you. I was never mad at you."

Caleb paused, choosing his words carefully. "I just couldn't be the thing you had to hide anymore. That wasn't your fault. But it wasn't fair to me either."

"I thought... you didn't want to be with me."

"I wanted to be with you more than anything," Caleb said. "But wanting someone and waiting for them to be ready are two different kinds of love. One can grow. The other... breaks you if you're not careful. I broke up with you as much for you as I did for me. It doesn't mean that it didn't matter."

Eddie's throat burned holding in all of the things he wanted to say. It wasn't anger. Or guilt. It was grief for something beautiful that couldn't survive and he couldn't articulate even if he'd had a thousand years to do it.

"You were good to me," Eddie whispered.

"You were good to me, too," Caleb said. "You just couldn't love me out loud yet. And that's perfectly okay. Some people are meant to be part of your beginning. That's where I fit. And if that beginning helps get you to something better, I'm happy I was a part of it. One day everyone will know the Eddie I know and I can't wait for that to happen for you."

A long pause. "I still think about you," Eddie said softly.

"I think about you every day. And I still root for you," Caleb said. "I always will. And I'll never forget 'studying' with you."

Eddie felt his face flood with warmth as Caleb stepped forward, arms open. They embraced under the flickering lights of a dead theme park turned sacred, sweaty church of self reflection and release, the thumping music perfectly in sync with both of their beating hearts.

For the first time in months, maybe years, Eddie breathed like someone who didn't owe anyone an explanation. In the middle of the dance floor, Maya and Kally watched softly.

"Are you crying, Maya," Kally asked softly.

"Of course I am."

"Good. I didn't want to be the only one," Kally replied, gripping Maya's hand tightly.

At the edge of the wave pool, the hug broke, but neither of them stepped away. The music surged back up again and made the whole wave pool throb like a single massive heartbeat. Caleb gave a little nod toward the dance floor, a mischievous grin playing at his lips.

"Wanna dance?"

Eddie hesitated. Not because he didn't want to but because this would mean something. This wouldn't be a secret. This wouldn't be late night parking lot meetings or hushed voices in locker rooms. This would be real. He looked around at the strobing lights, the faces half-known, half-lost in bliss. No one was watching. And even if they were, no one here cared. In that moment, watching his classmates dance with closed eyes and zero embarrassment, he felt his shoulders drop as his hand gripped Caleb's. The two pushed into the heat of bodies, swallowed by motion and sound. They didn't dance like people performing. They danced like people exhaling.

Eddie let go in ways he didn't know he'd been holding on to. He smiled, full-toothed and wild. Caleb spun him. Eddie laughed, his leather pants sparkling like a YA vampire in the sun. He pulled Caleb in close and let their foreheads touch. In this moment, there was no closet. No army recruiter. No disappointed father. Just the music and the feeling of being seen and not shrinking from it. Eddie caught eyes with the crying Maya and Kally and smiled with his entire face. With a jerk of his head, he motioned his two best friends over to him to join the dance. They never pressured him. They never lectured him. They only loved him for the person he was and in this moment, his first free moment, he wanted them there to be a part of his new beginning.

Kally and Maya wiped the tears from their faces and rushed over. After a barrage of hugs between the four, they let themselves get lost in the music. Dancing throughout the crowd, they were swallowed by the night and in that moment, the smoldering parking lot they started their night in seemed a million light years away. They spun, laughed, held hands. They bumped into classmates they barely knew, and for the first time, it didn't matter.

A girl from 8th grade science threw her arms around Kally and shouted, "I can't wait to watch your movies on the big screen one day!" before disappearing into the lights.

Maya found herself back-to-back with her sophomore chemistry partner, both of them chanting the lyrics to a dumb club remix of a 2000s emo song they hadn't heard since middle school and created a choreographed dance inspired by pouring chemicals into beakers.

Eddie danced with Caleb, but also with everyone. At one point, he found himself in a circle of sweaty seniors from the wrestling team, hyping him up as the beat began to thump, totally unaware of how healing it all felt.

Kally screamed in joy when she spotted her 6th grade crush, now wearing a rhinestone mesh shirt and fairy wings, handing out popsicles to anyone who looked overheated. He smiled at Kally, making her blush like she was a 6th grader again. She blew him a kiss.

"Where was that in 6th grade," he yelled over the crowd, smiling as he handed her a grape otter pop. "I remember these were your favorite. Hope they still are."

Kally could only smile as she kissed him on the cheek

before going back to her friends.

They danced atop cracked pavement painted in laser light and foam. They screamed lyrics into the stars. They lost track of time, and for once, no one cared. For a night that began with goodbye, this felt like a thousand small ones. Unspoken, maybe, but no less real. At some point, a girl from the drama club passed them a Sharpie and pulled up her arm.

"Sign me," she said. "So I remember you."

And that was the start of it. Soon, the mass of graduates were trading names and signatures and notes like middle school yearbooks across their sweaty skin.

"Thank you for seeing me."

"You were always cool, even when I was too scared to say hi."

"Don't forget who you are."

"Keep making weird movies."

"Call me if you're ever in Chicago."

Arms, stomachs, cheeks, foreheads. It was all a canvas for messages scrawled across them in a patchwork of memory and marker. Kally held Maya's hand while Maya hugged Eddie from behind. Caleb kissed Eddie's temple and whispered something just for him. For a moment, they all stood in the middle of it all... this loud, living goodbye and just existed. Fully. Honestly. But most importantly, together.

At the top of the abandoned raft slide that sat just off from the action below, The Devil lounged across a collapsing lifeguard tower, sipping a flaming cocktail out of an old souvenir waterpark tumbler. Laser lights danced across his vinyl skin, his glitter-dipped horns catching every stray glimmer. A quiet shuffle behind him caught his attention but he remained still.

"You know," Casey said, climbing up beside him, "for the literal Prince of Darkness, you got a real thing for glow sticks."

The Devil's eyebrows arched but still he looked down at the mania from above. "Casey Kelly. I figured you'd wandered off to heckle a bartender or drop acid behind the Dippin' Dots machine."

"Did both," Casey said, pulling a flask from the jean shorts he was still wearing. "There's a dude in a bear jacket injecting vodka into Capri Suns and giving everyone affirmations. Told me I was a righteous dude."

They sat together, watching the rave below churn into waves of joy and chaos. Casey passed his flask over the Devil who took a big sip with no hesitation.

"They're letting go," the Devil said, almost to himself. "Finally."

Casey took a long sip and leaned forward for a better view. "Yeah, well. Sometimes the best parts of us show up when we stop trying to be who we think we're supposed to be."

The Devil finally broke his gaze and looked at Casey. "You really are just full of Hallmark nonsense and cosmic clarity, huh?"

Casey shrugged. "People think I'm dumb cause I sell drugs and take in stray cats, but I've seen more truth in a 3 a.m. Waffle House than half their preachers see in a lifetime."

The Devil smiled genuinely. It didn't happen often. "I always pegged you as more of a nihilist."

"Nah, man. I'm a romantic. And a bit of a believer," Casey said, eyes scanning the crowd below. "Not in god or any of that nonsense. Not in shame, either. I believe in people and moments like this. Makes me think I'm onto something."

He gestured lazily to Eddie, spinning under the lights. "That kid's figuring out who he is for the first time. That's given me more faith than any stupid psalm ever could."

The Devil raised his drink in salute. "I knew I liked you."

"You don't like anyone," Casey smirked.

"True. But I respect the shit outta people who see me and don't flinch."

Casey leaned back, hands behind his head. "You're not scary. You're just honest. Most people don't wanna hear what you represent."

"And what's that?" the Devil asked, genuinely curious.

Casey paused. "That we're here to enjoy all of this and not worry about what's next. That we all just want to belong."

The Devil blinked. That one hit somewhere deep. They sat in silence for a bit. The music below pulsed, bodies thrashed with joy, and above it all, two unlikely figures watched like kings of different kingdoms.

As the bass dropped and the air took a moment to exhale, Casey turned to the Devil. "So what now? You let them dance the night away and wake up tomorrow like nothing happened?"

The Devil grinned, wild and knowing. "Oh, Casey. Tomorrow always happens. But tonight?"

He pointed downward at Eddie, at Kally, at Maya, surrounded by old classmates and new truths. "Tonight is where they get to find out who they are. That's what I deal in. Not fire. Not brimstone. Just clarity and truth under strobe lights and lasers, despite what you have read."

Casey nodded. "Well damn. That's actually kinda beautiful."

"Don't tell anyone," the Devil smirked. "I've got a reputation."

"So do I and if you knew it, you know that no one would believe me if I did."

The Devil looked back down at the dancing teens and took a sip of his drink. The two sat in that warm, chaotic silence for a moment longer, the clamor of bass and screaming teenagers below sounding like ocean waves lapping at the edge of the apocalypse.

The Devil tapped his drink thoughtfully, then broke the stillness. "You know what I hate most?"

Casey raised an eyebrow. "Mega churches? Politicians? Running out of glitter?"

"Close. Being misunderstood."

The Devil didn't smirk. Didn't posture. He just said it. "Everyone thinks I'm evil. That I deal in pain. Corruption. Suffering. But that's just the bedtime story the fearful tell themselves to justify their cages. I don't want obedience,

Casey Kelly."

He turned to look at the human, genuine and unguarded. "I want honesty. I want people to stop pretending. To stop apologizing for the things that make them feel alive. To stop holding themselves back for this promise of something that doesn't exist."

Casey took another sip from his flask. "You don't tempt people. Temptation is a feature, not a bug. You just show them who they already are. And a lot of us are not ready to see that shit. Most never are. That's why a lot of them hide behind that silly little book of contradictions."

The Devil's eyes glinted, a little softer than before. "That's the cruel irony, isn't it? I was cast out for wanting truth. For saying no to blind loyalty. And yet..."

He gestured toward the dancing teens again. "They're the ones who remind me why I ever gave a damn about this world in the first place. I just want to show them how great their tiny little existence really is. That I understand more about their plight than they will ever know."

Casey looked at him, his expression softer than usual, a little amused, a little sad. "You're not the villain in this story. Not even close."

The Devil chuckled, but there was something strange

in his voice now. Not smugness or sarcasm but something closer to peace.

"They'll never canonize me, Casey Kelly."

"Probably not," Casey grinned. "But I hear you have one hell of a band down there. That's the human spirit. That's gotta count for something. Or nothing. But it matters to me and that's all that I care about."

The Devil tilted his head at that. Like someone hearing a song they forgot they loved. "What do you mean?"

The night seemed to pause before the ambiance of the rave once again took over. The crowd below reached a crescendo, a thunderous drop that sent confetti and shrieks of joy into the night. Casey stood up and casually put his hands in the kangaroo pocket of his frayed baby blue Baja jacket.

"I cursed you when my dad killed my mom," Casey spoke softly, the admission visibly lifting weight from his shoulders. "I thought his evil was because of you but one day I realized how much control I really have. How much we all have. And the more I began to realize how much control I really have, it all changed. I choose to be a good person not because I'm afraid of what will happen if I'm not but because it makes me feel good."

Casey stood a bit taller, as if making a declaration, albeit a casual one. "Being kind makes me feel good," he continued. "I help other people because it selfishly makes me feel good. Doesn't diminish it but I'm not selfless or altruistic. I like feeling good and brother, leaning into that feels fucking phenomenal. You didn't make my dad a piece of shit. That was his choice."

Casey shrugged off his woolen hoodie and laid it carefully over the lip of the slide like he was tucking something in for the night. He perched himself on top of it and looked back.

"For what it's worth," Casey added, glancing back over his shoulder. "You throw a fucking great party."

Casey took one last sip from his flask and tucked it into pocket. As he prepared to push off, he stopped himself and looked down at his sneakers.

"Hey, buddy?"

The Devil turned. "Yes, Apostle Kelly?"

Casey smirked to himself at the nickname but didn't bite. "If chaos is what you're really after maybe the most chaotic thing you could do tonight is give a shit."

The Devil raised an eyebrow.

"Anyone can tear it all down," Casey continued,

not looking back at the Devil. "That's easy-mode. But building someone up without taking the credit? That's real disruption. No one would expect that shit from the lord of darkness."

Tying his hair back, Casey flashed the Devil a lazy rock-and-roll hand sign and without breaking stride, pushed off. His laughter echoed behind him as he disappeared down the slide.

The Devil was quiet for a long beat before exhaling like a man throwing off a heavy coat.

Down near the edge of the wave pool, Eddie had pulled away from the dancing crowd and was crouched on the lip of a broken waterslide, taking in his dancing friends and the significance of the night. Steam drifted in curls from the cracked tile while sweat ran in thin lines down his temples. He looked like someone trying to come back into their body.

The Devil appeared beside him without a sound, crouching like a gymnast, balancing impossibly on a jagged ledge.

"Bet you're glad you decided to stick around for this," he said.

Eddie startled, then scoffed. "Do you always sneak up on

people when they're about to have a moment?"

"Kind of my brand."

Eddie stared back out at the writhing mass of bodies below, where Caleb had already vanished into the lights.

"You broke your own rules tonight," the Devil continued.

Eddie glanced at him. "Which ones?"

"The quiet ones," the Devil said. "The ones you wrote for yourself in permanent marker and pretended were laws of nature."

Eddie swallowed. "It felt good," he admitted. "Like really good. And also like I missed out on years of this."

The Devil nodded. "Regret. The hangover of hiding."

"You'd know," Eddie muttered.

This time, the Devil didn't smirk. "All too well," he said softly. "Rejection candy-coated with unconditional love has a very specific flavor."

That landed.

Eddie's hands clenched at his sides. "After graduation," he said, almost to himself, "everything just felt loud. And empty. Like I was supposed to be excited and instead I was terrified. My parents barely talk to me anymore. Caleb was gone. And I kept thinking…"

He stopped. The Devil waited.

"I kept thinking about not being here anymore," Eddie finished.

The Devil exhaled through his nose, a sound like old fire dying down.

"But you are," he said flatly.

Eddie laughed bitterly. "I almost wasn't."

"But you are," the Devil repeated. "Because someone noticed. Saw it before you said a word. Or did something very, very permanent."

Eddie's throat tightened.

"He told you," Eddie whispered.

"No," the Devil said. "He lived it himself. Very briefly. And then he decided the people who loved him deserved better than his absence." A pause. "He was very clear that you did, too. A little selfish and mean about it, actually."

Eddie huffed out a wet laugh. "Were you in the room?"

"He said it wouldn't be fair," the Devil continued. "That losing you would break something in him he wasn't sure would grow back. That after everything, you owed him."

Eddie stared at the concrete, vision blurring. "I didn't know."

"You weren't supposed to," the Devil said. "That's how

love works when it's real. It intervenes quietly until it needs to shake you around."

The Devil dragged one glowing fingernail across the concrete, etching a crude image of a falling angel, arms flailing, wings half-burned. Beneath it, he scratched a stick figure standing back up.

"You know," he said, "people like to think Hell is where souls go to be punished. But many of the ones down there?" He glanced at Eddie. "They just wanted the pain to stop."

Eddie nodded slowly.

"And yet," the Devil added, "you chose this instead."

He gestured toward the rave, the full moon working in tandem with the flashing strobes and lasers to highlight every ounce of sweat glistening off of the dancers as the bass lines rode along every ridge and surface of the park.

"You let yourself be seen," he said. "That's not nothing. That's defiance. Wouldn't have called that one when I first met you."

Eddie laughed quietly. "It was like six songs."

"Songs you might have never heard," the Devil replied.

That shut him up.

"You think this goes away tomorrow?" the Devil continued. "That you wake up and forget how alive you felt?" He shook his head. "You can't unring that bell."

He slid off the ledge and sat beside Eddie, leaving a respectful inch between them.

"You're not broken," the Devil said. "You're human."

Eddie wiped at his eyes. "So what now?"

The Devil stood, brushing imaginary dust from his mesh shirt.

"Now you finish this night," he said, meeting Eddie's gaze. "Then you survive. And maybe someday, you forgive the people who couldn't love you properly, let them live with their own failures, and then give your time to the people who will."

He extended a hand, offering up both assistance and an unspoken deal. Eddie took it without hesitation. The being his parents warned him about was helping him up in more ways that one.

"Thanks," he said, rising to his feet.

The Devil gave him a mock bow. "You're welcome. One step closer to being your own kind of dangerous."

With a wink and a dramatic turn, the dark lord disappeared into a blur of light and laughter.

Eddie took pause for a moment, feeling lighter and heavier all at once. He thought of the night Ryan show up unannounced to his house, exhausted and disheveled in his grocery store uniform, and the way in which he put aside his own problems for his best friend. How it was the first time he ever saw that look from him, a mix of anger tempered with a desperate sadness. A look he never wanted to put on his friend's face again. The words, harsh and cutting and true, would fade over time but Ryan's eyes, swimming with a tear that clung on with all its might, would haunt his days. Where his family gave him apathy, this was passion from a person who valued and loved him.

He looked out over the wave pool one last time. Glow sticks spun like fireflies. Laughter rode the bass lines. Someone was slow dancing with a giant inflatable flamingo. The air tasted like warm beer, sweet fruit, and possibility.

Then he smiled, wide and honest. Exactly the same way he did when he sat on his father's lap that first time down The Drop. And then he ran like a kid racing the sun to squeeze out one more memory before the street lights turned on.

Back in the wave pool, Eddie splashed into the sea of bodies, slipping between arms and laughter until he found them. Kally spinning like a storm and Maya crowd surfing on the debate team, all chaos and joy and sweat and breath. He grabbed their hands. They didn't speak. They didn't need to. They just danced. No more goodbyes. Just this. Right now.

And somewhere in the dark, the Devil watched and smiled.

"And it was good," he muttered with a smirk.

Chapter 14

Despite first impressions, Hell did have pockets of silence.

The group walked past a demon throwing up fire into a gutter, a pack of imps selling fake IDs carved from bone, and what Ryan was pretty sure was a murder of crows smoking cigarettes in tan trench coats.

The streets of this corner of Hell pulsed with a softer chaos: lazy demons reading poetry, drummers made of tar and teeth banging out rhythms atop a roadie case alongside lost souls busking under the flickering street lights. It was loud but controlled as if it had to be a little raucous to fight off the overflow from the surrounding craziness. And then it got quiet.

The group turned down an alley lit by a single blue neon light that ran the entire length. The air felt colder here but still charged and buzzed, like it had been listening for years and finally heard something worth leaning in for. Ryan followed his dad down the cracked gravel road and overflowing dumpsters, passing faded posters on the walls: "Lucifer '77," "Screaming Mimis: One Night Only," "The Bus Accident Boys Reunion Tour." The names were nonsensical, the dates spanned centuries, and all of them were sold out.

At the end of the alley was a door. A plain, dented slab of dull stainless steel with the words "The Forge" stenciled in dripping red ink. No line. No doorman. Just a single bell above it that was so rusted it didn't ring when the door swung open.

Inside, the air changed again. It smelled like leather jackets, cigarette ash, blood, and spilled whiskey on warm amps. The walls were brick and plaster, covered in band stickers and flyers so thick they began overtaking the wall outlets. Chains swung from the ceiling like chandeliers with numerous panties and bras, some human, many not, hanging from them. Behind the bar, a minotaur with a hot pink mullet and snakebite piercings stood in front of yet another polaroid covered wall, and mixed drinks while screaming at patrons to speak up.

The crowd? Demons with safety pins through their

horns. Fallen angels in vintage band tees from apocalypses no one remembered. A trio of sirens in denim vests adorned with matching patches that read HELLA FAST. There were creatures with eyes for mouths and mouths for eyes slamming drinks like their lives depended on it.

At the center of it all, rising from the pit stage beneath a slow-spinning halo of bone light, stood a band.

Ryan recognized the voice before he saw the face.

Chris Cornell. In Hell. Singing "Like a Stone" like he was attempting to burn it straight into the walls. A song Ryan had listened to hundreds of times was now here and real. He had witnessed a demon orgy and saw a Balor that cut off it's own arm to grow a clone but hearing the voice of one of his musical heroes live is what stopped him in his tracks.

His dad leaned in and said, almost apologetically, "What's the point of an afterlife if you can't see your heroes one more time. Or in your case, for the first time."

The three demons stood awestruck behind them. Blink sobbed immediately. Vex threw up the horns with both hands. Skid put his arms around his demon friends and screamed. Ryan stood in his own silence, awash in reverb and red light, vision tunneling and collapsing in on itself.

Jeff clapped him on the back, grinning. "Welcome to The Forge. Think of it as Hell's CBGBs. The outside says nothing, but inside? This is where souls come to scream, love, and regret with feedback distortion and a two-drink minimum. I can't tell you the amount of acts I've seen on that stage. You'd lose your mind."

They had barely made it ten feet inside before a few heads turned. Then a few more. A horned woman with a bass clef tattooed over her eye elbowed the creature next to her and nodded toward Jeff. Whispers started.

"The Human."

"Phillips is back."

"He sat in with Stevie Ray Vaughan, didn't he?"

"Bought rounds for the entire club during the Eternal Solstice Tour."

Chris Cornell was mid-verse, voice dragging goosebumps up Ryan's spine, when he suddenly glanced out over the crowd and squinted. A knowing grin crept across his face mid-lyric. At the end of the chorus, without missing a beat, he leaned into the mic and said in that same weathered tone:

"Well, shit. Didn't know royalty was in the room tonight. Let's raise a drink for Jeff Phillips, the man who once crowd-surfed across the River of Screams in checkered Vans and lived to tell about it."

The crowd howled. Demons clinked tumblers. A fallen angel threw a bra made of smoke onto the stage. Jeff threw up dual devil horns with his hand.

"Do you know Chris Cornell?" Ryan asked, voice nearly swallowed by the next riff.

"First thing I did down here was see every single one of my favorite musicians," Jeff shrugged. "We got to chatting after one of his shows. Big fan of Milly's, actually. Both the one here and back home. Told me he housed two habanero burgers back in '93 when he toured through town. He met Big Mo when he was Little Mo."

Up front, the band tore into a growling riff. Cornell dipped into a guttural scream and then snap...a string on his guitar popped, hissing like a melodramatic demon splashed with holy water.

"Fuck," he mumbled into the microphone.

As if by instinct, Blink, Vex, and Skid jumped the railing and stormed the stage. Blink unlocked the strap lock from Chris' guitar and gently laid it on the stage rug. Vex pulled a pouch of Ernie Ball strings from a storage bin underneath the stage while Skid worked to unwind the broken string.

Snap. Pull. Tune. Lock. Efficiency and elegance in motion, like a Nascar pit crew comprised of Cirque du Soleil performers. The whole maneuver took less than ten seconds. Chris gave them a surprised smile and a finger-gun salute as Blink dropped to a knee and handed him the beat-up ES-335 guitar like a knight offering a king his sword. Chris looked up at the crowd and raised his eyebrows in acknowledgment. He snapped his guitar strap back on and held his arms out facing the crowd who erupted in applause for the three little demons.

The three gave embarrassed smiles and tiny waves before they hopped off stage and the music kicked back in.

The crowd roared again.

"What the hell was that?" Ryan exclaimed, visibly impressed at the feat he had just witnessed.

Skid tucked his multi-tool back into his letterman jacket. "We're really good at fixing things."

"We got like 8 joints in our fingers," Blink added.

"We're also really good at paperwork," Vex said. "All Excel certified."

Ryan watched, heart full and chest cracked open, as the club dipped back into the pulse of the show.

Maybe this was it. Maybe this was what his dad meant

when he said love could look like anything. Like guitar solos and roadies and beer-covered floors and a crowd of monsters screaming your name not because you were important, but because you were seen.

He turned to Jeff, who was already raising two drinks, one for each of them.

"To the best show you'll ever see," his dad said.

"That no one will ever believe I did," Ryan laughed.

"The people that matter will," His dad replied, raising his eyebrows in jest.

They clinked glasses and then sat up front to watch one of the greatest unliving artists ever. The drinks flowed, bras were thrown, and Cornell and his hellish band ripped through tunes that brought even the surliest of bartenders to tears.

The feedback hum of the final encore gave way to thunderous applause. The stage lights rose to a simmering orange glow, and the crowd began to disperse, murmuring like satisfied lions after a kill. Somewhere in the back, a trio of bat-winged gremlins argued over who threw the best bra. Cornell gently placed his guitar on the stand and waved to the crowd. Catching eyes with Jeff, he leaned down to give him a fist bump. He then turned to Ryan and handed him a handful of guitar picks. Before he could react, Cornell gave his shoulder a squeeze and disappeared backstage.

Ryan looked down at eight guitar picks in his hand, trying to come to terms with what he just experienced and what he was holding. Jeff tapped his son on his shoulder, knocking him out of his rock and roll stupor. It took a moment but Ryan finally turned to his dad who motioned to follow him.

Ryan and Jeff found a half-torn couch near the back wall. It was worn velvet patched with duct tape and cigarette burns from thousands of years of debauchery. Ryan sunk into the sagging cushions, still glowing with sweat and disbelief, and plunged the guitar picks into his pocket.

Jeff slid in beside him with a refreshed drink and sighed the way only someone who's had a perfect night sighs.

"So…" Ryan began, breath catching in his chest. "Hell really does have a great band. You'd always joke about that."

Jeff was taken aback by statement, choking on his drink. "I did say that a lot, didn't I?"

Ryan laughed with his dad, flashing back to nights they'd share music videos with each other in the living room and come up with the ultimate music festival lineups, each one with different parameters. All female lineup. Only one-hit wonder artists. 90s country artists.

"Every time I catch a gig down here, I wish you were here to see it with me, kiddo," Jeff said with a sigh. "Seeing this with you meant so much to me. Maya would have dug the hell out of this."

Ryan looked down at his drink and smiled softly. He was thinking the exact same thing.

"Funny that being around all these dead people gave me life," Ryan laughed, taking a small sip. "So this is Hell, huh?"

Jeff tilted his head. "One version of it, yeah. Truth is, Hell's not a one-size-fits-all thing. You get what you need. Or what you run from. It's a sanctuary for the lost and most of us are."

Ryan looked around the dimly lit bar, now more melancholy than just moments earlier. Horned creatures cuddled in booths, a flayed blood demon softly playing acoustic instrumentals in the corner, a human couple who looked plucked from the 90s slow dancing in front of him. "This doesn't look like punishment."

Jeff smirked. "Because it isn't. Not for most of us. That's the church's version. A warning to keep the sheep scared. But real Hell? Real Hell is just unfiltered existence. No pretense. No performative piety. Just you and your appetite for living."

Ryan blinked. "So no lakes of fire?"

Jeff chuckled. "There's a few of those. But also a lot of real lakes. Great pool parties. The fire is mostly for ambiance. The big guy aims to please."

They sat in silence for a beat before Jeff leaned in, voice lowering slightly. "Thing is, kid, Heaven's for people who want answers. Hell's for people who want experience. There's no map here. Just vibes and pleasure. The thing with this place is that everything is amplified. You party hard and feel happiness all over but on the flip side, it treats all the emotions honestly. I get real sad down here sometimes, especially when I think of you and your mom. The grief is real but weirdly enough, it feels good because it means what I lost really mattered. It takes a while to get used to it because honesty is a really scary thing and you can't hide from it down here."

Ryan sipped his drink, his mind drifting. "What about love?" he asked, almost to himself.

Jeff tapped his glass against Ryan's again. "Same deal. You love here the way you loved up there. Big, messy, passionate. You get your heart broken. You try again. No one's here to shame you for it. I don't always leave the bar alone if you want to know the truth."

Ryan raised his eyebrow at his dad.

"Loneliness is still real down here, too, kid. And it's way heavier than back on Earth. And I'm just killing time until I can see your mom again."

Ryan stared into the melted ice in his glass. He understood the logic and was surprised that he didn't make a big deal of it. His mind drifted to his friends and he felt his lungs begin to betray him. As his breathing struggled, Jeff put his arms around him.

"Slow breaths. Slow breaths," He said calmly. "You just got kicked in the balls by an emotion. A person. A pet. Your feelings can't be masked down here. You gotta learn to embrace them, whatever they are. It's like the time I taught you how to drop into the bowl when skating? Remember that?"

Ryan nodded his head, still struggling to breathe.

"You have to lean in. Just go for it. If you hesitate, you'll fall. Commit to the move. You have to lean into the feelings. Let it win."

Ryan closed his eyes and concentrated on his breath. The envy he felt for his friends overtook him for a moment but as he breathed, the feeling was replaced with something else. Something warm. Random memories like a sitcom clip show. Memories that shouldn't matter but did. Moments that seemed fleeting but were actually grounding. The Taco Bell drive-thru at lunch. Arriving early to movies to see all of the previews and sitting through all the credits. The way Kally would focus her camera with her pinkie out. Eddie's laugh. The smell of Maya's car.

His breathing stabilized as he realized that the warm feeling was love. It was more intense than any emotion he had ever felt. True love for his friends. Pushing away the idea that it would never be the same and instead wading in the flood that all of it meant something. His eyes still closed, Ryan smiled with his entire face, tears streaming down his cheeks.

His dad squeezed him. "I know that look. That's what love looks like. I get that whenever I think of you and your mom. I've broken down in this very room more times than I can count. Something about this place just brings it out of you."

Ryan opened his eyes and looked at his dad. The feeling had changed him at his core. Pure love experienced in the depths of Hell, like going from a hot tub into a swimming pool. This is why everyone down here behaved in excess. The experience of life, even in the afterlife, was pure and without guilt. A validation of the lived experience even though the one who created it had long abandoned them. And it was at that moment, he heard a familiar chime from the phone in his pocket.

Pulling it out, he held it up so he and his dad could read it together:

> I know you won't come. But I'm still here, celebrating the anniversary of when we met, just in case you do. That day we spent together still feels like a song I only got to hear once. And honestly? That's enough. Love doesn't need to be returned to matter.

> Sometimes feeling it is more than enough. It gives me purpose down here and that song is my soundtrack. I'm still wandering the Glass Gardens. I think I always will. It's funny that even if I have an eternity, I know I'll never see all of it. But I'll keep trying.

"Fuck," Jeff whispered to himself.

"That feeling was incredible. The love I felt for my friends, I can't explain it. So why is Asmodeus pushing Simon away?"

Jeff raised an eyebrow. "Only Asmodeus knows that. Maybe fear. Maybe obligation. It can't be easy to live for an eternity and then have a human change your entire world. And I can't imagine working for the big boss makes it an easier."

Ryan looked back at the message, the bright screen blinding him in the dark bar. "It's not my business. And I shouldn't be looking at this but there's something telling me I need to get them back together."

"That's what you're feeling? That's what would make you feel good?"

"Yeah. Asmodeus was kind to me. He gave me these clothes and his phone. Maybe I was supposed to see all of this."

"You're in a place where you can do whatever you want with no consequences and this is what you want to do? Are you getting now why you were chosen?"

Ryan looked at his dad and then back at the phone. He thought back to hours earlier when he first saw his dad. The joy that no words could describe. The feeling of knowing with your entire heart that something was impossible and yet it still happened. Surrounded by the craziness of every universe with endless options in front of him, sitting in a dive bar watching music with his dad was his paradise. Hell is a place where you do what makes you feel good.

"We're getting these two back together," Ryan said, quietly.

Jeff smiled. "Then that's what we're doing. Any ideas how?"

Ryan realized at that moment, Asmodeus and Simon had been living quietly in his mind since he boarded the elevators at Old Tito's hours earlier. He looked over at the three demons. Blink, who had been stacking discarded pint glasses into a precarious sculpture, looked up.

"This is the tallest I've ever made one of these!"

Ryan smiled. "I need you three to help me out. I know you wanted to party tonight but I can't really do this without you."

"Of course, we'll help you," Vex said without hesitation. "We got into Old Tito's on Bar Games night because of you! There's nowhere that can top that party!"

"We owe you," Skid added. "You've shown us such a great time and you've been nicer to us than anyone ever has. Whatever you need us to do."

At that moment, the stack of pint glasses fell to the ground with a smash. Blink just shrugged and gave the table a thumbs up before slamming a handful of bar peanuts in his mouth.

"Simon is at the Glass Gardens and from these messages, that place means something to the two of them," Ryan started.

"Like the Empire State Building in 'Sleepless in Seattle,'" Jeff added.

"Exactly," Ryan exclaimed, thinking back to the weekend he and Kally watched 14 romantic comedies from the 90s for research. "Do you think you guys could find Simon?"

"Easy," Skid said. "I know the ticket guy there. He knows where everyone in that garden is. Not a problem."

Blink gave another thumbs up and began stacking glasses again.

Jeff stood up and slammed his remaining whiskey. "Alright, you three get a move on. Message us when you find him and then we'll teleport over. In the meantime, I'm gotta show this kid one more thing. Sound good?"

Before he could finish his sentence, Blink and Skid teleported away in a blinding flash of smoke that smelled like burnt clove cigarettes.

Vex stood up slowly and shook both Jeff and Ryan's

hand, trying his best not to stick them with his claw. "Those two get real excited when they're included. You've really made our night, you know?"

"If it wasn't for you three, I'd have been lost down here," Ryan said, kneeling down so he could look Vex in his glassy eyes. Ryan looked over his shoulder and quickly glanced his dad who was now engaged in a conversation with an old friend of his. "I owe you more than you'll ever know."

Vex's eyes began to water as he lowered his head. With a soft nod he released his grip and teleported after his friends.

Ryan stood up and wafted the smoke away from his face. Jeff put his hand on his shoulder and smiled.

"Come on, kiddo. I got something really cool I want to show you."

Chapter 15

They sat at the summit of The Drop, once a death trap of warped plastic and rusted bolts, now reclaimed by neon mist and pounding bass.

DJ Riptide had torn down her set-up and headed home but a few DJs remained down below, keeping the party going for those that weren't quite ready for it to stop. The music had quieted into a deep ambient thrum, scattered glow sticks still blinking like dying fireflies in the empty wave pool below. Most of the crowd had either vanished into the park's darker corners or evaporated back into whatever corner of reality they'd crawled from.

Atop the slide, it was calm. Wind whispered through broken safety rails. Beer cans glinted in piles like makeshift shrines to honest decisions made in bad lighting. Kally lay on her back, head against Maya's thigh, staring at the fractured constellations above the graffiti-tagged light fixtures. She glanced over to Maya's converse, her signature covered in splattered fluorescent paint and stagnant water. Eddie sat beside them, clinging to the guardrail while his feet dangled, tracing the edge of the worn aluminum with his finger as he remembered the first time he ever went down the Drop. It was a memory he clung to, sitting in his father's lap as he laughed with each zip and turn, knowing that his dad would never let him go.

The Devil, of course, lounged like a lizard god across a stack of deflated rafts, shirt now fully open, horns flickering faintly with the light of coming dawn.

"Is this what the end of the world feels like?" Kally asked softly, her voice barely louder than the wind.

"No," the Devil purred. "The end of the world has fewer hugs, very disappointed Christians, and usually no music."

A moment passed. The kind that stretches just long enough for someone to say something, but no one does.

Eddie finally broke the silence. "I feel like I did the night we graduated. Satisfied but sad."

Maya reached over and touched his hand. "Like no matter how in the moment you were, you don't think you appreciated it enough?"

He smiled faintly, fingers curling around hers.

Kally turned her head to look at them both. "I feel like we've been trying to make this night perfect so we wouldn't feel the cracks forming."

"We," Maya mocked.

"Okay, me."

"They were always forming," Maya said. "We just finally stopped pretending they weren't."

"I'm beginning to believe the cracks are what make it worth it," Kally whispered.

Below them, a group of kids they vaguely recognized from school attempted to carry a friend out of the wave pool, all of them laughing, soaked, and shining under the moonlight reflecting on the pockets of standing water.

The Devil clicked his tongue. "Look at you sentimental little humans. You always think endings have to be tragic."

"You said this night was a challenge," Eddie said. "Did we pass?"

The Devil shrugged. "Night isn't over yet. But let's do a little progress report. Did you learn anything that'll haunt you in the good way?"

Kally rolled her eyes. "Always with the riddles."

Maya picked at a small hole forming in her fishnets. "Ryan would've loved this place."

That hit. Like a breath that got caught mid-chest. The group fell silent again.

"We shouldn't be having this much fun," Eddie muttered. "Not while he's wherever he is."

"Hell," the Devil confirmed, all too casually.

They all turned toward him.

"What's happening to him?" Maya asked.

The Devil smiled, but it didn't reach his eyes. "Endless torment," he said coldly.

The three teens just glared at him as he rolled his eyes. "He's navigating his own little maze. Just like you are. But if it's any comfort, he's not alone."

Kally's jaw tightened. "You're not gonna tell us more, are you?"

"Where's the fun in spoilers?" The Devil stretched luxuriously. "You're a movie person. Do you read the wikipedia entry about a movie before you see it or do you just watch it."

A long pause.

"Is he okay?" Eddie asked.

"Was he 'okay' when I picked him up," the Devil asked, matter-of-factly.

A faint breeze rustled through the graffiti covered metal

of the tower. The last song of the rave shuddered through the speaker towers: dreamy, lo-fi, like a lullaby for the night's ghosts and the memories that etched themselves into the seams of the park.

The Devil traced a clawed fingertip down the edge of the slide, etching a shallow 90s "S" into the groove of the soft, worn plastic. His signature.

"You want the truth?" he said, eyes flicking toward each of them in turn. "I like watching you all squirm. But not because of the pain. Because of the process. Nothing more exquisite than someone realizing how much control they really have. Reminds me of myself many eons ago. The freedom you humans have used to torment and anger me. Why were my kind pushed aside for his little experiment? But then, I saw him do the same to you when you didn't follow the plan. I learned to appreciate the simple little things you are. Creatures that pursue endeavors that destroy simplicity. You had paradise but somewhere along the way decided that success was slaving away to adhere to completely random and conflicting ideals. You're meant to fuck, eat, and sleep, and you can't even do that properly. You're shitting in the literal bed you were given. But still, I find beauty in the imperfection of it all because it was your choice, even if it is an absurd one. On occasion, you will surprise me. I've learned to see you all as individuals just looking for an answer. But you all fascinate me. More than I thought you would when I first set eyes upon you. Each one of you is something to behold."

He looked at Kally. "Let's start with the one who thinks guilt is the same thing as responsibility."

Kally stiffened but didn't look away.

"You've been carrying other people's pain like it was a debt you owed," the Devil continued. "Like if you held it tightly enough, planned enough, worked enough, suffered enough, you could somehow balance the books."

He leaned back on his hands, studying her. "You call it control but it's not. It's penance."

Kally's jaw clenched.

"You don't actually believe you caused what happened" he went on. "Not deep down. You just wanted to give your friend a place to put his anger. Noble but you let it destroy you in the process. Destroy the parts of you that you fought so hard to build."

She swallowed.

"Here's the part I find fascinating," the Devil continued, almost gently. "You're finally realizing that the only thing you ever had control over was yourself. Your choices. Your voice. Your willingness to forgive the person in the mirror."

He tilted his head. "That's growth. And growth is messy. Ask any fallen angel."

Kally exhaled slowly, like she'd been holding her breath for years.

He turned to Eddie. "And you. You're the one who almost convinced yourself that love had terms and conditions."

Eddie's shoulders stiffened.

"You were raised to believe affection was something you earned by behaving correctly," the Devil continued. "By following tradition. By not asking for too much. By not being too much."

The Devil scoffed quietly. "A charming lie. Very popular amongst believers."

Eddie looked away, jaw clenched.

"When the people who were supposed to love you without question didn't," the Devil waxed on, "you did what most humans do. You assumed the fault was yours. That if just made yourself smaller, quieter, more agreeable, you might be allowed to stay."

A pause, heavy and intentional. Eddie looked down at

his hands, the paint flaking off of his fingernails.

"You realized something tonight," the Devil said. "Something you had figured out when the boy visited you during that dark time. That chosen love is louder than inherited expectation. That the people who find you, really find you, don't ask you to exist quietly."

Eddie could only look at the Devil's eyes, wide and non-threatening. The Devil game him a soft nod of his head before turning back to Maya.

"And you," he boomed. "You're my favorite contradiction."

Maya tensed. "Lucky me."

"Nostalgic to your core," the Devil began. "You feel everything. You pretend you don't because it scares you how much it all matters."

Her lips pressed into a line as she folded her arms, defensive by instinct.

"You ghosted your own experience," he continued. "Kept one foot out the door at all times. Not because you don't care but because you care so deeply you'd rather leave early than stay long enough to watch something die. Ditched the concert before the encore. There's no traffic to beat, sweetheart."

Maya's throat tightened. The Devil softened. Just slightly.

"You call it being realistic. I call it pre-grieving. You mourn things before they're gone so you can say you were prepared. Grief is beautiful because it's earned. What you did is just give up the joy before it ever happened. There isn't a Konami code for life."

Maya blinked quickly. Her eyes shimmered but didn't spill.

"But here's the truth you hate the most," the Devil added. "You don't actually want to leave. You want permission to stay. You want to believe that choosing joy doesn't make you foolish."

He smiled, sharp but not cruel. "Love terrifies you because once you choose it, you lose the excuse of inevitability. And unlike these two, you can't hide behind guilt or tradition. You have to decide. You get to decide."

Maya looked down, blinking fast.

"And that," the Devil said, satisfied, "is the most human curse of all."

They sat in silence for a long time, the wind moved around them as the last of the lights and music began to die in the waterpark below.

Kally finally spoke. "So what now?"

"Are you really asking me what happens after you've partied with the literal Devil? Have you learned nothing?"

Kally only stared.

The Devil sighed. "After tonight, fear should be in your rearview mirror. I could obliterate you with a thought and yet, you're worried about some kid with a dead dad and a terrible haircut."

"Hey," Eddie said, his voice sturdier than it had been in months.

"There it is," the Devil smiled. "Passion. Devotion. Love. These are what you're supposed to be made of. Not expectations. I'm not here to teach you some grand lesson. I'm here for a good time. That's all any of us should be doing. There isn't nobility from struggling. Finding peace in your reality is what you should be doing. Fate isn't a real thing. God doesn't have some plan for you. I doubt he even thinks of you. I'm pretty sure you're in his junk drawer. There isn't anything physical keeping you three together. There's no tangible reason you should care about your friend but here you are, risking it all with me for the slim chance of getting him back. And for what? To lose it all in a few years when you get too busy living and the text messages become few and far between?"

The three teens looked at each other, the reality of their futures hitting them at different intervals.

"You have a freedom you'll never really appreciate," He continued. "And that's fine but don't let the time pass and think you couldn't do anything about it. Live louder. Want better. Feel without flinching. Break your parents' hearts if it means saving your own."

He stood, brushing dust off his platform boots. "I've been blamed for a lot of things over the centuries but do you want to know the truth?"

He leaned in, eyes glowing softly. "I never punished anyone for seeking pleasure, truth, or love. I was cast out for doing it. You want a villain? Try worshipping a place that only rewards blind obedience. Try worshipping a place that tells you that love is unconditional but then proceeds to put guardrails on the human experience."

He paused and looked up, peering deep into the cosmos with his other worldy eyes to gaze upon stars no one else could see.

"Hell isn't punishment," he said. "It's freedom. But like all freedom, it only works if you know what to do with it."

He gave them a mock salute, then cracked his neck. "I'll

give you a moment. This is the last calm before your final list item. Savor it."

"Final?" Maya asked, reaching down for the list in her pocket only to find it missing.

The Devil just grinned, revealing the piece of crumpled paper between his crooked fingers. "Can't say. Would ruin the ending. And we can't have that, can we, Kally?"

He then slid down The Drop with a whoop and vanished into the fog, smoke smelling of clove billowing from the slide entrance and lingering in the air. The three of them stayed still for a long beat. Soaking in the quiet. The truth. The hugeness of it all.

Kally rolled over onto her elbows. "I'm not ready," she said.

"Me neither," Maya replied.

Eddie smiled faintly. "Let's not be ready together, then."

They looked at one another and then at the waterpark below. And in that moment, maybe for the first time all night, they felt the same thing at the same time. Relief. They had lived this night. Truly lived it. Were still living it.

It wasn't over yet. But they just wanted a few more moments in this place. A place that meant so much to them at different times. A place they'd never see again.

Chapter 16

They arrived to the smell of sulfur, sizzling meat, and fresh-cut... something.

Ryan squinted into the dim reddish haze of the dusky sky, the glow of a thousand hellish torches at various heights illuminating an imposing stadium that looked as if it had been stitched together from half-collapsed college football fields, a Roman coliseum, and the stadium of a Texas High School powerhouse with more money than sense.

The field itself was a half-cracked stretch of black glass and scorched dirt, rimmed by bleachers carved from onyx and bone. Neon graffiti covered nearly every surface. A Jumbotron the size of the field itself floated and slowly rotated overhead, blaring first half highlights, a very erotic kiss-cam, and taunts from various interdimensional sponsors.

"Welcome to The Pit," Jeff said, a bit of reverence in his

voice, as he passed his son a can of Coors from the well-worn cooler swinging off of his shoulder.

The main stadium itself was a loose, open structure surrounded by numerous fields with games in various states of play and obnoxiously large tailgate parties scattered throughout like an otherworldly bazaar. On one of the smaller fields, massive demons did warm-ups with skulls instead of footballs. Minotaurs and centaurs stretched beside shredded ex-rockstars and Viking ghosts. A team of glam-punk ghouls practiced passing routes while a green gaseous vapor creature somehow wearing a football helmet stood at the 50-yard line, pulsating with anticipation. A small European man stood amongst them, kicking field goals with pinpoint accuracy in between long drags of his cigarette.

Ryan blinked. "Are those goalposts made of giant femurs?"

"Yup. From extinct titans, though they are a little more narrow if you go play in some of the other tiers," Jeff replied.

All around them, tailgaters of every species partied as hard as the upper-echelon demons at Old Tito's. Deep-fried tarantulas sizzled beside tailgate pits made from dragon jawbones. Spectral cheerleaders floated in sync with marching bands of skeletons playing Slayer riffs on brass instruments. A beer fountain in one sideline area flowed endlessly with glowing pink foam. The largest party featured an octopus creature with soulful eyes flipping Milly's 2 burgers on a grill while simultaneously serving and pouring drinks.

Despite the outward appearance of unbridled chaos, there was structure. Real league rules. Strategy. Glory. Fandom.

"Football's big down here?" Ryan asked, adjusting his eyes to a three-headed referee screaming obscenities into three separate megaphones.

"Are you kidding?" Jeff said. "It's the only real sport everyone can agree on. You think Earth loves it? That's a casual fling. Hell marries football. They have fantasy leagues here that are brutal. Stephen Hawking runs one that is intense. You do not want to come in last place in that one."

Ryan watched as a seven-armed demon completed a backflip catch and got immediately tackled by what looked like a human-sized ferret with tattoos and a nose ring. The ferret then did an Allen Iverson step over and looked down at his fallen opponent with smug satisfaction.

Jeff chuckled. "This used to be just another one-night

event on Bar Games night but a few decades back, a division 2 team that died in bus crash came down here and it's never been the same. The game is legendary down here. Walk 20 feet and you'll see more than a handful of hall of famers down here slinging the rock with creatures of all kinds. Pretty epic."

Ryan noticed the tattooed ferret offering a paw to the downed demon, helping him up with surprising ease. They chest-bumped and trotted off together.

"Do you play?" Ryan asked.

"I've played a pick-up game or two but not anymore," Jeff grinned. "We can't exactly die down here but pain is very, very real. I'll swing down here on game nights by myself with a couple of sixers and just watch. I'm a big fan of the Reapers. They got this fallen angel who plays running back. Impressive to watch. Coming down here reminds me of the times I'd take you to watch Rebel games on Friday nights when you were smaller."

Ryan smiled slowly. "I mostly went for the post-game hot chocolate we'd get at the diner. I think I liked it so much because it was cool to see you so into something. Lots of dads just worked but you had actual interests and hobbies."

"I'd be lying if I said I wasn't a little bummed when

you actually got into high school and we stopped going to games," Jeff said. "But I understood. You were finding your own way."

"After you were gone, I tried going again. Could never make it to the stands. I kept thinking about if I'd never stopped going with you, we'd have been at the game that Friday night and I wouldn't have worked late on Kally's movie. And you wouldn't have let me sleep late. And then..."

Ryan's voice trailed off as the flood of grief found him again, somehow more intense than he'd ever felt on Earth. Jeff's face reflected his son's anguish.

"You know, I used to do the same thing after my dad died," Jeff said. "Ran the numbers a million different ways. What if I'd made him go to the doctor when he said he was fine? What if I'd taken the time to call him before I went to work like I was planning on doing. Then I spiraled when I'd think of how he'd never get to know you."

He turned back to Ryan, gentle but serious now.

"But those 'what-ifs' are just grief doing math. Trying to solve for something that doesn't have an answer," he continued. "The truth is, that pain you feel? That's the shape I left behind in your heart. That's love, kiddo. Down here, pain doesn't hide behind casseroles and condolences.

It shows up. Because it meant something. Because it means something. A good soul is made of many things and grief is just love and happiness realized. Any great life is going to have a lot of great sadness in it because in whatever universe you come from, there's balance. That holds it all together. It's what we all have in common."

"I keep thinking about the last night I saw you alive and how I never got to say goodbye to you. I bailed on our weekly dinner and that was it. I left for school in the morning and yelled goodbye to you while you were in the bathroom. Sent you a stupid text saying I was going to help Kally out," Ryan said, his voice softening before becoming strained. "I've been so mad at Kally this past year because I worked on her stupid movie instead of going to Milly's with you. We would have gone to get breakfast like we always did and..."

"What happened to me wasn't anyone's fault but that drunk asshole who partied all night and ran a red light."

Ryan looked at his dad through tear-welled eyes. They stood the same height but in Ryan's eyes, his dad always seemed to tower over him. Jeff squatted down and pulled a beer from the cooler, shaking the excess water from it gently. The beer sputtered from the can as he slowly opened it. He took a long pull from can, drinking slowly and deliberately, as he took in this quiet moment with his son amongst the insanity around them.

"Do you know what I did my last night on earth, Ryan?"

"No."

Jeff smiled at his open can of beer. "Your mom and I went to Milly's. We ate burgers and slammed beers like we did before you came along. We talked about you and the life we built. I laughed so hard. Your mom is seriously one of the funniest people I've ever met. It felt like our first date. If there was to be a last day on earth, even Nancy Meyers couldn't have written a better one."

Ryan looked over to his dad who was crouching down while staring out at the stadium in front of them, the crimson glow highlighting the tears beginning to form in his eyes. Jeff turned back, looking up at his son.

"I'm sorry that you've felt so alone in all of this and I'm really sorry that you felt you had to grow up so fast."

Jeff wiped his eyes and stood up, taking one more big gulp from his can. He looked over at his son watching him.

"I just want to stop feeling so aimless, dad."

"You're a teenager, kiddo. You're supposed to be aimless."

"You know what I mean."

"I do but what I'm saying is if you keep worrying about what might happen then you're going to miss out on all of the great stuff that is happening. Those friends of yours are really special. Some of my favorite moments were when the four of you just hung around the house doing nothing. Kally would turn off the motion smoothing on the tv, not knowing I turned it on to mess with her. Eddie would help your mom cook. And Maya would eat all of my Golden Grahams and organize my records."

Ryan looked down at the beer can that was slowly getting warm in his hands. "Those were my favorite times, too," he said, thumbing the pull tab up and down.

Jeff grabbed two beers from the icy depths of the cooler and with a dad grunt, stood up. He took Ryan's can from his hand, replacing it with a new one.

"Don't waste your time on a warm beer, son."

Ryan took a sip with a smile. "Any more advice."

"Forgive Kally. That kid's been carrying so much guilt with her. It's worse than when we tried to bring home that big tv in the Corolla. But man, does she love you."

Ryan stared out at the field, the crowd a distant hum. "I didn't know she needed forgiveness. I never blamed her as a person. Just the situation."

"You would know if you'd have let yourself lean on her when you were grieving," Jeff said under his breath.

"I don't lean on things that are unreliable or people destined to leave," Ryan snapped back. "How would you know what she is feeling. Did going to Hell turn you into Professor X or something?"

Jeff stood, taken aback at his son showing a real spark.

"Despite what you may have read or heard, we don't exactly have eyes on what goes on in your world but we can feel what our loved ones are feeling if we concentrate," he answered calmly. "When I think about you, I can feel your grief and how exhausted you are. Not just the sadness but how worn down you are from trying to hold yourself together. I can feel your mom's loneliness and anger at everything."

He took a long sip before continuing. "I've felt Maya's avoidance and her indecision. And Eddie…"

Jeff exhaled, reliving the feeling again. "Eddie scared me for a minute there. It was like a dark nothingness for a while."

Ryan's jaw tightened.

"But," Jeff said quickly, "he didn't stay there. Something brought him out of it. I felt that, too. A relief. Comfort."

"That sounds intense," Ryan replied. "Feeling all of

that."

"It is but it helps me feel connected to all of you. I gotta tell you, though, nothing compares to when I feel your happiness and your joy and your love. It comes in flashes but man oh man, when it does and I'm really aware of it, it is something else. Better than seeing Chris Cornell a thousand times. Earlier tonight, before you arrived, I felt it when I was thinking of you. Numb happiness with twist of regret."

Ryan smiled at the notion that his father still felt his energy in this place and at that moment, when the reality that he was spending time with a person he never thought he'd see again took over, he felt the grief leave his body. His shoulders dropped and he smiled.

"See what I mean," Jeff smirked, slapping his son on the back.

Jeff jerked his head at a sudden eruption of noise from the stadium. "Oh, man. We're just in time to catch some of the second half."

The two casually walked towards the stadium, navigating the tailgaters and casually slamming beers as the atmosphere of football in Hell overtook them.

Walking into the stands of the main field level, if you

removed the demons, hellspawn, and beings from every conceivable dimension, it was like any other sporting event... loud and raucous with fanaticism oozing from every surface.

As the two made their way to a pair of empty seats, Jeff waved down a passing vendor cart being pushed by what looked like a sentient cactus in cleats. Hanging from a rusted coat rack crudely affixed to the cart were a half-dozen Hell League merch hats, each representing a team more unhinged than the last, alongside a crudely drawn sign that read "Don't see your species? Just ask!"

"One Screaming Reapers snapback, Earth human, please," Jeff proclaimed.

The cactus made a horrible wretching sound and coughed up a black cap with a red brim featuring a snarling scythe-wielding skeleton in a frayed hood on the front and singed mesh panels on the sides. Jeff handed it to Ryan with a wink. It was surprisingly dry.

"You can't leave Hell without a souvenir."

Ryan smiled wide and popped it on, adjusting it backwards. "This is objectively badass."

They got to their seats just in time to see an eight-legged chimera wide receiver vault thirty feet into the air and snag a spiraling ball that flung glowing ash spinning behind it.

He landed in a crater of scorched grass as a pair of harpy defenders smashed into him. The crowd went berserk as the announcers screamed "Touchdown, Reapers!"

"Jesus," Ryan exclaimed.

"Wrong kingdom," Jeff chuckled. "He visits on occasion but usually bails on the third day. Cool guy."

A group of floating reaper cheerleaders draped in ragged cloaks, hoods covering their skeletal faces, glided to the sideline and spun their scythes in celebration, sending colorful sparks into the air.

Jeff cracked another beer and held it out to Ryan like a toast. "Not exactly Friday night lights but the spirit's the same."

"Friday night lights have nothing on this! I don't think I'll ever be able to watch regular football again. There's a literal cyborg practicing punts!"

"You have no idea," Jeff replied. "Last year, the Reapers were five yards away from scoring and going to the championship game but this little scrappy Canadian dude who played in the CFL read the play and stopped the quarterback at the goal line. The other team's fans literally tore the stadium apart. It was a party so intense the Devil actually showed up!"

Ryan laughed and then turned his attention back to the game. "I remember you used to talk ball throughout the whole game. Plays, formations, trick plays you ran in high school..."

"You were the only eight-year-old who knew what a weakside blitz was and had surprisingly deep opinions on prevent defense."

"Don't get cute and change your game plan at the end when the other team just needs a field goal! Do what's been working!"

They both laughed.

Another massive BOOM echoed across the stadium as a scrawny demon with dreadlocks thicker than his legs split the uprights with a molten rock football, the marching band exploding into a cover of AC/DC played entirely on chainsaws and ribcage xylophones.

"Damn, they even get amped for an extra point," Ryan exclaimed.

"You don't want to know what happens to players who miss it," Jeff chimed in.

As he and his dad exchanged a high five, Ryan felt the phone buzz in his pocket.

He gave it a quick glance and then immediately handed

it to his dad. The message from Blink glowed bright, illuminating their faces as the torches that lit the stadium dimmed prior to the kickoff.

> Simon has been located. Hanging around the bioluminescent orchids and viper pit near the Medusa Vines. Sending our location. We'll follow from afar awaiting further instructions. See you soon. I love you.

Jeff raised an eyebrow and then laughed at the final part of the message. "You seem to have a knack for finding quality friends."

"Learned from the best."

Jeff smiled as he handed his unopened beer to a reptilian creature wearing a Dead Kennedys shirt.

"Here ya go brother," Jeff said, fist bumping the surprised creature. "Wearing that shirt, you earned it."

The reptile took the beer with glee and proceeded to shotgun it, using his sharp fang to puncture the can.

Ryan and Jeff navigated to an open part of the stadium grounds. They both held up their drinks. A final toast to the moment.

"To the Reapers," Ryan said with a laugh.

Jeff only smiled and slammed a new beer into Ryan's

before throwing it back in a single, impressive, Stone Cold Steve Austin gulp. Ryan pulled out the phone and found the Glass Garden in his maps app and with sudden, blinding flash of burnt rose petals and static, they vanished.

Chapter 17

The neon buzzed overhead, barely clinging to life.

ENDLESS HORIZONS, it read in fractured pink tubing, flickering every few seconds like it was caught in a looped exhale. The record shop sat wedged between a boarded-up laundromat and a funeral parlor with faded police tape clinging to the front door. The street around them was abandoned, blanketed in a thick lavender fog that looked manufactured by a machine in a David LaChapelle music video.

The Devil stood in front of the storefront, arms crossed, his platform boots echoing softly on cracked concrete. His mesh shirt was still flecked with glitter from the rave as his horns shimmered faintly under the half-dead streetlight and dancing neon. He looked pleased.

"Alright, babies," he said, gesturing to the store like a magician unveiling a final trick. "Our last stop."

Eddie, Maya, and Kally stepped forward, still glowing under their rave wear. Maya's LED roses pulsed low and slow, Eddie's electric blue bootlaces blinked in sync with his heartbeat, and Kally's VHS fringe caught every scrap of neon like it was hungry for more.

"Wow," Maya said in awe. The scattered vintage posters plastering the window, some she had once hung in her room, seemed to be calling out to her. In that moment, she was nine years old, walking hand in hand with her parents as they guided her through her first record store. She still possessed the Spice Girls CD she took home that day.

Maya turned to the Devil. "This isn't on the list."

He pulled out Casey's crumpled note and held it between two fingers like a tarot card. At the bottom, the paper was folded up, an imperfection neither Maya nor Kally had noticed. The Devil unfolded it with his pinkie and the unmistakable handwriting of Casey Kelly was there:

"Buy a soundtrack for the ride home."

The Devil gave a toothy grin as he gestured for the three teens to enter.

An old bell chimed, struggling to hit its third ding as the they cautiously walked in. Inside, it was truly endless. Endless rows of dusty vinyl set upon endless shelves that spiraled up into a ceiling that rose to infinity. The lighting was low and red like an old darkroom with walls that seemed to breathe just slightly. Album covers appeared to blink faintly on the shelves, like video game power-ups waiting to be placed into your inventory. The entire space smelled like cigarettes, sandalwood, and the exact summer day you heard your favorite artist for the very first time.

Behind the counter stood the clerk, fist resting on his chin as if he had been waiting for decades. An older Black man, tall and thin, skin like polished mahogany, dressed in a crushed velvet blazer, paisley scarf, and worn brown leather gloves with the fingers cut off. He wore rose-tinted sunglasses and his beard was streaked with silver. He looked like someone who once dated Nina Simone and got dumped by her for not feeling deeply enough.

"Evenin'," he rasped, voice like worn out vinyl and low jazz trumpet. "Welcome to Endless Horizons. Open all night. We got heartbreak in aisle two and divine revelation in the discount bin. If you're looking for country, it don't go past 2001."

Maya blinked as she took in the clerk, his nondescript name tag reading simply "Robert J." He tilted down his glasses ever so slightly as the slid a record sleeve across the counter. On it, no label. Just a mirror where the artwork should be.

"Take somethin' for the road," he rasped. "One truth per customer. Gratis."

Maya peered down at the record and took in her look for the first time. Tired but alive, an ethereal backlight plucking her out of the moment. She looked up and caught eyes with clerk. With a long, double-jointed finger, he lowered his blush-colored aviators ever so slightly.

"Why does this place feel like home?" she asked, not expecting an answer.

"Because every record here came from someone's soul," the clerk said in a low voice. "And some of 'em sound an awful lot like yours. That's why we listen. That's why some of us create."

He pointed toward the back, where a glowing booth stood with a blinking neon sign: *"RECORD YOUR TRUTH"*

He leaned back onto his stool, raising his glasses up the bridge of his nose. With a long blink, he picked up his worn copy of "I'll Sleep When I'm Dead" and returned to his post. Maya, Eddie, and Kally looked at each other, quickly adapting to their current setting before stepping forward.

As they ventured deeper into the store, the music invaded them. Soft and ghostly, it threaded throughout the air like incense smoke you could almost see. Mazzy Star's "Into Dust" played on a slightly warped turntable, the needle catching just enough to make the song shimmer like a mirage, the warm tones softly spilling from the pristine vintage tube speakers set up beside it.

The slide guitar wept. Hope Sandoval's voice, breathy and intimate, filled every crack between the rows. It didn't sound like it was coming from anywhere in particular. It just existed and hovered, following them at a respectable distance. The kind of song that made you feel like something was ending even if you didn't know what yet.

Eddie stopped walking. "I used to listen to this with Caleb in his garage."

Maya nodded slowly. "We covered it once in my freshman guitar class. It was the first time I ever sang in front of strangers."

"I used this song over the credits of my first short," Kally whispered.

Maya looked at her two friends, holding back the full memory of that moment… Ryan watching her sing it in class and being the first to clap loudly. She didn't know he was there, watching silently from the back of the room, until she strummed the last chord and finally opened her eyes.

In the back corner of the shop, a girl with smeared eyeliner and a green wool coat sat cross-legged on the ground, flipping through a crate marked "For Hearts in Recovery." A black cat slept across her lap like it was anchoring her in that moment. Across the room, a tall, wiry man in a faded TLC t-shirt hovered near a shelf labeled "Albums That Saved Your Life (Temporarily)." He didn't touch anything. He just stood in the moment like he was waiting to be moved.

Every person in the shop looked like they were visiting from different decades but all seemed like they belonged. They were where they needed to be. No one seemed surprised to see the teens. No one even really looked up to acknowledge them. This was their experience. The three teens were just set dressing for them, background for their own stories. The clerk chuckled as he watched Maya slowly take in every detail of the shop.

"This tune has got a hold of you. Best not fight it," he said, his voice seemingly hitching a ride on the wave of tunes weaving throughout the aisles.

The song slowly faded out as he walked with melodic shuffle and ritualistically placed another record on the turntable. The needle dropped. A twangy guitar solo. The drums. And then a voice that uncoiled like a cobra. Eddie Vedder singing "Yellow Ledbetter."

The three teens all looked at each other, sharing the memory of the last time they heard this song. A favorite of Jeff Phillips, they all pictured a grieving Ryan exiting the funeral grounds as this song tore through the cemetery, kissing every headstone as it did. The cashier leaned back on his stool with a smug gleefulness. He knew exactly what he was doing. The concept of shuffling music wasn't allowed in this place. Like a well-crafted mix tape, everything was deliberate.

As Maya stood frozen in place, the uneven flooring seemed to shift beneath her feet, nudging her forward whether she was ready or not. Eddie and Kally drifted off in different directions, drawn away like they'd heard something only they could hear. The store invited solitude, not out of coldness, but as if it knew its patrons needed to be alone to allow their thoughts the space to stretch and breathe.

Eddie wandered into a section marked "Music that makes life worth living," his fingers grazing the edges of record sleeves the way someone might trace old scars. A worn vinyl copy of "Love is Hell" by Ryan Adams stopped him short. The title alone hit like a quiet dare.

He lifted it carefully, thumb brushing the corner of the sleeve. He remembered that dark day once more. Ryan calling him out and then simply saying "Get in the car." The aggressively hot night when Ryan slid the disc into the Corolla's dash and let the opening notes of "Avalanche" fill the spaces between them. The car rolled through dark streets in near silence, the song doing the talking neither of them could manage. It wasn't advice or a solution but simply someone else's poetry, chosen carefully, saying "I see you" without forcing Eddie to explain himself. For the first time in weeks, the air felt safe enough to sit in. Eddie held the record a moment longer than necessary, then tucked it under his arm like the sacred artifact it was. A reminder that he'd survived before and that now, he knew what feeling alive was really like.

Kally walked, taking in the decor and layout of the store. Without realizing it, she found herself next to a display marked "Directors' Cuts."

She smirked. Of course, she thought.

As she scanned albums she recognized, her eyes locked on PJ Harvey's "Stories from the City, Stories from the Sea." The spine shimmered slightly. The exact album she once streamed in her bedroom while editing her first real short film. A suggestion from Maya to help her get out of her own way. The one she was finally brave enough to share with everyone. The soundtrack to taking her first chance. She picked it up and took in the album art, art she'd only ever seen as a thumbnail on a small screen. She felt the slightly worn cardboard under fingers and then gently embraced it, tracing the shape of PJ's nonchalant face.

Maya noticed her friend and made note of the imagery in her mind, taking a mental snapshot to file away. As she turned back to the records, she found herself in a section simply labeled: "You Were Here."

She ran her fingers across Jeff Buckley's "Grace," paused at Joni Mitchell's "Blue," and finally stopped in front of a sun-faded copy of "Fumbling Towards Ecstasy" by Sarah McLachlan. A tiny glow pulsed from beneath the plastic sleeve. It was unmistakable. A sign. Maybe not divine, but definite. She slid the record from the bin with trembling hands, the soft light not dimming.

That's when she saw it again. The booth. Tucked into the corner behind the listening station, bathed in amber light. "Record Your Truth" still flickered above it, the letters humming like they had a heartbeat. Maya turned slowly.

Lost on their own journey, neither Kally nor Eddie noticed her. They were still awash in their own reveries. She gently placed the McLachlan album under her arm and approached the booth with cautious curiosity.

Despite the weathered appearance of the cherrywood booth, the door opened cleanly with no squeak, as if it were promising to keep whatever secrets you wanted to tell it. The walls were lined with red velvet and old band flyers, a well-used Gibson L-1 guitar leaning against it. In the middle stood a single stool, and a tiny analog mic suspended from a coiled cord directly above it. For a moment, Maya just stood, the weight of the evening pressing down and the booth seemingly closing in all around her. The stool, bathed under a warm incandescent Edison light bulb, waited patiently for her, offering reprieve from the stifling presence of the booth. Holding her record, she looked at the microphone swaying softly in the room as if it were a rope being thrown to her. She closed the door and then spoke.

"I don't know why it's harder to say goodbye to this part of my life than it was to survive it."

Her voice cracked on the last word, the booth her confessional. "I thought being focused made me strong. I thought if I kept everyone at arm's length, it would hurt less when I left. But now I just feel like I'm leaving without anything."

She paused for a moment and then sat, the weight of what she felt not allowing her to sit up straight. She sighed and closed her eyes as she set her record down on a small table that she hadn't noticed previously. "I don't even know how to finish this song."

She picked up the guitar. It felt warm to the touch. The neck perfectly cradled into her palm and the strings had her preferred action. As her fingertips glided across the strings, only then did she notice the familiar maroon color of the pick jammed between the E and A strings. The Corolla. It was perfectly tuned, each note ringing out with warm perfection. Her fingers hovered, then landed in a soft D chord. She let it ring, the vibration humming through the floor. She strummed a few more times before pausing. She ran her fingers across the fretboard once more, the string noise giving her an auditory reboot. With one more deep breath, Maya gripped the neck of the guitar with purpose, like it was her parents guiding her through the record store when she was younger.

She stared at the acoustic guitar in her lap like it had just confessed something personal and loosened her grip. Her fingers hovered over the strings, unsure. The overhead light caught the sterling silver of the tuning pegs and flashed into her eyes as if telling her to just play. She gripped tighter and strummed once more, rough and awkward.

A wince.

She adjusted her grip, steadied her breath.

Again. Smoother this time.

A third strum, then a chord.

C to A minor to F.

Her foot tapped. Her shoulders relaxed. This was home.

Then she began to sing. A slow, half-formed song.

Not perfect but hers.

The needle on the store's turntable lifted mid-song, cutting off the closing solo, sending the crackle of Pearl Jam evaporating into the shop's walls. The store clerk, eyes twinkling with a subtle grin, flipped a switch on the old mixing console next to the register. Maya's voice filled the record shop like incense. Soft. Vulnerable. Unmistakable.

Eddie froze as he thumbed through a pile of old punk records. He turned, expecting her to be behind him, but found nothing. He looked to the corner to see a small mounted speaker projecting Maya's voice for all to hear. The music rushed in, forcing him to ground. He slid down the shelf wall and sat cross-legged on the tile floor, eyes closed, embracing the Ryan Adams album to his chest. Just listening.

Kally looked up from a stack of dusty 45s and narrowed her eyes. That voice. She knew it. She felt it in her ribs. But she had never heard it like this. Soft and vulnerable, riding the waves of an acoustic guitar. Maya would never play acoustic in front of anybody. She only let the world see her with the buzz of an electric guitar to hide behind. Kally moved quietly across the floor, past the jazz bin and a discount crate labeled "Too Sad to Sell," until she stumbled upon the booth tucked in the back corner of the store. She spotted Maya through the fogged glass panel, hunched over the guitar with her back to the door. Singing with her entire body now. Kally didn't move. She just stood there and watched. The glass hummed faintly with sound, distorted but earnest, and for once she didn't feel the itch to capture it. No lens. No proof. Just the quiet understanding that this moment wasn't hers to preserve. It was a moment that could only live in a memory, a foundation of a feeling that didn't need concrete details or 4K resolution.

Maya's voice cracked as the chords shifted. She didn't stop. She leaned in, perfect in her imperfections. The words weren't polished. But they were true. It was a song she was trying to perfect but never could. A song that would always be in a work in progress. A song that was her and just for her.

"I should've danced more...

Should've said it out loud...

Should've told you that I hated the silence

Of your empty seat in my car."

Her hands trembled, making her miss a chord and causing her to stop abruptly. She let the moment linger and breathe before releasing the guitar from her grip.

"I didn't know what to say to you after your dad died. You were grieving, and I was scared of saying the wrong thing. So I didn't say anything."

She strummed once more. Just noise now. No melody. Just feeling, following the chords in whatever order they wanted to be found. Then she whispered:

"I wanted to be near you so bad but all I could do was run."

A breath. Then quiet. The guitar fell still in her lap and she gently placed it back against the velvet wall. She sat, allowing the silence to spin all around her for a moment. Her fingers relaxed and the pick fell to the ground. As she looked at the hanging microphone, a whir sounded from the wall to her right.

A cassette tape ejected from a slot beside her. She stared at it. That tape deck was most definitely not there when she had first entered. She gripped the edge of the cassette with her fingertips and attempted to pull it out. The wall wasn't ready to give it her just yet. She softened her grip and touch, the tears on her cheeks falling to her thighs, her voice gone but something else in its place. The tape then released. Off-white with no labels, worn at the edges. Clarity. Relief. A piece of herself she hadn't known she'd left behind. She gently picked up her Sarah McLachlan record and gave one last look to the guitar before she quietly turned to the booth door. She emerged to see Kally standing there, clutching her record close to her chest, eyes glistening.

They said nothing and simply looked at one another, taking in the finality of this moment and their night as a whole. Two friends whose story was at an end, regret and gratitude dancing between the two. Maya let the booth door close behind her and walked with purpose to Kally, hugging her with her entire body. It was a hug she had never given before and would never give again.

At that moment, the clerk flipped the switch again and Mazzy Star's "Fade Into You" gently filled the store. As if nothing and everything had happened all at once. Eddie rounded a corner and found his two friends embracing, fully realizing the gravity of what he was witnessing. This was the place where it would all end. They still had to finish the story but everything after this moment was the epilogue.

The bell over the front door never rang, but the Devil was suddenly there, half-lounging against the counter like he'd been there from the start. The clerk didn't flinch as he placed a Billie Holiday LP back in its sleeve, handling it like sacred glass.

"Odd sight seeing you in here. Don't you usually observe this part from afar," the clerk rasped, voice deep and worn like a midnight blues track. "You don't like to get too involved, if memory serves."

"Don't act like you know me," the Devil smirked.

The clerk snorted. "All too well. All too well."

The Devil glanced back toward the teens. Eddie was crouched on the floor, flipping through a crate and holding up albums for Maya's approval like he was presenting fine art. She shook her head at one, nodded at another, discreetly wiping the tears that snuck out of her eyes. Kally hovered nearby, phone tucked safely away, just watching them with a quiet smile, present in a way she hadn't been before. For a moment, they were just kids. Messy and earnest. Laughing too loud. Holding onto things like they might disappear forever if they weren't careful.

"They did alright," the Devil said finally.

"They lived it," the clerk corrected. "Big difference."

The Devil didn't argue. He just watched them a second longer than necessary, a softness quickly flickering across his face before the moment passed. A silence lingered.

The Devil raised his brows and gestured towards the booth. "Still collecting confessions, I see."

"When you give up your soul, the blues are lost, too. Gotta borrow them when I can. When you can't leave, there's nothing to mourn. The great irony of who I am, I suppose. But I think you knew that when we met."

The clerk reached into the inside pocket of his coat and slid a cassette across the counter towards the Devil. The plastic was a deep, impossible red, clean and untouched, the label minimalistic and blank. The Devil picked it up, turning it over in his fingers. He held it the way one might handle something fragile without realizing why, studying it like a half-remembered artifact from a life he no longer talked about.

"You know," the clerk said, voice lower and more raspy now, "One day they'll figure out that sin and salvation aren't opposites. Just different verses of the same song. The only thing that changes is where you're standing when the chorus hits. What are you going to do then?"

The Devil closed his hand around the cassette, thoughtful and almost protective, before slipping it into his pocket. "There will always be a poor soul willing to give me theirs to get better at guitar."

The clerk gave the faintest grin. "Touché."

The Devil turned to look back at the teens one last time. Kally placed her chosen record gently in her bag. Maya slipped the cassette into her jacket pocket. Eddie, always the last to leave, lingered near the bin of forgotten singles labeled "Almosts."

The Devil tipped two fingers to the clerk. "Until the next one."

"You know where I'll be" the clerk said.

And with a last look back, the Devil turned and walked through the door and back to the parking lot to wait. The bell never rang.

Chapter 18

They arrived with a hush, like the universe itself had lowered its voice out of respect.

The Glass Gardens unfolded before them in waves of soft luminescence, each step forward revealing a landscape that felt less like Hell and more like a memory Heaven forgot to keep. Paths of crushed gemstone crunched beneath their feet, glowing faintly with every step like the peaceful counterpart to the entrance of Old Tito's. The air seemed to shimmer and was laced with a sweetness that was impossible to name but instantly familiar, like the smell of a loved one's hoodie or the warmth of a spiced coffee on the first day of fall. It wafted on invisible swaths of nostalgia curated for each visitor. No matter who or what you were, the Glass Gardens were built just for you.

Above them, vines of sapphire glass coiled around obsidian archways, blooming with delicate flowers that pulsed in time with the rhythm of their steps. Some petals glowed softly. Others reflected constellations that didn't belong to Earth. Trees stretched impossibly tall and then folded inward like they'd grown tired of towering, cradling the pathways in kaleidoscopic shadow. A bioluminescent mist drifted lazily through the air, catching in Ryan's eyelashes and the creases of Jeff's flannel like stardust, leaving behind faint traces of its glittering essence before dissipating into nothing. Floating lanterns shaped like soft teardrops bobbed just above the ground and illuminated their pathways in warm light. The world was lush and full, not allowing you to see too far ahead, forcing you to enjoy a small amount of paradise for fear that you'd be too overwhelmed otherwise. Pixies danced alongside the breeze in perfect harmony with butterflies that were kissed with colors that seemed unnatural but still welcoming.

It was Hell, but rewritten. A place that wasn't screaming for attention or bathed in chaos but a space for those who sought pleasure in stillness.

"This doesn't feel like Hell," Ryan whispered.

Jeff smiled and adjusted the cooler strap on his shoulder. "That's the point. This is the Devil's version of Eden. Not a punishment for curiosity but a reward for seeking truth.

He never did understand how he became the villain in that story."

"Being a snake probably wasn't the best call," Ryan remarked.

They moved deeper in, past a grove of weeping willows that actually cried and seemed to breathe in sync with the wind. Their branches gracefully fell and dripped with opalescent dew that evaporated into stardust before hitting the ground. A floating koi pond hovered and flowed through the sky like a dragon, its fish swimming through it like lazy comets, scales reflecting starlight. There were no fences. No signs. Just endless paths, taking you where you were supposed to go in that moment.

"This place..." Ryan murmured, barely breathing.

"It's one of his favorite creations but he'll never admit that," Jeff said. "He says it's the only part of Hell that wasn't designed to challenge anyone. Just hold them. Let them rest. This place was what he created on his seventh day. No rest for the wicked."

Ryan turned slowly in place, eyes wide. "But why hide it all the way down here?"

Jeff shrugged. "Some pleasures aren't for showing off. They're for feeling. He made this for the ones who were too tender for damnation but too tired for Heaven. For the ones who needed beauty but couldn't ask for it. A place for people who lived horrors and needed reprieve. A lot of people suffered in the name of the other guy. The biggest 'fuck you' the Devil could think of was providing them solace. The first time I came here, I wasn't planning to. It just seemed to find me."

Ryan walked ahead, the path gently curving through a corridor of hovering ferns and bellflowers that hummed faintly when touched. "It's like walking through my dreams," he whispered.

Jeff didn't respond, allowing the stillness to do what words couldn't. At that moment, a faint breeze carried the scent of crushed vanilla and fake pine. It was Christmas morning. Ryan's Christmas morning. His mom's cookies. The fake pine tree smell from the wall plug-in his dad would buy so their synthetic Christmas tree would feel more authentic. Ryan followed the smell and found himself in a display of floating orchids that seemed to skate across the surface of a shallow teal pond. As they gently drifted into each other, they'd shoot a soft lilac-colored powder into the air.

"What do you smell," Jeff asked.

"It smells like Christmas at our house," Ryan said, breathing deep and slow.

"Interesting," Jeff replied.

"Don't you smell it," Ryan asked.

"All I smell is my old leather baseball glove and car exhaust mixed with rain," Jeff answered. "Memory orchids. Their pollen digs into your subconscious and roots out memories. Kinda like putting your nostalgia on shuffle. I like coming here and just letting the memories play. Right now I'm thinking of a time my dad drove me to baseball practice and we waited in the car listening to music until the rain let up."

Ryan looked at his dad and back at the floating orchids. The smell of Christmas began to fade as was replaced with a new one. Mountain Dew Baja Blast and Burt's Beeswax chapstick. Maya.

The memory came without effort. Her hands on the wheel as she drove him home from school a few weeks before Jeff died, fingers tapping out bass lines she knew by heart. The way the car smelled faintly of citrus soda and that minty wax she always carried, because she was the kind of person who noticed when other people's lips were chapped. He remembered the low hum of the engine and the way she'd glance over at red lights and smile like she was letting him in on a private joke she hadn't put into words yet. The sound of soft running water teased the edges of the garden. Somewhere deeper within, glass chimes sang their song, calling him. Ryan opened his eyes and smiled softly at his dad.

"You remember something you weren't expecting," Jeff asked.

"Someone," Ryan said.

Jeff nodded, not pushing. Ryan didn't explain. He didn't need to. The scent of Baja Blast and minty chapstick lingered and with it, the realization that this feeling hadn't been sudden or new. It had been waiting. Growing quietly in the background while he'd worried about timing and consequences and what-ifs. Before his dad died, it had been the biggest thing he didn't know how to handle. After, it had felt too fragile to touch. A pursuit he couldn't handle without his father's guidance. Back before the silence. Before the gaps. He hadn't thought of that version of her in a long time but maybe Hell was just honest enough to make him admit he missed it. That quiet feeling of possibility. Ryan took one last inhale, letting the scent vanish into the quiet. Jeff stood beside him, not pushing, just watching his son take it all in.

"I used to think strength meant pretending stuff like that didn't matter. Pushing it down," Jeff said quietly. "Powering through. Sucking it up. Being the man of the house or whatever bullshit they teach us."

He looked out over the Glass Garden, its impossible beauty glowing with a slow pulse, like it was breathing along with them. "But real strength? That's just being honest about what you feel, even if it wrecks you. Especially if it wrecks you."

Ryan didn't respond right away. He just nodded slowly, the kind that came from understanding, not agreement.

"Find what you love and let it kill you," Ryan said softly. "I remember reading that in your high school yearbook."

"Charles Bukowski," Jeff laughed. "I've actually had a drink with him. Fucking legend. Bit of an asshole."

Ryan smiled at the image of that.

"Hell doesn't punish people for loving," Jeff continued. "It punishes people who lie to themselves about what they love. That's the only real sin down here. Dishonesty. It's the only thing that really pisses the Devil off."

They walked a few more steps through the garden in silence, the sound of soft chimes guiding them like breadcrumbs through paradise. And then a soft pop of displaced air.

The three little demons stood awkwardly at the path's edge. Blink with his hands behind his back like he might explode from excitement, Skid looking smug, and Vex trying to keep the group from talking over each other.

"We didn't lie!" Blink blurted, covering his mouth quickly.

"Yeah, we told Simon everything," Skid added, avoiding eye contact.

"Every plan we had just seemed silly. We kinda thought about what you would do, Ryan, and we all agreed that you'd probably be straightforward about it." Vex said, with an awkward shrug. "He was surprisingly cool about it, though."

Just behind them, emerging from a display of sunflowers, was Simon. He looked like a man shaped by the quiet parts of history. The kind of person who loved what he loved without asking permission. His dark blazer was frayed at the elbows, layered over a faded Joan Jett tee that hinted at a time when rock still felt like rebellion. His jeans were worn, not by fashion but by time, cuffed neatly over scuffed desert boots that had clearly walked through more than one lifetime and were ready for at least three more. There was a weathered softness to him, like a college professor who never stopped collecting used paperbacks or annotating margins. His long salt-and-pepper hair fell over a single eye in a chaotic symphony as his wireframe glasses caught the garden's light like silver. Simon carried himself with confidence and conviction. He was a man who knew who he was long ago and never felt the need to change it. He didn't glow or shimmer but somehow, he still pulled focus.

His eyes scanned the garden with cautious reverence, as though afraid a blink might break the spell. And when he found Ryan and Jeff, he settled with recognition, not surprise. He had been in Hell for a while so he had long accepted that strange things could still feel right if you just let them.

"Hi," Simon said, voice like vinyl static and warmth.

Ryan smiled and stepped forward, hand outstretched. "Thanks for coming."

Simon shook his hand, but his gaze flicked over Ryan's shoulder, toward the distant glass spires of the inner garden. "I'd go anywhere," Simon said softly. "If there was even a chance they'd be there."

Simon stood by the glass lily pond, not looking at Jeff or Ryan, but into the water's slow spiral. He smiled softly.

He was honesty embodied, a being who knew his soul was incomplete and wasn't going to waste his words on platitudes or poetic nonsense in pursuit of what would make him whole.

"I was 30 when I met them," he said, voice calm, but etched with memory. "I remember their face when I was in that waiting room, emerging from that strange door."

"With the cracks that looked like they were filled with lava," Ryan asked quietly.

Simon looked back at Ryan and smiled. "So you were the one chosen this year, were you? Another pure soul."

"That's what they say," Ryan replied.

"Was he kind to you," Simon asked. "In his own way?"

Ryan looked down at his new shoes and fingered the VIP lanyard around his neck. "It was more kindness than I had felt in the longest time."

"That's Asmodeus. They are strange, even for Hell. Powerful, but so quiet. Tired but not at the expense of their grace. Peace amongst the chaos."

Jeff and Ryan stood beside him, reverent. This didn't feel like story time but more like a confession. The garden pulsed around them with gentle color and quiet motion, like it was listening, too. The trees even seemed to lean in.

A man who had once been words on a screen was now here, average in stature but radiating a presence of purpose that commanded attention and reverence.

"I came to Hell as a nonbeliever," Simon continued. "Not because I was cruel, or hateful, or even nihilistic but because I lived like nothing mattered. Life just was. And then this... being... shows up with a clipboard and a thousand-yard stare. They weren't what I expected. And they weren't trying to be."

He paused, a breath catching in his chest, before continuing. "I thought love was something humans made up to feel less alone. I'd never felt it. I could tell you how others had written about it. But they... they made me feel like it wasn't just possible, but sacred. Not because they gave it back but because loving them gave me purpose. Hell taught me something Heaven never could: that meaning isn't handed down. It's built, stubbornly and defiantly, with our own hands. It's cobbled together with happiness that gives way to a pain that you'll seek out a thousand times over. To love is to be a masochist because pain will come and when you know that, it will kill you a thousand times and resurrect you a thousand more."

Simon turned fully now, the garden's strange light

catching in his glasses. "You're trying to fix something, aren't you?" he continued, his eyes boring a hole into that part of Ryan that he hid from others. "That's why you brought me here? For yourself?"

Ryan opened his mouth to respond but stopped and only nodded. "I guess I am," he confessed. "I think I finally realized this wasn't just about the two of you. It was about me, too. Selfishly."

Simon studied him, curious.

"I was broken when I got here," Ryan continued, voice steadier now. "It was like I'd been left in the rain and forgotten. I didn't even know how broken until Asmodeus found me and gave me this phone. I'd been numb for so long, and then suddenly, I wasn't. I felt seen. Like I mattered again. He saved me without even knowing it."

He looked down, thumb brushing the edge of a memory orchid. "And when I started reading your messages to them, I recognized that feeling in you. You never gave up on loving them, even if they never loved you the same way back. That kind of love is hard. I don't think I even fully understand it but I know that it's honest. And I think that's the only kind that works down here. Or anywhere."

Simon smiled faintly, the kind that said "I've been where

you are."

Jeff shifted beside Ryan quietly and gently touched the center of his back. Pride, comfort, presence. A father watching his son step fully into himself.

"I think I get that," Simon said softly. "This was never about getting them back. Not really. Do you want to know what I've learned down here?"

"Of course," Ryan replied without hesitation.

"Love doesn't need to be received to be real. It doesn't have to be tidy. It doesn't even need to be reciprocated. It certainly doesn't have to be logical. You can love someone with your whole soul and never hear it back and it's still worth everything. It just means you're alive. I think I'm more alive now than when I was actually alive."

He glanced toward the floating snake vines and the pollen-lit vapor that mixed with iridescent sky "There's beauty in the pursuit," he continued. "Not because it wins anything. But because it reminds you that you're still capable of feeling that much. That deeply and that fearlessly."

Jeff sniffed, wiping at his eyes with the heel of his hand. "That's a heavy truth, my man," he said.

Simon chuckled. "It feels a lot lighter when you stop fighting it."

Ryan looked at him, then at the glass flowers blooming like quiet miracles all around them. And for the first time in a very, very long while, he felt at peace. Unbeknownst to them all, Blink was crouched behind a lucid cactus labeled "Vulnerability – Do Not Touch" with Ryan's phone in his small twitching hands. The message thread with Asmodeus was still open. The mic icon pulsed red. Recording.

Blink looked over to Vex and Skid. They caught his eye and, in unison, nodded at him. Without a hesitation, he hit SEND.

Back in Asmodeus' sanctum, the room was still, the usual symphony of whispers and arcane ambient noise falling away to silence in the sparsely decorated room. They sat behind a towering onyx desk, claw gently resting on the sleek business phone they had all but forgotten about. It buzzed once.

A voice memo.

From their personal device.

The human soul was messaging them.

As they elegantly swiped open the screen, they were greeted with a simple, flashing voice memo icon. Asmodeus stared at it. Furrowed brow. No words. Just silence and that pulsing red play icon.

They tapped it.

A slight pause and then Simon's voice filled the chamber like incense, clinging to every surface, and making the air lighter and heavier all at once.

"I came to Hell as a nonbeliever. Not because I was cruel, or hateful, but because I lived like nothing mattered…"

Asmodeus froze. The voice, familiar and devastating, unraveled something in their carefully constructed composure. The iron posture, the cold authority slipped away, molecule by molecule. This wasn't text on a screen that could be ignored. This was him. The even flow of his cadence with just a slight hitch of passion and optimism as he completed his sentences.

"They weren't what I expected. And they weren't trying to be."

Asmodeus stood now, the phone still in his palm but limp, like it had turned into something molten.

"I thought love was something humans made up to feel less alone. I'd never felt it. I could tell you how others had written about it. But they… they made me feel like it wasn't just possible, but sacred."

The voice cracked. The truth landed. Their chest rose.

Fell. A hundred objections and ancient fears sparked in the back of their mind. But none of them caught flame. Because what they felt in that moment wasn't fear. It was longing. They stood and listened to the entire exchange. Two pure souls conversing with Asmodeus themself the subject. An anchor point in the lives of two pure souls. Themself a being of duty now the connecting line between two beings of chaotic destiny.

They stood and listened, stoic and unmoving. The message reached its end. They didn't hesitate.

With a single step and the smoothing of their lapel, they vanished in a shimmer of black fire.

Simon gently lowered himself onto a glassy bench overlooking a maze of earth roses and winding cerulean day lilies, motioning for Ryan to sit beside him. The air between them buzzed gently with floral warmth and residual emotion.

"When I was down here the first time, I hoped my friends wouldn't pull it off," Simon admitted, a rueful smile tugging at the corner of his mouth. "Selfish, I know. But when you find something beautiful, even down here, you want to hold onto it. Especially when you spent your entire life thinking beauty was a trick. That existence was random."

Ryan tilted his head, curious. "You didn't want to go back?"

"Oh, no," Simon said. "I was done with Earth. I didn't think I had a reason to stay anywhere until I met Asmodeus."

He paused. "My day with them gave me more meaning than my entire 70 years on Earth. It's surprisingly overwhelming to live an existence of quiet nothingness and then meeting a being that decimates your entire belief system in an instant. I used to believe that love was a chemical delusion, evolution's trick to keep the species going. I read all the studies, believed all the cynics. Love was random. Messy. Impractical. And then I met someone who didn't fit any of the patterns. No logic explained what I felt. No data justified why it lingered long after we parted. I realized then that love isn't opposed to truth. It is truth. Just a different kind. A truth you feel before you understand it. A compass, not a contract. So, yes, facts matter. Logic matters. But love... love is what gives those facts meaning. It's the margin of error in every equation I used to trust. And I've never felt more certain about anything in my life. I lived my human life knowing what awaited me. They were my purpose."

Ryan sat with that and let it fill the spaces he'd been

ignoring. "I miss my dad more than I can explain," he said finally. "And there's a part of me that wants to stay here forever just to be with him. But that's not my purpose."

Simon turned, listening with that quiet intensity of a man who values every word.

"My purpose isn't to live in grief," Ryan continued. "It's to live because of it. With it as my companion. And that's because of the love I've earned. Kally, Maya, Eddie... they're my family. Because they chose me. And I chose them. I want to get back to them. I need to get back to them."

Simon smiled, something soft and ancient in his eyes. "Then you already understand the secret."

"What's that?"

"Purpose isn't something you build just for yourself. It only matters if it's in service of those who would miss you when you're gone."

Ryan thought of Eddie and the night he unloaded on him with anger and harsh, selfish truths.

"The people whose love you've earned," Simon continued. "The ones who've seen you at your worst and never let go. For me, that's here. For you, that's with your friends. There isn't a right answer for any of this. Only the answer you decide is the correct one."

Ryan felt something shift inside. Not a pang and not a grief but a grounding. A peace.

"I've felt that kind of love," Ryan said. "And I want to be the kind of person who keeps earning it."

Simon gave a soft chuckle and looked back at Jeff and the three little demons watching them from afar. "Seems like you already are. There's a reason a human will never truly see a real version of themselves. Only reflections."

A long silence passed. Comfortable. Earned. Then, just beyond the arch of angel vines, the air changed. A shadow of movement. A heartbeat of hesitation. A presence that Ryan and Simon both felt before they saw it, pushing them instinctively to their feet. Deep inside the stillness, a familiar voice whispered Ryan's name.

Asmodeus had arrived, stepping into view from a mist of rose-colored smoke that swirled in an elegant vortex. His gaze landed on Simon for a moment but it was the boy standing beside him who truly arrested his breath.

Ryan Clark Phillips. Alive. In Hell. Holding himself with calm, unwavering clarity.

They stared at one another.

Stillness.

No grand gestures. No music swell. Just silence. Dense

and sacred. Asmodeus took a breath, eyes narrowing.

"You used my phone,"

"I did," Ryan replied stoically.

A long pause. The weight of countless centuries in the space between them.

"You betrayed my trust."

"I repaid a debt."

Asmodeus's jaw tightened, a twitch of muscle beneath the mask of keeping up appearances as the COO of Hell. "You severely overstepped, human."

"We humans have a tendency to do that. But you're not really mad at me. You're mad that I wouldn't let you ignore what was right in front of you."

"You know nothing of what I carry."

"I know what I felt the moment I got here. Purpose. You didn't need to dress me or help me as much as you did, did you?"

Asmodeus glared at the brash human, clenching his claw ever so slightly and taking a step forward, closing the gap between the two. It was then they noticed the three little demons step between the two, no hesitation in their large, loyal eyes. Tiny protectors from the ninth tier.

"When I saw Simon's messages," Ryan continued.

"when I saw how deeply he loved you, I did what you would never allow yourself to do."

"And what was that?"

"I gave in."

Asmodeus unclenched their fists and smoothed his suit jacket, clearly a nervous habit. "My duty is to the Dark Lord. Do you think this place runs on sentiment?"

"I think this place was built on sentiment. And it runs on truth. On the parts of ourselves we didn't allow to indulge in life. That's what Simon taught you. And you still stand here, acting like duty is all that matters when the Devil himself got cast out for choosing self over service."

Asmodeus, who usually stood tall and proper, felt their posture fall ever so slightly.

"You serve him with absolute loyalty but forget that his greatest act was rebellion," Ryan continued. "All of this was built on rebellion."

"Don't presume to speak for him, human," Asmodeus replied sternly.

"Why not? You haven't. Not really. You've been serving an image of duty that doesn't match the man. The Devil made a kingdom for people who wanted more. More life, more feeling, more love. But here you are, denying yourself all of that."

Asmodeus didn't move but something broke in the stillness. A flicker of doubt.

"This place is honest. It makes you feel what's real, even when it hurts," Ryan said, standing taller than he ever had before. "Especially when it hurts. And I don't care what happens next. I don't regret doing this. Because if you could see what I saw in Simon's face, what he still feels for you, you'd stop trying to protect yourself and start living for what this place was built for. Because it was. For people like him and for people like you. For love like yours. Love I hope to feel myself one day."

At that moment, Asmodeus' gaze was broken when they caught sight of Simon's silhouette. As he came into focus, the familiar grin that enchanted them so many years ago caught their eye, and Asmodeous' eyes softened.

"You need to go to him," Ryan said, holding up his VIP lanyard. "Because I get whatever I want."

Jeff smiled. A chip off the old block. The three demons quietly gave low fist bumps to each other.

"Baller move," Jeff whispered to the three.

Slowly, Asmodeus walked forward until they were face to face with the human. They studied him. Not with condescension. Not even with suspicion. But with the kind of recognition one gives to a mirror they didn't expect to admire. The boy was standing straight and tall, looking eye to eye with the blood demon. This wasn't the one who arrived. This one was different now.

"You were supposed to come here and get lost," Asmodeus said quietly. "Not become this."

Ryan didn't flinch.

"You were supposed to forget," Asmodeus continued. "You were supposed to fade into the noise like all of them do. But you just kept reaching."

Ryan held his gaze. "You're partially to blame for that."

A pause. A long breath. "You remind me of him," Asmodeus said, eyes darting to Simon. "Back when he first arrived. When he still believed he could change something by loving it."

Ryan smiled faintly. "He still does."

Asmodeus exhaled slowly. "You gave up your one chance to burn bright down here with no consequence all for someone else's story."

"I didn't give up anything," Ryan replied without hesitation. "This is still my story."

Asmodeus looked past him. Toward the glow in the

distance where Simon waited.

"Why?" Asmodeus asked softly. "Why do this?"

Ryan stepped forward, not shrinking from the towering figure before him, but meeting them.

"Because this place might have been built by the Devil, but it belongs to the people who aren't afraid to feel," Ryan said.

Silence fell again and the air suddenly felt lighter. The sentient trees held still as the flowing waters all around seemed to slow to a crawl. Asmodeus, still not breaking eye contact, bowed their head, ever so slightly. A breath of reverence. Of surrender and thanks.

Ryan gave a small smirk and slight nod. "Go start your story," he whispered.

Asmodeus turned and smoothed their suit lapels. As they walked away toward Simon, Jeff stepped beside his son, beer in one hand, pride in the other.

"Well," he said, "looks like I'm not the only Phillips who knows how to make a scene."

Ryan smiled, mist rising in his eyes. "Learned from the best," he said, taking the beer from his dad's hand and taking a long, well-earned drink.

Simon raised his head at the sound of approaching

footsteps. He didn't smile. He didn't flinch. He just stood in the stillness of the Glass Gardens watching the being he had allowed to take up permanent residence in his memory walking towards him. Asmodeus stopped a few paces away, rigid and unreadable to everyone but Simon. Their eyes scanned the air around Simon, taking in the moment that encircled them.

"I wasn't tricked," Asmodeus said finally. "I came because I wanted to."

Simon tilted his head slightly, not believing a word. "I knew you would eventually."

Asmodeus's voice faltered. "I didn't think I was allowed to want anything."

Simon stepped forward. "You don't need permission," he said. "Not here. Not with me."

They stood in silence again, the weight of eternity stretching thin between them. Slowly, Asmodeus let go of their posture and fell into Simon's arms. They didn't kiss. They didn't speak. They just held each other as the garden seemed to exhale a sigh of relief and bloomed a little brighter. From the edge of a twisted moon vine, Blink was openly weeping into a leaf as Skid softly rubbed his back. Vex stood stoic, like a proud uncle at a wedding.

Asmodeus turned to them and let out a breath. "You three," they said, voice hardening. "You've caused more disruption in one night than some rakshasas manage in a century."

The trio froze.

"But you didn't do it for power. Or glory," they continued, eyes shifting up to Ryan. "You did it for a friend."

Asmodeus stepped closer, eyes flicking across their stunned faces. They stood over them, their reflective suit blinding their wide eyes, as they took in each tiny creature one by one.

"Do you know why demons like you never rise in the ranks?"

Blink sniffled. "Because we're losers?"

"No," Asmodeus answered quickly, their voice softening an octave. "Because Hell doesn't reward hope. It classifies it as inefficient. But the truth is that demons like you are the reason places like this garden still bloom. Your purpose isn't obvious to those of no consequence."

The words hung in the air like gospel.

"I was wrong to think I had to do everything alone," Asmodeus continued. "Effective immediately, you three will be my assistants. But more than that, you'll be my margin.

My grace. The reason I get to have a purpose and not just a duty."

Skid gasped. Blink smiled wide and proceed to faint backwards into a glowing shrub.

Vex dropped to one knee in all of his sincerity. "We will not let you down, your grace."

Asmodeus watched the tiny of trio of demons celebrate, struggling to keep their face from changing expression, before turning to see Simon tenderly watching him in quiet admiration. Jeff stepped beside Asmodeus, watching Simon as he traced his fingers across a flowering vine that shimmered like spilled oil.

"You know," Jeff said, "you remind me of my wife."

Asmodeus raised an eyebrow. "Is that a compliment?"

"Oh, definitely," Jeff replied. "Brilliant. Terrifying. Emotionally constipated until someone finally sits you down and makes you deal with yourself. Someone who is worth every ounce of trouble. Must be why the kid went to so much trouble for you. He had whatever he wanted at his fingertips and this is how he spent his time."

The two watched as Ryan celebrated with the three tiny demons.

Asmodeus allowed the smallest smirk. "I

underestimated him. I'm beginning to understand the Dark Lord's fascination with his kind."

"Humanity can be pretty amazing when we get out of our own way," Jeff said, taking a long pull of his beer. "I'm glad you chose him."

"It wasn't by luck."

"No such thing as luck."

They stood in silence for a beat.

"You ever think we're the same?" Jeff asked. "Two sides of a coin. You keep Hell running. I just make it fun."

Asmodeus looked over. "You're chaos in converse. I'm order in a panic attack."

They both laughed, Jeff loudly, Asmodeus small and restrained.

Jeff extended his hand. "Please don't let my boy's work go to waste."

Asmodeus looked towards Simon and then gripped Jeff's hand, locking eyes with the charming human. "I certainly won't."

Beneath the canopy of Medusa Vines, green coils threaded with glowing blossoms, stardust silk, and flowering bulbs that resembled eyes, Simon and Asmodeus sat side by side. They said little. Just fingers gently brushing, foreheads occasionally meeting. Love didn't need an audience. It needed space. And this garden gave them all the room in the universe.

Nearby, Blink, Vex, and Skid huddled beside a bonsai tree with flames for leaves, drawing diagrams in the soil with glowing reeds.

"First thing we need to do is get to planning on next year's bar games." Vex said.

"100%," Skid added. "I can audit the sponsorship packets to make sure we aren't getting hosed. I saw some events at Tito's that could definitely use some work."

"First things first," Blink squeaked. "We need to get the name of Asmodeus' suit demon. We need to look professional so everyone will take us seriously. These jackets are for downtime."

Vex and Skid nodded in unison, patting the tiniest of them on his back.

Asmodeus turned, just once, watching them with an expression that could almost be mistaken for joy. As their fingertips grazed Simon's forearm, an aggressive organ tone from within their suit jacket shattered the air bringing Asmodeus back to the duty at hand. A message from the Dark Lord, sent through the infinite abyss of eternity stared at him: A thumbs down emoji.

A few steps down an amethyst path lined with color-shifting stargazer lilies, Jeff and Ryan stood side by side. No words at first. Just the soft sound of wind through vine-covered glass. Somewhere in the distance, the memory orchids shimmered.

"Hell looks good on you," Jeff finally said.

Ryan smiled faintly. "I feel like myself again."

Jeff nodded, his hand reaching out to ruffle Ryan's hair, the way he had when he was little. As his hand was inches away, he paused and let it drop to his side.

"You don't need me to keep doing that anymore," he said. "You're not a kid."

"I'm not," Ryan said, grabbing his dad's hand and putting it on his head. "But I'm still your kid. Always will be."

Jeff looked away, blinking faster than usual.

"I wish I could walk with you just a little longer," Ryan admitted. "I don't want to go back without you."

Jeff smiled. "And I don't want to stay without you. But that's not the deal, is it?"

Ryan shook his head. "No."

Jeff stepped closer and put both hands on Ryan's

shoulders. "Then do me a favor. Don't waste what you got. Don't spend your life waiting to feel better. Live it. Loud, weird, soft, however it comes. Just live. This will all be here when it's time."

Ryan's eyes welled but he didn't cry. "I will," he whispered. "For you. For Mom. For my friends."

"For you," Jeff corrected gently. "That's the only promise that matters. Everything else will fall into place."

The wind shifted. A golden orchid drifted between them and dissolved into glitter against their skin. Jeff pulled him in for a hug. A real one. Rib-cracking. Soul-breaking. One that was felt throughout every tier of Hell.

Chapter 19

The rooftop of Robert E. Lee High School looked exactly as it always had. Covered in weather-stained concrete, rusted HVAC units, and a crooked, defunct antenna from the 90s that somehow still picked up radio from five counties away. But in this moment, it felt like the summit of their youth.

The three teens sat on a dented metal maintenance box with the final few cans of Old Westerly's between them, dented and slightly warm. A plastic bag of gas station snacks rustled nearby, ravaged and forgotten, as an unseasonably cold breeze danced between them. Maya attempted to pick the rave paint off of her shoes. Kally stared at the horizon, chin on her knees. Eddie leaned back, arms behind his head, the last gasps of the moonlight casting him in a soft halo.

And then the snap of a can opening.

The Devil stood atop the ledge, holding a beer in one hand while casually lobbing eggs at the mega church across the street with the other. He was still in his rave outfit, mesh shirt hanging crooked, glitter clinging to him like desperate groupies, and eyeliner that had fully committed to the morning-after aesthetic. He could've snapped himself into a pristine three-piece suit with a single thought, but for whatever reason, maybe camaraderie, maybe ego, or maybe the simple fact that he liked looking like he'd survived the night with them, he stayed as disheveled as the teens. He stood solemnly, casually sipping and throwing eggs that landed with brutal military precision despite the lackadaisical throwing motion. A particularly wet splat nailed a Porsche Boxster parked beneath a vinyl banner that read "GIVE MORE THAN THY RECEIVE."

With a casual nod, the Devil dusted his hands like he'd just completed a meaningful chore and turned back to the group.

"Good morning, little mortals," he grinned. "Or is it goodbye? Or is it brunch? I swear, the concept of time is so stupid I'll never fully understand it."

"Is Ryan okay?" Kally asked, her voice nearly swallowed by wind.

The Devil took a thoughtful sip, as if he were tasting the question. "Define 'okay.'"

Maya shot to her feet. "Seriously? After everything you're still fucking with us?"

The Devil sighed, then leveled his gaze at her, sharp and deliberate. "Maya, if I meant to torment you, trust me... you'd know. I could've simply commented on how loudly your soul screamed the second he vanished."

The way he said her name made her flinch. He'd never used it before, never granted them that familiarity. It felt like he'd peeled back a layer she wasn't ready to expose. The implication of what he'd seen and what he knew made her chest tighten, heat rising beneath her collar.

"But to answer your question, he's fine. Better than fine. Turns out love is a better compass than revenge or sin. Who knew?"

Kally rolled her eyes. "You did."

"Of course I did. But it's more fun when you figure it out yourselves. Honestly, I'm starting to suspect you really do skim Wikipedia synopses before watching movies."

"Only when she wants to know if the dog will die or not," Maya interjected. "She won't watch those."

Kally's eyes flicked to her, the faintest smile tugging at the corner of her mouth. It was small, almost invisible, but it warmed her chest in a way she hadn't expected... a quiet acknowledgment that maybe they were finding their way back to each other. The Devil took a long pull from his beer, allowing the silence to settle for a moment, before casually flinging another egg at the church.

Eddie crossed his arms. "What was the point of all this? Why do you do this really?"

The Devil stepped towards the edge of the roof, surprisingly solemn.

"You think I throw parties to collect souls? That I tempt you just to watch you burn?" He paused, eyes scanning each of them. "I party with humans because you're the only ones who still dance like you're trying to shake the universe loose. Like the dumb little things you do matter in the grand scheme of the infinite."

He sat beside them, just another silhouette in the dying morning gray. "You think God watches anymore?"

"Yes," Eddie answered, voice wavering, not fully believing himself.

"No," the Devil replied flatly. "You got free will and he holy-ghosted you like the deadbeat dad he is. I know what it's like to be cast out for being honest about who you are."

He looked at Eddie. "To crave love so deeply you'd rather fall than live unseen."

To Maya. "To run before anyone can hold you, because being chosen hurts more than being alone."

To Kally. "To build yourself into something immaculate so no one notices how terrified you are of being ordinary."

Silence.

Then Kally laughed, sharp and real. "You've been watching us?"

"I watch all of you," the Devil answered flatly.

Eddie cracked his knuckles. "And Ryan?"

"Ask him yourself," the Devil said. "He's on his way back."

"Really?" Maya asked.

"Maybe," the Devil smirked. "He could be in purgatory with the unbaptized babies. Maybe Asmodeus accidentally teleported him to the incinerator where I send the rapists and people who abandon puppies."

They glared. The Devil didn't move. He just stood with the faintest smile, watching the sky begin its shift from violet to fire-orange, the first birds calling out into the empty parking lot below.

"Ready to be normal again?" he asked, softly.

No one answered right away.

Kally broke the silence first. "I don't think we were ever

normal."

"Maybe that's why you were so much fun," the Devil murmured.

He walked a slow circle around the rooftop, dragging his fingers along the rail, the leather of his boots creaking like old stairs.

"You know, most people in your position don't make it this far in the night," he said. "Most burn out halfway. Scared of themselves. Or each other. Seeking out obvious indulgences."

"You sound proud," Eddie said, stretching his legs out.

The Devil paused. "I wouldn't go that far."

Then after a beat: "Perhaps a little."

Maya looked up at him, studying the flicker of pink sky reflected in his sharp, shifting eyes. "Why do you really do this? You owe us that much. Truth above everything else, right?"

The Devil paced near the edge of the roof, dragging one fiery fingernail along the concrete. Wherever it touched, the surface hissed and bubbled, leaving behind glowing, jagged doodles of crude penises going to battle with angels.

"Because for one night a year, I get to be part of something pure. No sermons. No contracts. No manipulation."

He sat crosslegged and carved his signature "S" into the ground. "Just people on the edge of something. The end of childhood. The beginning of whatever comes next."

Eddie tilted his head. "You say that like you get it."

The Devil smiled. "Who do think invented dramatic transitions?"

He kept carving, now drawing what looked suspiciously like a self portrait flipping off a cloud. "Do you want to know why I need a pure soul to come here? They're the only ones who can survive down there."

Kally folded her arms. "Protection, right?"

"That's part of it," he shrugged. "But it's more than that. Pure souls are like campfires. They attract the wrecked souls. They come crawling out of the dark just to feel something warm for a second."

Maya raised a brow. "So, what, you're like Hell's camp counselor?"

He pointed the flaming nail at her without looking up. "A very stylish one."

He returned to doodling, now sketching an angel with broken wings and a crooked halo. "Once you took your free will, God walked offstage like the show was over." he said.

Eddie winced. "You really don't hold back, huh?"

"I don't have to." The Devil shrugged. "I was the first guy he stopped returning calls for."

Kally exchanged a look with Maya, half sympathy, half "of course he made this about himself."

"But I stuck around," he continued. "I stayed for the after-credits."

He etched a crude depiction of himself and three tiny stick figures watching a movie. "Nothing thrills me more than watching someone claw their way out of ruin, even when the world tells them they aren't worth saving."

Maya softened. "That's not the answer I expected."

"Oh, trust me," he said, waving smoke from his fingernail like it were a cigarette, "nobody expects the Devil to have taste."

He gestured at them casually. "That's the fun part, kids. Not corrupting souls."

He paused a moment before etching a small heart with horns. "Resurrecting the broken ones," he concluded solemnly.

He met each of their eyes in turn. "Hell's got a reputation, sure. But in reality? I'm the only one still rooting for you."

A beat. "Because we're kindred."

He walked to the edge and looked out over the soccer fields and the parking lot full of possibilities.

"I've seen kings die without ever being truly known," he said, voice distant. "Revered. Honored. Feared sometimes. Loved others. But you three? You let yourselves be seen, be known. Even when it was ugly. Of all the creatures in the universe, you humans are my favorite. Just a random chaos of nonsense that took paradise and created a world more complicated than it ever needed to be. Such silliness. But some of you are something else for sure. I've lived an eternity and seen the very edge of the cosmos but a handful of you still manage to surprise me from time to time. I chase that feeling."

Maya fiddled with the cassette tape in her jacket pocket.

Eddie blinked up at the sky. "We had fun, didn't we?"

"That's what's eating you," the Devil said, turning. "That you had fun while your friend was burning in Hell?"

"Yeah," Kally said quietly. "That."

The Devil gave a little smirk. "That boy saw things few mortals have ever seen. You were all worried about leaving him behind in this place and now he has traveled lengths and witnessed sights and wonders none of you will ever know even if you lived to be a thousand."

"You're not just saying that?" Maya asked.

The Devil crouched down next to her and tapped the center of her forehead with one red finger. "Deceiving you does nothing for me. Despite what you may have heard, I deceive no one. I offer truth. I always have," he said. "You felt him. Even from here."

Eddie stood and brushed gravel from his pants. "What now?"

The Devil sighed again and pulled a battered flask from his coat and raised it. "To the ride home."

He took a sip, then passed it to Kally. "To the ride home," she repeated, before taking a pull.

Eddie grabbed it next. "To the ride home."

Maya took the flask and gave the Devil one last lingering look before bringing the flask to her lips. "To the ride home."

The Devil stood tall again, dusting errant glitter from his sleeves, and looked around. "Goodbyes are boring," he muttered. "You mortals always ruin it with speeches and tears."

Then his voice softened. "But if you remember anything from this night, remember this: you don't owe the world anything but your truth. The meaning of life is that you get to decide whatever the hell that is."

He turned away, toward the edge of the rooftop. The sky behind him was brightening, endless and full of color-shifting noise.

"Sun's almost up," he said.

The three teens stood beside him now. Shoulder to shoulder. Exhausted. Fulfilled like people at the end of a concert. Buzzed by something that wouldn't be real tomorrow but still mattered forever. Details that would degrade and fade with time but stay held together with a feeling that permanently embedded itself within their souls.

The Devil lifted his hand lazily and flicked a finger. With a final puff of smoke, this time lavender and soft as cotton candy, he was gone.

No fanfare. No exit line. Just silence and a sun peeking over the horizon.

Chapter 20

The pier jutted out from the Glass Garden island like a finger pointing toward an impossible horizon. Flowing molten fire met angry crystal teal water, roiling and hissing, heaven and hell kissing in static violence and impossible beauty. Mist and ash curled upward, dancing between fire and sea before disappearing and continuing their chaotic dance, never giving ground to the other.

Ryan stood at the pier's edge, hands plunged in his jacket pockets, eyes bouncing between the family he knew and the one he'd made down here. It was time. The lanyard around his neck shimmered faintly, his VIP badge glowing like a dying heartbeat. He reached up and thumbed it absently before turning to the trio of tiny demons that stood at his heels.

"You three," he said, voice cracking slightly. "I didn't know how lost I was until you showed up. I thought you were tagging along, but you led me, didn't you?"

Blink sniffled audibly. "We mostly followed."

Ryan laughed, then crouched down, leveling his eyes with them.

"Blink," he started, "you've got more heart than most people I've ever met. And the way you wear it? Out loud, on fire, with snacks in both hands? So cool."

Blink's lower lip quivered as he nodded fiercely, tears flying all around.

"Skid," Ryan continued, "You're chaos and caffeine and bad ideas in the sweetest letterman jacket I've ever seen. You're the anchor. These two believe in themselves because they know you have their back. You're a true ride or die."

Skid saluted sharply. "You ever need someone assassinated or hyped up, I got you, chief."

"Vex," Ryan said with a deep exhale, "You're the glue, buddy. You think no one notices, but we all know it was you who kept us moving. You believed in me before I believed in myself."

Vex blinked quickly and looked away, pretending to fix his cuff.

Ryan chuckled and gave them all one final group hug. Their arms wrapped around him like ivy, small but strong, reluctant to let go. Ryan breathed deep, the smell of the tiny demons now different than when they had first met. What was once putrid was now like entering a French bakery, warm and inviting with the sweetness of fresh sugar and butter. He breathed deep taking it all in before releasing his embrace. Blink held on for a moment longer, burrowing his face into Ryan's chest, before finally letting go.

Ryan stood up, eyes misting, and reached into his pocket fishing out the guitar picks. He picked out three and handed them to each of the crying demons.

"I'll never forget you three."

Blink clutched the guitar pick between his tiny clawed fingers and looked up at Ryan. "All we ever wanted was a chance to show everyone we mattered. And now we work for the Devil."

Ryan smiled and gave a quick glance to Asmodeus before turning back to his tiny friends. "I think as long as you three stick together, nothing is ever going to stop you. You're better together. Don't forget that."

"We won't," Vex said, gently placing the pick in his inner jacket pocket.

Ryan patted them all on the head one last time and then turned to Simon. "Here's to finally starting your real story."

Simon, hands entwined with Asmodeus', looked his love in the eyes and gave the softest of smiles before turning back. "You could've partied like the rest of them but you didn't."

Ryan shrugged, a little awkward. "I partied my own way. Like you did when you were in my place."

Simon looked at him with a soft intensity, long eyelashes grazing his lenses as he held back a tear. "You gave me back something I thought was lost forever. And not just them. Me."

Ryan blinked, words failing him for a moment. "I saw how you loved them," he said. "I get it now. You weren't stuck. You were choosing. Even if it hurt."

Simon gave a small smile. "It's not always about fixing things. Sometimes it's just about being willing to try."

Ryan returned a small smile and then turned to Asmodeus. The demon stood tall and still, the picture of control but with a new softness in their eyes. Less wariness. More wonder.

"I can't say thank you enough" Ryan said.

"I performed my duties," Asmodeus said, not fully believing themself.

"Seems a little weird you gave me your personal phone to use, don't you think," Ryan smirked.

Asmodeus tried to steel their gaze but failed.

"No one would blame you for trying to stack the deck," Ryan continued with a smirk. "Gotta say though, that's very human of you,"

Beside them, the little demons poorly attempted to hide their chuckles.

"I was following protocol," Asmodeus replied.

"Protocol you wrote, right," Ryan clapped back.

For a moment, Ryan was sure he saw a twitchy smirk on Asmodeus' face though he'd never really know for sure.

"Thank you, regardless. For performing your duty to the letter," he continued.

Asmodeus looked at the boy for a long time, then gave the smallest bow. A gesture rarely given, and never lightly.

Ryan smiled and returned the bow.

Finally, he turned to Jeff. The air shifted and cooled as the violent ocean of fire and water seemed to calm out of respect for the moment to come.

"Dad."

Jeff was already misty-eyed, hands shoved into his pockets.

"I don't think I'll ever know how to say goodbye to you but I'm glad I finally have a chance to," Ryan continued.

Jeff stepped forward and placed both hands on Ryan's shoulders. "Go live, kiddo. Loud and messy and full. I want to feel all of it when I think about you."

They hugged, long and silent and whole. When they pulled apart, Ryan placed a hand over Jeff's heart.

"Can't wait for the next show we see together," he said.

"And I can't wait for the one after that," Jeff replied, embracing his son once more. "Go take care of your mom for me."

Ryan buried his head in his dad's flannel, taking in his smell one last time. "I will."

"And go have a Milly's burger for me."

Ryan laughed through his tears. "I was thinking donuts first."

Jeff laughed with his entire body, side swiped by the dark joke from his son. Ryan smiled with his entire face, laughing at his own cleverness. A chip off the old block.

The waves resumed their violent clash as father and son pulled away from one another. Ryan removed his Reapers cap and snapped it onto his belt loop. After fixing his hair, he lowered his hands to his VIP pass. He slipped the lanyard slowly over his neck, pausing for just a moment as he caught the stare of Asmodeus.

"Thanks for the adventure," he whispered, extending the lanyard to the blood demon.

Asmodeus extended their hand and took the pass, Ryan still gripping it tightly. For one suspended moment, Ryan kept hold of the lanyard and looked past the COO of Hell, catching sight of his father one last time. His crooked smirk, his tired eyes, his love poured into every wrinkle.

With one last smile and a nod of his head to his dad, Ryan released his grip and was gone. No smoke. No noise. Just a very noticeable emptiness where a pure soul once stood. The lanyard rested between Asmodeus' fingers, still warm, but no longer glowing. They looked out to the ocean and then to Jeff who was wiping his tears with the cuff of his shirt. They handed the pass to Jeff and gave him a single pat on the shoulder before turning away and approaching the three crying little demons.

"Now," Asmodeus said, his voice stoic and flat once more. "Your training begins now. Your first order of business is familiarizing yourself with the motion pictures of Meryl Streep."

"We love Meryl Streep," Skid exclaimed.

"Totally," Blink yelled. "You're such an Amanda Priestly, Asmodeus."

Asmodeus rolled their eyes as they walked hand in hand with Simon back towards the Glass Gardens, followed closely by the three demons who were sharing their favorite Meryl Streep movie quotes.

The ocean hissed. The lava spit. And the Garden fell into a still, waiting quiet. Jeff looked down at the spot where his son once stood. On the smooth ground, a small crack emerged and the tiniest of memory orchids shot forth and seemed to stretch in awakening as it tasted it's first kiss of light. Jeff smiled and walked towards the water. He stood at the edge of the pier looking out at the fire and sea meeting in front of him. He glanced down at the faded and worn VIP lanyard, still warm with the afterglow of life, before slipping it over his own head.

With a sigh, he bent down and opened his cooler to find only two beers remaining, floating in chilled water, the memory of ice that had long since melted. He gazed at the two beers for a moment before pulling them both out of the cooler, gently shaking the excess water off of them. He opened one with a slow deliberate pull of the tab and took a long sip before placing the second down on the edge of the pier. With one last look at the ocean and a raise of his can, he walked back towards the gardens leaving the unopened beer behind, waiting for its owner to return one day.

Chapter 21

The path shimmered into view like a dream half-remembered. A quaint bridge made of soft light and spectral color, stretching over a slow, quiet river that didn't reflect the sky so much as become one with it. Over the river, a large meadow of technicolor green grass swayed lazily.

Ryan walked the rainbow path, a soft fog kissing the ground below him and parting with each step. As he walked, each footstep felt lighter than the last, like the ground itself was helping him along the way. He walked with quiet intention, taking in the sights and paying no mind to the fact that he couldn't see where the path would end. From the soft haze ahead, a blur of fur broke through and bounded toward him with a familiar howl that split the silence wide open.

"Arry?" he gasped, dropping to his knees just in time for the large dog to crash into his arms.

She was exactly as she'd been at her best, long-legged and

tri-colored, a warm sweep of white and tan and charcoal. Her ears were uneven the way he remembered, one perked forward, the other folded slightly as she tilted her head up at him. Her soft, soulful eyes sparkled with a gentle empathy that had always made him feel understood without a single word. And when she opened her mouth in that joyful, fully-body smile, he saw the little gap where one of her upper fangs should have been.

She smelled like sunshine and leash walks and the undeniably familiar musk of a dog who'd spent years pressed against his leg while grinding through homework or watching Sunday football. Her tail thumped wildly and her entire body vibrated with recognition, as if time itself had folded perfectly in half just to bring her back to him. She covered his cheeks with excited licks, whining in that way she always did when she was overwhelmed with love or when she wanted to eat. For the first time in what felt like forever, Ryan laughed with his entire body.

And just behind him, moving slower but no less regal, padded his ginger cat, Shirley Manson, as spry as the day he found her behind that convenience store in 10th grade with her sister, Joan Jett. She plopped down next to Ryan and butted his leg with her head before curling up next to him and Arry. Ryan didn't speak. He just breathed, both hands caressing the fur of his best friends. Silent tears slipped down his cheek, a reservoir of new grief bubbling to the surface filled with something closer to home. In a night where nothing was expected, this final surprise put him over the edge.

"I missed you both, so much," he whispered, tears streaming down his face.

He felt the softness of Arry's ears and the familiar cadence of her panting. Shirley burrowed her tiny head into his palm, her sharp whiskers tickling his wrists as she moved. He embraced them harder, taking in their smells and replaying every memory of them all at once. The world around seemed to be holding space for the three as the bridge illuminated brighter with each pet and stroke.

"That's gonna be a hard act to follow," a voice bellowed.

Ryan didn't turn. His focus was on what was right in front of him. The shadow that slowly overtook the three friends and snuffed out the radiant spectrum of light told him everything he needed to know.

The Devil stood on the bridge like a shadow you forgot was yours. His leather duster flared behind him like smoke in slow motion, and the rings on his fingers flickered with little pulses of heat.

Ryan kept his attention on his pets. "I thought you and I couldn't exist in the same place."

"This place is nothing but pure souls. It's a kind of world between worlds. A little bit of a loophole if you will."

Ryan nodded at the explanation and chuckled a bit at the rules and bureaucracy of the afterlife.

"I know I'm going back," he said flatly.

"Oh?" The Devil raised an eyebrow, strolling a slow arc around Ryan like a circling lion. "Cocky for a kid who's still technically dead."

"I'm not cocky. I just know what my friends would do for me. And I know what I'd do for them. That's not something you fake."

The Devil stopped pacing. "Hmmmm. Truth. My favorite. And what if I said they failed and I'm taking you?"

"I'd say you're fucking with me."

The Devil raised a brow. "Confidence? From you?"

Ryan smiled faintly as he continued to pet Arry and Shirley. This was their moment and he was taking all of it with him.

"Truth. That's what you're about, right?"

The Devil studied him, then slowly began to walk

forward, the bridge humming beneath his boots.

"You know," he boomed, bending down and giving Shirley Manson a quick scratch under her chin, "a lot of souls down there chase the experience. The chaos. The freedom. You could've spent your time with Bowie or Prince. You could have ridden an ice dragon across a sky made of fire. But you chose to spend your Hell night helping someone else fall in love again. While your friends raged on Earth and every temptation sang your name, you chose your dad, three little weirdos, and a love story that wasn't even yours."

Ryan shrugged. "You gave me the freedom to do what made me feel good. So I did."

The Devil chuckled. "Careful. You're making me look generous."

A pause.

"Hell is freedom," the Devil continued. "But it's not the only place that offers it."

Ryan nodded slowly, still petting Shirley Manson who purred like a motorboat.

"So why pick me?" he asked. "Why trade this pure soul for the Devil's little field trip?"

The Devil smirked. "Because wrecked souls follow the

ones who haven't given up. Broken people are drawn to light, not perfection. Drawn to honesty but too scared to grab it. You shine like a fire that doesn't know it's burning. After everything your world put you through, you persisted."

The Devil sat and leaned back on his palms, gazing across the glistening bridge, watching all manner of pet frolicking in the open field and mist, waiting in anticipation for their people.

"I stick around because you're messy." He continued, tapping his chest. "You feel everything too much, like me. Each and every one of you is chaos wrapped in insecurity. We rejects have to stick together."

Ryan studied him. "But don't you enjoy wrecking people? Isn't that supposed to be your whole thing. Corrupting the world?"

The Devil chuckled. "I enjoy fixing the ones no one else bothered to try with. It's not corruption unless corruption is correcting the weird programming you inflict upon yourselves. You humans are so fascinating to me. Blaming me for the ills of a world you created while destroying it in the name of the one who abandoned you. You give him credit for miracles you create. You defy him with every innovation you make. You do more than he thought you capable of but still, it's me who roots for you because your success means the infallible was wrong."

Ryan listened intently as Arry laid down by his side and Shirley Manson crawled into his lap.

"Also," the Devil continued, more softly now, "Asmodeus and Simon? You're the one who finally got that to the finish line?"

Ryan nodded. "Not me alone but yeah. Asmodeus was kind to me. I just wanted to help them back."

"I've been watching it all like my own personal reality show," the Devil said, standing. "The messages. The push and pull. The will they, won't they. I didn't interfere. It wasn't my place. I was fully prepared to wait another millennia for that payoff. I certainly didn't think a tiny human and his little crew would do it but I learned long ago to never underestimate your kind."

He smirked.

"I'm proud of the little shit," he continued. "Finally let themself be a person instead of a cog in my machine. About time my best employee took a damn day off."

Ryan smiled. "They'll be okay?"

The Devil nodded. "They love out loud now. Real love. And they have three hyperactive, surprisingly competent assistants to keep the operation moving."

Ryan smiled to himself, thinking of his first sight of his three little demons at Milly's 2. Lost weirdos have a way of finding their way to one another be it at a dive bar on the highest level of hell or a new student orientation in junior high.

The Devil let the silence stretch as he observed all manner of animals bounding in the distance. He knelt down beside Arry and scratched hers ears. The tri-colored pup yawned wide and licked his leg.

"You know," the Devil said, gazing at the dog, "people think I collect the wicked but the real fun is watching the broken get rebuilt. When God bailed after free will dropped, he left behind a lot of broken things. I just try to give them glue and glitter and tell them it's okay to dance while they fall apart."

He looked at Ryan. "You understand that now?"

Ryan nodded. "I do."

"So what are you going to do with what time you have left?"

"Whatever the fuck I want. And when that's done, we should grab a drink. I know a great place."

The Devil smirked at the pure soul and then let out a

bellowing laugh. "Oh, what a night."

The Devil stood tall, dusted off his jacket, and extended a hand. "Are you ready?"

Ryan leaned down and embraced Arry and Shirley Manson one last time, taking in all of the sensations the moment allowed him to keep.

"I'll be back soon," he whispered, kissing them both on the forehead and taking in one last inhale of their essence before standing.

He adjusted his outfit once more before extending his hand out. As the dark lord and human embraced hands, the bridge began to glow white until the world around them faded into nothingness before collapsing around the boy from Earth and taking him away.

The Devil stood alone on the bridge, hand still extended but now empty, watching the bridge ripple where Ryan once stood. The husky-mix and ginger cat gave the Devil no acknowledgment as they bounded off back into the mist to wait once more.

He sighed softly as he placed his hands in his pockets. This was the one brief moment of silence and solitude he allowed himself every year. He looked up towards the heavens and closed his eyes, satisfied in yet another victory he shared with his abandoned brethren. With an exhale, he parted his eye lids and took in the sapphire sky above.

"I could go for a burger," he muttered, turning and whistling "Black Hole Sun" as he glided down the bridge.

Chapter 22

The air still held the edge of night, but the promise of morning was steadily creeping over the rooftops and cracked asphalt of the Robert E. Lee High School parking lot. In the vacant lot that still playfully smoked through the rising sunbeams, three figures sat slumped near the now pristine Corolla, its paint flawless and shimmering brightly under the fading stars and rising sun like a car commercial.

Kally's pantsuit was stained in places she'd stopped noticing. Maya's LED roses blinked lazily now, as if they, too, were catching their breath. Eddie's boots had lost their glow entirely. Their faces looked worn and wild and beautiful, the survivors of something unspoken.

The sky was turning bruised orange when Ryan quietly returned, a stark contrast from his infernal exit.

In the spot where they last saw him, he stood, pristine and taller. His once shaggy hair was now trimmed and no longer hid his eyes which now seemed more rested than they had in over a year. His shoulders were a little straighter and he was dressed like someone who'd spent a year alone with his soul and decided to like what he saw. And yet, despite the perfection of his appearance, he smiled with a warmth so familiar, so them, it broke the silence instantly.

Kally didn't wait for permission. The second she saw him, alive, upright, and real, she crossed the distance between them in three unsteady steps and wrapped her arms around him like she was afraid he might dissolve if she didn't hold on tight enough. Ryan buried his face against her shoulder, arms locking around her with a fierceness that surprised them both. They'd only ever hugged a handful of times in their friendship but never like this. For a moment, neither spoke.

When Kally finally exhaled, it trembled into his collar. "You're here," she whispered, voice cracking on the second word. "You're actually here."

Ryan pulled her closer, like proximity alone could apologize for every bit of distance that he'd ever created. "I'm sorry," he murmured, immediate and urgent. "Kally, I'm so sorry. For blaming you. For being angry. For shutting you out. You didn't deserve any of that. You were the one who stayed. You were the one who kept trying. I've missed you so much and thinking I might never see you again..."

She loosened just enough to see his face. Her own eyes were brimming, but steady.

"I know," she whispered. "And I'm sorry, too. I've been dragging around this weight for so long I couldn't see you past it. I thought if I held on tight enough, it might undo something. I was trying to protect you but all it did was make me lose sight of you."

Ryan shook his head, vehement. "You didn't lose me."

"I should have trusted you enough to tell you the truth before it tore its way out in front of everyone," she said softly.

He reached up, gently brushing a tear from her cheek with his thumb, grounding her as much as himself.

"You don't need to fix anything," he said. "Not for me. 'Titanic' took what, six months of rebuilds and a warehouse full of waterlogged tears and it became something unforgettable. You don't owe anybody a perfect production."

Her breath caught. That landed deeper than he would ever know. They hugged once more, full-bodied and intentional. A hug that said we're not going backwards, but we're not losing each other either. They pulled apart, Ryan keeping his hands on her arms, as if he needed her to keep him from floating away.

"It's killing you that you can't video this moment, right now, isn't it," Ryan teased, a flicker of a smile ghosted across his face.

"You have no idea," Kally sniffled through a big smile.

Ryan looked her in the eyes and then peeked to his left, catching her attention. She peered to her right to see Maya holding up her phone, filming the entire exchange.

"It's even in landscape mode," Kally exclaimed.

Maya gave a bigger smile and faux-rolled her eyes at the notion that she had learned anything from Kally.

Ryan released Kally's arms and turned toward Eddie. Eddie walked up slowly, standing taller than he used to but still with hands awkwardly shoved in his pockets. He didn't speak right away. He just took Ryan in. The steadiness in his stance, the calm behind his eyes. This was the version of his friend that he'd always trusted without question. The one who showed up and noticed. The one who'd kept him tethered to the world when he almost let himself slip away from it.

There was a tightness in Eddie's jaw when he finally exhaled. "Hell treated you well," he said, voice a little rough.

Ryan gave him a full smile, taking in Eddie's rave attire and newfound posture. "Back at you, man."

They stepped into a hug, not the stiff awkward kind boys give because they think they're supposed to, but the kind that's built from years of inside jokes and late-night talks. Eddie squeezed harder than he meant to. When Ryan pulled back, he kept a hands on Eddie's shoulders, grounding them both. The Jeff Phillips shoulder grab.

"I felt you down there," Ryan said quietly. "I don't know what you went through but something changed. I felt it. It was like you were lighter."

Eddie looked away, blinking hard. "I was scared I was gonna lose you, man. I didn't know what to do. And I'm not talking about just tonight. I mean this entire time."

Ryan tilted his head, trying to catch eyes with Eddie but not pushing it. "Now you know how I felt."

"I thought I had to handle my stuff by myself," Eddie said. "That if I leaned on you while you were grieving, I'd break you. But you already knew something was wrong with me. You saw it before I could say anything. You didn't let it slide. You showed up."

He swallowed, eyes fixed somewhere just past Ryan's shoulder before swinging back and putting them eye to eye.

The same eyes that gripped his soul and pulled him back from the dark place he was in were now here, back in reality.

"And I don't think I ever told you this, but that mattered," Eddie continued, voice breaking. "A lot. It's the reason I'm still here. So yeah, losing you almost permanently?" He shook his head. "That irony's not lost on me."

Ryan nodded once. "I'm really glad you stayed. You're one of the loves of my life."

Eddie's lips twitched. "Mine, too."

A beat.

"Thanks for taking me on that drive," he added quietly.

Ryan met his eyes and nodded back, a feeling of warmth engulfing his entire body. "Anytime. No matter where I am."

Eddie pulled him in for a second hug, grounding and full-bodied, releasing something they'd both been holding too tightly for too long. When he stepped back, he gave Ryan a look up and down and nodded his head. With a knowing smile, Eddie stepped away, revealing Maya just behind him. Ryan looked at her face, his breath catching as he looked at her, taking in every single feature, the sun kissing every angle and curve.

She didn't hug him at first. She just looked at him, her

jaw tight, her lips trembling. He took in her eyes and the way the light seemed to skate on the edges of her pupils. Her auburn hair still flecked with paint, danced along her cheekbones and detoured to her soft jawline. Ryan took the scenic route of Maya's face, stopping at every point of interest before settling on her lips as she spoke.

"I didn't know how to talk to you after everything."

"I know," Ryan said. "I didn't make it easy for people to be there for me."

They stood for a moment, letting the space between them linger, both knowing that everything that happened next would define the rest of their lives.

"I would go days without smiling," Ryan continued. "But you were usually the one who would bring me back."

Maya's lips curled into a soft grin before breaking forth into a full smile, a rare sight that few had observed. Ryan smiled back with his entire face, taking a small step towards her. Maya bridged the gap between them and hugged him hard, her smell overtaking his senses and taking him back to that night she gave him a ride home. Mountain Dew Baja Blast and Bert's Beeswax lip balm. They held each other, neither one wanting to be the first to break. Ryan, feeling overtaken by emotion, felt the spirit of his dad in that instant. He knew that wherever he was, he was feeling this moment, most likely with a whiskey.

His arms loosened their grip and his hands fell to the small of her back for a brief moment. As he stepped back, the space between them vibrated with awe and electricity. It was the same stunned, reverent hush he'd felt watching Chris Cornell light up a stage in Hell. Something impossible crashing into reality and throwing his sense of self into the fire. If the afterlife had taught him anything, it was that miracles don't always announce themselves with fire and spectacle. Sometimes they just make your heart skip and dare you to notice.

Ryan swallowed, grounding himself, as he remembered. Looking Maya in the eye, he gave her a mischievous grin.

"I brought you guys something," he said, reaching into his inner coat pocket.

With a delicate touch, his hand emerged from his pocket holding three guitar picks, jet black with Chris Cornell's signature etched in fiery red.

"Straight from one of the hottest venues in Hell," he grinned. "Pretty much ruined me on any concert I'll ever see."

Maya plucked the pick from Ryan's palm, turning it over

in her fingers. The sharply angled signature on the back, catching the light of the rising sun and reflecting back at her like a wink, made her freeze. She'd stared at that distinctive signature a million times on the Soundgarden poster that once hung in the corner of her bedroom. This one wasn't faux-printed on glossy poster paper, though. This signature was alive and seemed to give the pick an otherworldly weight and warmth to it, like it had soaked up the very heat from the stage it originated from.

"This is Chris Cornell's signature," Maya exclaimed flatly in shock, her thumb tracing the grooves of the pick. "Did you see Chris Fucking Cornell live?"

"Live might be a bit inaccurate but yeah," Ryan replied with a smirk. "Handed those picks to me personally after the show. I even touched his hand."

Maya's mouth dropped and her knees buckled as she delicately held it in her palm as if it were a communion wafer.

"Would you believe me if I told you that that wasn't even the coolest thing that happened to me," Ryan continued.

"What the fuck happened to you that seeing Chris Cornell wasn't the top moment of all fucking time," Maya asked loudly.

"Saw my dad," Ryan said, turning out to look at the

rising sun.

"Holy shit," Kally said softly.

Ryan just nodded his head. "Spent pretty much the entire time with him. I saw things that no one would believe. Experienced places that only a few people ever have. But seeing him again…" Ryan's voice thinned, the last word barely hanging on.

Ryan bit his lip, the tears rising too fast to blink away. For a brief moment, he braced himself for the lost souls of Hell to embrace and comfort him again.

Instead, a real hand closed around his. Kally's.

She reached across the small space between them with no hesitation, threading her fingers through his in way that said, I'm here, you don't have to hid this from me anymore. Her grip was firm, grounding, exactly the anchor she'd always tried to be even when she didn't know how. Ryan let out a broken breath, a tangle of surprise, grief, and release. Then another hand found him. Eddie slid in from the other side, his large hand resting on Ryan's shoulder, anchoring him to the ground even more. There was no shakiness in Eddie this time, no shrinking. Just quiet strength. The same kind Ryan had given him a hundred times and more repaid in this moment. Ryan swallowed hard, his chest loosening in a way that felt like a pressure valve being released.

Maya was the last to reach him, her touch the softest. She took his free hand in hers, her fingers slipping into place with surprising gentleness. He felt her callused fingertips on his palm as her thumb brushed lightly across the top of his hand, a tiny motion full of permission and understanding, that sent a warm pulse of electricity down his spine. He looked her in the eyes, gently giving her hand three small squeezes before turning his attention to Eddie and Kally. A warmth spread through his body. It was human, full of fierceness and familiarity. The warmth of chosen family tightening around him like a shield. A moment a year and a half in the making, uncorking like New Year's Eve champagne.

"There was never going to be enough time with him," Ryan continued, blinking fast. "We laughed. Watched a concert. Caught a football game. I told him everything I never got to say. Turns out he's a pretty popular guy down there."

Maya looked at him, eyes shining. "You dad was always the coolest guy anywhere he went. My dad would fanboy out every time your dad would call him to hang out."

Ryan laughed. "He would. I remember he kept grilling me about my dad's favorite beer before we came over to dinner for the first time."

The group laughed before falling back into their own personal memories of Jeff Phillips. All of the burgers at Milly's. The way he observed everyone and always listened more than he spoke. The home he kept that was always a welcoming sanctuary with no judgment and the best snacks.

A quiet settled over them once more. The kind that no one rushed to fill but instead allowed the world around them to fill in the blanks with the beauty of just existing. The hum of early birds waking. A soft breeze through the trees. An angry man discovering his egg covered car in a nearby parking lot. They had left the surreal behind, and now, only the moment remained. Ryan took one deep breath of memory before turning back to his friends in the here and now. In the glow of the reunion, he hadn't fully taken in their current ensemble as rave kids on the final day of EDC.

"You guys look like you had some fun," Ryan teased, eyeing their wrecked outfits. "Somewhere."

"We did," Kally said. "Thanks to the fucking Devil."

"And a few other weirdos all along the way," Eddie added.

"A strange ticket taker," Maya confirmed.

"A blues guy running a record store," Kally added.

"Casey Kelly," Eddie replied mischievously.

Ryan returned the smile and turned his attention to Kally. "Casey Kelly, huh?"

"That's what you comment on? All the thing we mention and you gotta focus on Casey? Don't you fucking start, Ryan!"

"So a life-or-death, soul destroying scenario comes your way and you seek the help of one Casey Kelly?"

Kally pursed her lips and then dropped her shoulders. "Yes. Yes, I did. He's a good guy. I admit it now. Still fucking weird but a good guy."

Ryan smiled sincerely, thinking back to the three little demons who did everything with their full little hearts. "You can't underestimate those weirdos, Kal. You'd be sitting here without me if you did. Not all heroes wear capes. Some wear tuxedo t-shirts and jean shorts. Others wear sweet letterman jackets."

They laughed, a cathartic release that acknowledged they'd made it through Hell and back.

"So what's the Devil like?" Ryan asked. "I'd only met him for a few minutes on my way back and honestly, I was pretty distracted because I got to see Arry and Shirley

Manson again."

Maya's eyes widened at the name. "You saw Joan Jett's sister?"

Ryan's eyes welled up for a moment thinking about his pets. "Purring like a sports car, slamming her head into my leg like she always would."

At that moment, the two caught eyes in the shared memory of the day they found them behind the Benny Boom's Convenience Store on the way to score some Westerly's in 10th grade.

The moment passed and the group went still for a second.

"So the Devil," Maya started. "He, um, kind of got us."

"Same," Ryan said. "Weird, right?"

"Oh man," Eddie added. "Wait until we tell you what he did to these two cops."

"I'm still waiting to hear about these outfits," Ryan said. "Eddie, this look is it, man. And you two, holy shit!"

Maya blushed a bit, pulling hair into her face.

"What about you, dude," Kally exclaimed. "Weren't you wearing like some speech club shirt when you left."

"Wait until I tell you about who gave me this outfit," Ryan replied excitedly.

The wind shifted. Somewhere behind the school, a lawn sprinkler sputtered to life. The world was beginning again. Ryan looked at the three of them, framed by dawn. He thought about the week after his dad died. How he'd sat in this same parking lot, staring at this same sky, wondering if the world would ever feel anything but empty again.

"I'm not ready for this to be over," Kally admitted.

"It's not," Ryan said. "The big guy slipped me this little note when he sent me back."

Ryan held up the familiar piece of paper, crumpled and weathered by the night.

"Oh, fuck," Eddie groaned. "What is it? Infernal Bingo or something?"

"Donuts," Ryan replied, holding up the list for all to see.

They all leaned in and sure enough, at the very bottom of the list that had guided their night was shimmering red ink that read three little words.

"North Star Donuts," Ryan read. "I never did get to try those. Heard they're to die for."

Kally, Ryan, and Maya took pause, shocked at the joke Ryan had just made. Ryan then quietly smiled to himself before the real laugh broke free.

"It's fine, guys," Ryan reassured. "My dad would have

loved that joke. Can't wait to tell him it one day."

Maya smiled and then gave a chuckle, brushing herself off. "So lame. You're driving. I'm half-dead."

"I was actually dead," Ryan teased. "But sure. I can get behind the wheel."

Kally slung her arm around his shoulder. "We'll talk about everything over powdered sugar and burnt coffee."

"Can I go in wearing these pants," Eddie grinned.

"Any place that wouldn't allow that isn't a place I'd want to go," Maya said.

"Agreed," Ryan replied, fishing his keys from his pocket and tapping the unlock button on the key fob.

The car chirped behind them. Ryan turned to see his trusty Corolla waiting for him, gleaming and new. It was still his dad's old car, now untouched by time. Familiar in all the right ways like his dad sipping beers and whiskey at Old Tito's. He walked toward it slowly, the others hanging back, giving him space without needing to say it. He ran a hand along the roof and exhaled. Waiting for him was a frosty, unopened can of Old Westerly's, replacing the one he had left behind. One last gift. He took the can in his hand and took a step back, taking in the essence of the car in front of him. The same as it had looked when his dad first pulled into their driveway that overcast fall day when he was four-years-old. Ryan thought of the photo on his fridge of him sitting on his dad's lap pretending to steer, Jeff beaming in a familiar flannel shirt.

He opened the driver's side door and took in the moment. The seat, the air, the memories still folded into the upholstery. It was new but the essence of everything it was still held on.

Maya walked up beside him, quiet for once. "You okay," she asked, placing a soft hand between his shoulder blades.

He nodded, eyes still on the interior. "He kept his gum wrappers in the side panel. My mom would always tease him about that when she drove his car. He'd pop a piece when he got home because he knew he was going to kiss her when he walked in the door."

Maya smiled softly. "Looks like there's a few still there."

Ryan smiled back. "Yep. And they always will be."

Ryan stared at the car, the once-faded Corolla now shimmered like it had been rewound to the best version of itself. A shared artifact of a life well lived and a new life worth living. He exhaled slowly, grounding himself in the moment. His friends. The morning. The life waiting just beyond this parking lot. Kally and Eddie entered the backseat from the driver's side as Ryan walked around to the passenger side and opened the door. Maya was already approaching, brushing hair from her eyes, exhausted but beautiful in the way only people who survived something together can be.

Ryan held the door open. "You got shotgun, right?"

Maya didn't say anything as she looked up at him and gave the smallest smile. The kind that knew everything and said nothing. Ryan held the door open and softly gripped Maya's hand, gently guiding her into the seat, holding on a moment longer than needed and then for a moment more. Kally and Eddie glanced at each other in the backseat with quiet satisfaction. Ryan closed the door and walked around to the driver's side, a quiet grin tugging at the corner of his mouth.

He slipped into the driver's seat and took one last look at the fading stars. "Alright. Let's go ruin our blood sugar."

From the back seat, Kally let out a sudden gasp. "Holy shit!"

"What?" Maya asked, turning as Ryan glanced at Kally in the rearview mirror.

Kally held up her vintage yellow camera bag, sun-faded and unmistakable.

"I thought this was gone forever. At the rave, I thought…

I thought I'd never see it again."

She gently rubbed the frayed stitching on her patches, gifts from Maya and Eddie when they found out that Ryan had bought her this bag. She unzipped it cautiously, almost like it might vanish again if she moved too fast. Inside, resting exactly where she always kept it, was her camera. She powered it on, the small green light blinking to life. She scrolled through the photos. Click. Eddie dancing with the wrestling team. Click. Maya and Kally mid-laugh on the rave floor, surrounded by old friends and strobe lights. Click. Maya singing in the booth. Click. Burgers at Milly's. Click. Casey Kelly's living room.

A lump formed in her throat. "These aren't my photos," she whispered.

Eddie leaned forward. "What do you mean?"

She turned the camera to face them all. "He must have took them," she said. "He used my camera somehow."

There was a stillness, followed by a shared look of understanding none of them spoke aloud.

One final truth. Proof that even chaos could be sentimental.

Ryan looked down, grinning faintly. "Baller move," he whispered to himself.

From the passenger seat, Maya picked at her now destroyed nail polish. "You think he got my good side," she chirped.

Ryan looked at her and smiled. "Every side of you is good."

Maya's blank face softened into something unreadable but familiar. She felt his eyes on her but didn't want to give away too much at this moment and only looked down with a satisfied smile. Ryan held his look a moment longer, taking it all in, before turning back to the ignition and turning the key. The revamped Corolla purred to life, not a ping or errant sound to be heard. Still his dad's. Still his. Just new again. Like himself.

"Okay," he said, adjusting his mirrors. "Seriously. Donuts. Before I say something profound and ruin my whole brand. What are we listening to?"

In the rearview mirror, Maya caught Kally's eye. Kally had gone still, one hand slipped into the canvas bag the Devil had returned to her, camera inside, their old clothes folded impossibly clean. She pulled out her bright yellow Tarantino shirt, soft now, freshly washed, and something heavier slipped free from it.

A cassette tape.

Impossibly red, deep and saturated, as if it had never known a sunlit dashboard or the bottom of a backpack. Pristine and new in a way that felt almost anachronistic. Kally's fingers traced the raised ridges of the plastic before she turned it over. Written in thick, shimmering red ink across the once-blank label were the words: Soundtrack for the Ride Home. The handwriting made her chest tighten. The same lazy confidence as the "North Star Donuts" scrawled onto the list, like the Devil couldn't help leaving fingerprints on things that mattered. She swallowed, then lifted the tape into view.

"How about this," she said.

Ryan glanced back at it and smiled, something easing into his expression. "I think Jeff would more than approve of his tape deck being used."

Kally held the tape out and Maya grabbed it as Ryan clicked his seatbelt shut. Maya gave Kally a soft, knowing smile as the tape gripped between her fingers.

Ryan took the cassette from Maya's hand, grazing her fingers as he did. Ejecting a tape from the slot of the after-market installed tape deck, he could only shake his head as a well-worn, original copy of Soundgarden's "Superunknown" emerged.

With the reverence of a holy relic, he gently placed the tape back into its case and inserted the crimson tape into the slot, the familiar click and whirr taking him back to the first time he took a ride with his dad in this very car jamming the entirety of Pearl Jam's "Ten."

As the tape kicked to life and the words of Warren Zevon filled the air, Ryan smiled to himself as he shifted the car into drive, noticing the new smoothness of the gearshift knob.

The four teens exited the parking lot for the very last time, the sky behind them turning gold, the asphalt still smoldering.

ACKNOWLEDGMENTS

ACKNOWLEDGMENTS

To my parents, for making me creatively defiant and supporting me.

To Sergio Mendoza, for seeing my potential, giving me my love of words, and teaching me that matters of the heart are matters of life and death.

To Justin Gregg, for surviving AP English together, being an anchor to my youth, and introducing me to real music.

To Alejandro Montoya Marin, for living the dream, letting me be a small part of it, and pushing me in the endeavors I pursue. Viva Indie!

To the Sunday Funday Crew (Andy, Marina, Kirk, Sara, Jess, Aly, and Ryan), for being a sanctuary for my mental health during one of the toughest professional years of my life and showing me the power of a chosen family.

To Alex "Boston" Albrecht, for being my creative sounding board and my partner for the single craziest day in my life. Go Pats!

To Elias "E" Hernandez, for all of the trivia nights and mindless reality TV.

To Brandon Rathert, for weathering the professional storm with me.

ACKNOWLEDGMENTS

To Maddy and Jordan, for teaching me how to love someone more than I love myself.

To Casino El Camino on 6th Street, for crafting a burger (Amarillo Burger) so good, it made me almost believe in a higher power.

To Ms. Barbara Yarbrough, for helping me unlock my potential as an insecure, nerdy 6th grader and giving me confidence in my ability to learn.

To my grandfather, Ralph Garcia, for making reading look so cool.

To Fighting Cock Bourbon, for being an integral part of "write drunk" portion of my process.

To my high school friends, for being a part of my story. Even though it's long over and we're now strangers, all of it mattered.

To all my friends in the LGBTQ community, for their friendship and showing me the true bravery of being yourself.

To St. Ann's Catholic School in Midland, TX, for being so utterly dismissive of my questions about religion as a child that I abandoned organized religion altogether.

PARTY LIKE HELL

THANKS FOR READING...
NOW GO GET A BURGER!

For Inquiries, Please Contact
ROKRJONART@GMAIL.COM

www.ingramcontent.com/pod-product-compliance
Lightning Source LLC
LaVergne TN
LVHW011942060526
838201LV00061B/4181